WITHOUT
BORDERS

AMANDA HEGER

DIVERSIONBOOKS

Diversion Books
A Division of Diversion Publishing Corp.
443 Park Avenue South, Suite 1008
New York, New York 10016
www.DiversionBooks.com

This is a work of fiction. Names, characters, places and incidents either are the
product of the author's imagination or are used fictitiously. Any resemblance to
actual persons, living or dead, events or locales is entirely coincidental.

For more information, email info@diversionbooks.com

First Diversion Books edition April 2016.
Print ISBN: 978-1-68230-054-1
eBook ISBN: 978-1-68230-053-4

For Matt,

I love you and I like you.

DAY ONE

It had been a peanuts-for-dinner, vodka-for-dessert kind of flight.

Annie stumbled down the plane's narrow steps into the sweltering night air. The humidity weaved spider webs in her lungs, and a film of sweat coated the back of her neck as she trotted into the brittle chill of the air-conditioned airport. Inside, she fell into a crush of recently deplaned passengers, their elbows and quick-clipped Spanish jostling first her bags, then her mind. She found an empty corner, pulled out her phone, and sent a text to Marisol.

I'm here! Can't wait to see you.

She put the phone away and waited at the crowded luggage carousel, straining to make out the conversation around her. But the Spanish flew by faster than anything she'd heard in her classes, each misunderstood word threatening to chip away at her excitement. *I'm tired. I'll understand more tomorrow. Please let me understand more tomorrow.*

As she tapped her foot to the feisty music playing on the airport's speakers, a large, nondescript black bag shot onto the conveyer belt, followed by a small blue duffle. Next came Annie's beautiful crème leather suitcase, barreling down the carousel, wide open and overflowing with its once carefully packed contents. She scrambled forward to snatch a stray t-shirt from the belt before pulling the bag to the ground. Her belongings scattered in a wide arc at her feet. *Shit.*

She shoved shirts, skirts, and bottles back into her suitcase, pushing piles of underthings beneath the heavier items. Finally, she pulled the zipper and dragged her luggage behind her to the nearest bench, all the while praying that no one had witnessed her underwear raining down from the conveyor belt.

She scanned the crowd for any signs of her friend and jotted off another text. **Where are you?**

Annie was certain she'd recognize Marisol, even if she hadn't seen her in person since they were fifteen. They'd spent a single year together in St. Louis, gossiping about teachers, the other girls in their freshman class, and what it would be like to French kiss boys. But in that year, they'd bonded for life. And even though their communication became sporadic after Marisol returned home to Nicaragua, Annie knew there was no way she'd miss her friend's impish grin.

In the month since Annie had decided to take this trip, they'd Skyped a handful of times. During their chats, Marisol rambled on about her job as a nurse and the men she dated, dodging all but the most basic questions about what Annie would do as member of the medical brigade—teach a sex ed course and shadow Marisol's brother, Felipe, the doctor in charge of the clinics.

The phone buzzed in her palm. **Am late. Sorry. Meet in bar.**

"Which bar?" she muttered, craning her neck to see over the crowd.

The airport was small but full of flickering, buzzing fluorescent lights—an open room with lines of weary travelers zigzagging across the floor. Dusty yellow letters above the entrance to the only restaurant in sight proclaimed "El Bar."

Inside, she sank onto the nearest stool and pulled out her phone. Her fingers itched to send another text, this one to America—to Mike, the solid, blond fraternity boy in Missouri. It had been two weeks since he'd dumped her. Fourteen days, three hours, and two minutes since he told her he didn't want to sit around waiting for her to come home.

I made it. She shot off the message as she ordered a beer.

Several bitter swigs later, the phone buzzed with Mike's reply. **Ok.**

She knew she should let it be, cut her losses and save her precious air time for someone who mattered. Like her father. Or the woman who took care of her bikini waxes. Anyone mattered more than this asshole.

Annie suspected he spent at least half an hour in front of the mirror each morning, adjusting every strand of his stupid, perfect hair to look like he rolled out of bed and walked straight into class. And he'd always pretended to be some kind of Scotch aficionado. But Annie knew, away from the bravado of his frat brothers, he'd choose a glass of Boone's Farm over a pricey single malt any day.

I should call him. Let him know how great I'm doing. Let him hear how I'm not missing him. At all. She plugged in his number.

One ring. She ran a finger along the outside of the bottle, tracing an M in the condensation. *Breezy. Be breezy.*

A second ring. She took a long drink to calm her nerves.

Voicemail.

He's ignoring me. She set her bottle on the glass bar top, took a deep breath, and put on her best carefree, I-don't-give-a-damn-about-how-you-dumped-me voice. "Hey, it's me. I know—"

"Welcome to Nicaragua," a low voice interrupted.

She swiveled to discover a man smiling at her, revealing a deep dimple in his right cheek and a few crinkles around the eyes. They left Annie unsure whether he was twenty-four or thirty-four, but the tilt of his chin was so familiar. She stared into his face, her forehead crinkled with confusion. *Don't be one of those people, Annie. Not all Hispanic people look alike.*

"I think this is yours, yes?" He slid onto the stool next to her and held out a small wad of purple polka-dotted fabric.

As soon as the soft cotton hit Annie's palm, she knew it was one of the many pairs of underwear she'd strewn across the baggage claim. She couldn't hit end on the voicemail to Mike fast enough, and she shoved the boy shorts into the nearest bag. "Thanks. Uh, I mean *gracias.*"

"*De nada.*" His eyes stayed on her as he scooted his stool closer. "How was your flight?"

She shrugged. "The usual. Hot, crowded, only peanuts to eat." Her stomach grumbled at the thought of food. The tiny bag of peanuts was the only thing she'd eaten all day.

"Do you want to order something to eat?"

She shook her head. Marisol would be here to whisk her away any minute. "No thanks."

"A drink? We should celebrate your arrival."

She shifted her focus between the bottle in her hands and his face. He was cute, with his short, messy black hair and squared jawline. A pair of sunglasses hung from the neck of the simple, white V-neck he wore. The starkness of the shirt set off his copper skin. He smiled, bringing out the dimple again, and her world shifted. That smile transformed him from cute to *yes, please.*

He's already seen my underwear.

"Sure." She pushed the hair from her face, wishing she'd bothered to wear something better than yoga pants and an old Tri-Delt t-shirt. **Found cute guy at the bar**, she jotted off another text to Marisol while he ordered.

He turned back to her, a shot glass in each hand. "*Salud.*"

"What's this?" She took a glass from his wide, dark fingers and wondered what those fingers would feel like against other parts of her. Parts not accessible in this tiny airport bar.

"*Limón sorpresa.*" He pulled a phone from his pocket, and his eyes locked on the screen. A second later, another universe-wrecking smile lit his face.

Taking "surprise" shots from strange men in a foreign country wasn't Annie's modus operandi. She was the mother hen who steered her sorority sisters away from creepy middle-aged men at the bars. The one who patrolled her friends' drinks when they went to the bathroom, keeping away guys with roofies and beer bellies. *I am supposed to be having an adventure.*

"Cheers." She knocked her glass with his and took the shot. It tasted like key-lime pie and burned on the way down. It was almost enough to make her forget she was about to spend the next month without access to electricity or running water. Maybe another would let her forget Mike's face altogether. She looked at her phone. Silence, but she was certain Marisol would arrive at any moment. *And in the meantime…* "One more?"

This time the bartender poured a single shot, and Señor Smile set it in front of her. "I have to drive," he said.

"Where?" Annie opened her throat and downed the alcohol. Her eyes were slow to focus, but she thought he was trying to look down the V of her shirt. At home, this would be enough to send her tearing in the opposite direction. But something about the thrill of a foreign place and a cute, interested guy made her a little reckless. *Also, alcohol.* Her insides fluttered as she leaned forward.

He shifted in his seat. "I have to take you back to the hotel,"

God, that dimple. She rested a hand on his knee and bit her bottom lip, wanting nothing more than to forget her ex. "That's forward."

He blinked at her.

"A friend is supposed to pick me up," she said.

"You *are* being picked up, no?"

Through the fuzzy glow of the shots and the beer, Annie laughed at his bad pick-up line. *I'll let that one go. Language barrier.* She teetered forward on the stool, her cross-shoulder bag throwing her off-kilter. He put a hand on her arm, and she used his thighs to find her balance. The way his muscles tensed under her fingers made anticipation gurgle in her chest.

"I think we should go," he said.

She wasn't about to leave with this sexy stranger, but she scooted closer, until her upper body perched between his legs. Each bit of stubble in his five o'clock shadow stood out in infinite detail, and her eyes shifted from his full bottom lip to his dark eyes. *Adiós, Mike.* She let her left hand slide further up his leg. For the smallest second, he leaned into her space, and she was certain their lips would meet. But then Señor Smile sat back, concern muddling his features.

"Annie, this probably is not a good idea. I—"

"Wait, what?" She pulled away, shaking the rum-fog from her brain. "How do you know my name?" It took her two tries to stand, weighed down by her bag and the booze. "Are you some kind of creep who picks up American girls at the airport and sells them into slavery? I saw that episode of *Law & Order.*" She stumbled away from him, yanking out her phone.

"I think you are a little *borracha*."

"What?" She didn't know what *borracha* meant, but disappointment was written all over his face. *Sorry pal, but I'm not about to star in some twisted, ripped from the headlines abduction tragedy.*

"Annie—"

"How do you know my name?"

"How do I…You know who I am, yes?"

"I just met you." She took another step away, and her fingers jabbed at the screen. **Where are you?**

The man grabbed his own phone off the bar, typing furiously.

Annie's phone buzzed, and she glanced at the message. **In front of you.**

Her eyes scanned the crowd, searching for any of sign Marisol. Any trace of a petite, raven-haired beauty. Nothing. Her gaze landed on Señor Smile, who still stared at her, his head cocked toward his right shoulder. *So familiar.*

Annie's hands went ice cold. The aftertaste of the shots still lingered on her tongue, now stale and sour. Her mind raced, searching for an answer. Any answer other than the one glaring back at her. "Felipe?"

"Mari did not tell you I was coming?"

"No." Annie wanted to sprint across the airport and onto the closest plane. She didn't care about the destination—it had to be better than here. "Where is she?"

"She had to work. I thought you knew." He shook his head. "Because of the text messages."

"No."

Marisol had sent the number just before Annie left St. Louis. *Just in case*, the email said. That was it. No further explanation.

Annie had a few vague memories of Felipe, with his floppy dark hair and perma-scowl. During the year his family had lived in St. Louis, he mostly stayed in the basement, blaring the television and playing guitar while the girls got ready for parties and football games. Annie never suspected that, six years later, he would look like some kind of sex god.

"Are you ready to go?" He took her suitcase and beelined for the exit, not waiting for her answer.

Annie slunk through the parking lot behind him, all her pride left behind in El Bar. When they reached the car, she opened her mouth to apologize, but both her mind and her mouth felt packed full of cotton. "Thanks for the ride."

For the first five minutes of the drive, she stared out the open window at the ramshackle houses and the legions of Ché Guevara graffiti covering nearly every flat surface. Talk radio blared through the old Corolla's speakers and filled the silence, saving her from small talk. A breeze rushed in and cooled her sweaty skin, but it couldn't blow away the raw sting of her mortification.

They stopped in a dim parking lot, surrounded by a rusty iron fence and topped with spiraling razor wire. Without a word, Felipe shut off the engine and hopped out of the car. She followed and stared at the ground as he plucked her bags from the trunk.

"So," Annie fumbled for words, "when you said you had to drive me back to the hotel… this is what you meant, huh?"

He nodded.

"And tomorrow we're flying to the other side of the country? With Marisol?" *Please say yes.* The thought of spending an entire flight alone with him made her stomach ball up into a hundred tiny knots.

He nodded again, and Annie was desperate for him to say something, anything, to relieve the tension stretched between them.

Nothing.

"So we'll drive to the airport in the morning?" she asked.

"I have some things to take care of at the hospital. I will send a taxi. Noon."

"Okay." She grabbed her luggage and lumbered toward the front doors of the grenadine-red hotel. A long staircase twisted its way to a second floor balcony, and above it a hundred shards of broken glass were glued to the flat roof.

Felipe's stare bored into the back of her head, and she couldn't move herself or her belongings fast enough to get away.

"Annie—"

"Yeah?" Her shoulders sagged, and she kept her eyes down. *I can't believe this is happening.*

"I—" he started. He ran a hand through his hair. "Never mind." He climbed into the car. "See you tomorrow."

DAY TWO

Annie stood in front of the blue and yellow La Costeña Airlines sign, waiting for Marisol. This section of the airport was nearly empty. Even the kiosks with snacks and knick-knacks were closed, shuttered by a fortress of wire fencing. She fixed her stare on the entryway, wound tightly as she waited under the harsh, too bright lights.

Footsteps shuffled along the tile. "*¡Mi Anita!*"

"Marisol!" Annie's eyes went wide, and she knew she probably looked like a feral cat, all puffed up with the excitement of seeing someone. But she couldn't stifle her crazed relief. After a day and a half of scrambling through airports and struggling to wrap her mind around unfamiliar words and sounds and faces, the comfort of a friend sent Annie spinning into overdrive.

"I'm so glad you're here. I was starting to worry." The words spilled from Annie's mouth, crammed together and a half-octave too high. "I missed you so much! Is everything okay? When you didn't come last night, I thought—"

"Breathe, Annie." Marisol laughed. She wrapped her arms around Annie's midsection and squeezed. "Everything is fine." For a moment Annie let Marisol's musical voice ease her neuroses. "I am so happy you are here."

They parted, and Annie took in her friend's round face and sheath of long, black hair. She was even prettier than Annie remembered, but the sparkle of adventure in Marisol's eyes was unchanged. It was contagious, and for the first time since last night's fiasco, Annie began to feel excited about their plans.

"How long is this flight?"

"Maybe one hour. That will be plenty of time to tell me about your travels, yes?"

Annie squirmed. No way was she going to recount her drunken misadventures. "We'll head out for the brigade tomorrow? I'm still not sure what I'm supposed to be doing."

Marisol was quiet. She frowned at the luggage piled at Annie's feet. "You have not checked these yet?"

Annie shook her head.

"Are they all yours? Did you get the packing list?"

That packing list needs work. "They told me to take them to the gate. There wasn't a place to check them at the ticket counter." Marisol's face scrunched, and Annie knew she must have misunderstood the attendant's instructions. "What do I do?"

"It is okay. Come." Marisol stalked toward the main entrance, and Annie scrambled behind her. They rounded a corner and hung a right before hitting an intricate maze of people and luggage. She pulled her arms in close, trying to make herself smaller against the buzz of the crowd and the press of bodies invading her personal space.

Marisol weaved them in and out of the lines, muttering the same Spanish phrase again and again. Annie couldn't tell exactly what her friend said, but based on the glares she received, she imagined it was "Make way. Idiot American coming through."

Marisol pushed them both to the front of the line. Her friend's hands flailed, explaining their predicament in rushed Spanish to the dull-featured man behind the counter.

With a grunt, he motioned to Annie and then to the scale next to him. Panting from the cross-airport sprint, she used both hands to drop her largest suitcase onto the scuffed metal surface. She followed with the two smaller pieces and waited for some type of identification tag. None came, and she plastered on the brightest smile she could muster. "That's all," she said. "*No mas.*"

Marisol placed a hand on the small of Annie's back and pushed lightly. "You too."

"Me?" Her eyes darted between Marisol and the scale, trying to make sense of the instructions. When she couldn't figure out anything else to do, she stepped next to the bags.

"No." The man took one look at Annie's blank face and shook his head.

"Too heavy." A low, familiar voice came from behind her, and Annie's insides constricted until she couldn't breathe. "There is a weight limit for the small planes." Felipe stood less than a foot away, his brown eyes and dark, rumpled hair set off by the baby blue shirt he wore.

"A weight limit?" She remembered the two bags of chips she'd inhaled the night before, still half-drunk on booze and shame. *Dear God.*

"*Sí.* Do you have extra things?" Marisol asked.

"Extra things?" Frustration rolled off the people behind her, but Annie couldn't imagine getting through an entire month without everything she'd packed. She put a lot of time and effort into her packing list—it held only the most necessary items.

"Is there anything you can throw out?" Marisol asked.

The man behind the counter smoothed his thick, graying mustache, and Annie's mind spun, composing a list of her belongings and ranking them from most precious to slightly less precious.

"I can check one. I only have this." Felipe held up a small duffle bag then reached for the bag on top of her mountain of luggage.

She pulled it out of his reach. That was the bag with her underwear, and she wasn't about to risk another disaster. "Thanks." She handed him the rolling suitcase full of first-aid supplies and extra socks and prayed that would be enough.

"*Bien.*" The mustached man began pulling Annie's luggage into the mountain of bags behind the counter.

For the first time since the El Bar debacle, she forced herself to look Felipe in the eye. "Thank you."

· · ·

Felipe heaved Annie's suitcase onto the scale and tossed his duffle bag into the mix. He stepped onto the scale, sliding under the limit by two kilos. *How can anyone need so many things?*

Annie's silhouette headed toward the gate, and he followed. Her face looked the same as it had all those years ago, the upturned nose and the wide brown eyes. The same untamed red curls. But the way her body had filled out was something new; the curve of her hips and the way they swayed the slightest bit as she moved had drawn his attention from across the airport the night before.

She never tried to kiss me when we were kids. And Felipe would have remembered, because his teenage crush on Annie was so charged and full of fervor. Instead, he spent his year in the States alone in the basement of their rental house, watching old *Roseanne* reruns and trying to get a handle on the strange Midwestern accent. Meanwhile, his sister and Annie flitted in and out between houses and social extravaganzas. Marisol's classmates saw her as an exciting and extroverted freshman. He was the short senior with a weird accent.

Outside the window, their small plane waited, and his stomach threatened to revolt. The flight from Managua to his mother's house in Puerto Cabezas never failed to turn him into a wobbling, nauseated mess. Most of the time, the other passengers pretended not to notice the dark patches of sweat that bloomed beneath his underarms. But every once in a while, the tiny fourteen-passenger plane would lurch and shift just right, and no one could ignore the retching noises he made as he filled the tiny paper bag tucked into the seat pocket.

Please do not let me vomit this time.

"*Buenos días, Doctor,*" the pilot called as Felipe climbed the unsteady steps. The man didn't look up, arranging newspapers along the windshield for easy reading. It was the same pilot from the last flight. The flight when Felipe didn't quite get the bag open in time. He muttered a quick response and kept his head ducked low.

He shuffled down the narrow aisle. On both sides, the plane brimmed with people. Children sat on parents' laps, smacking and slobbering on the windows. The recycled air was chilled, and already the beginnings of motion sickness churned inside him.

"'Lipe!" Marisol called to him from the last row, gesturing

toward the spot next to Annie.

His eyes darted around for another option. *Nada.* Of the fourteen seats, thirteen were already filled. He scooted in front of Annie without meeting her eyes, and their knees collided. It sent an ugly ache through his leg, and he doubled over, practically landing in her lap. "Sorry." He scrambled for his cracked vinyl seat and pressed his forehead to the cool glass, suddenly feeling more like a bumbling adolescent than a medical professional.

Annie's ears flushed a deep red. "It's okay."

"He is not usually such a mess," Marisol said.

Felipe kept his eyes on the seat in front of him, wishing he could crawl over the other passengers and into the fresh air. "I do not like to fly."

"Is it safe?" Annie asked.

"These are Sandinista pilots. The best in the world. Our trip is like a smooth baby's bottom."

Marisol laughed as the plane's engines roared beneath their feet. "Smooth as a baby's bottom."

Felipe waved his sister off, pretending not to care about the way the plane rocked as they moved toward the runway. Inside his chest, a familiar embarrassment flickered to life.

He hated the way Americans looked at him when he butchered their language. He hated the way his job—even after years of medical school and some of the top grades in his class—depended on their donations. He hated that, within a week of setting off on one of the brigades, Americans were beaten down by the rain and the bugs and the never-ending procession of poverty. Then, they became dead weight. One more piece of equipment for him to haul in and out of the boat. Necessary liabilities.

Annie would be no different—even if he couldn't stop thinking about that almost-kiss.

The plane taxied and took off down the runway. Felipe's insides pushed against his spinal cord, and the familiar jerk of panic grabbed him. He reached for the armrest, hoping to steady himself, but Annie's arm lay there. He yanked his hand away and mumbled an apology, but not before he noticed her hands were as clammy as his own. The brief touch allowed his mind to forget the heights and the swell of nausea threatening to overtake him.

Willing to do anything to keep his mind off the flight, Felipe focused on the smattering of freckles across her bare left shoulder. For the next half hour, he counted each of them out of the corner of his eye—an entire universe's worth. Lost in the constellations, he barely noticed the lurch of the small plane.

"Look." Annie leaned over him, her eyes fixed on the window.

The objects below grew as the plane eased toward the empty field. There was no landing strip. No giant tower full of air traffic controllers guiding their way. Only a few brown, spotted cows dotted the field, barely looking up from their grazing to acknowledge the plane—as though the aircraft belonged there as much as any heifer.

"We're landing in a cow pasture?" Annie's guffaw escaped between her words. She returned to the confines of her own seat.

Felipe closed his eyes as the plane's wheels hit earth. Already her superiority was showing. "You should not use that soap," he said, ignoring the way her coconut scent reminded him of those moments at the bar when he'd nearly leaned in to kiss her. "You will attract mosquitoes."

"What?" Annie stared out at the field, and he could tell she barely registered his words.

"*Nada.*"

• • •

Annie stepped through the door of *Ahora* headquarters—a modest two-story house with white iron bars in the windows. Fans whirred in every direction, and her gaze oscillated with them, taking in every detail of the place where Marisol grew up. The front room had been converted into office space, and towers of paper fluttered in the fake breeze. On the far wall, mismatched picture frames and awards hung in long, perfect lines. A far cry from her father's office, with its plush chairs and serene elevator music being piped in over the waiting room speakers.

A bright American accent interrupted her thoughts. "I'm so glad you're here." Marisol's mother wrapped her arms around Annie's shoulders, swaddling her in the scent of patchouli. The sixty-something woman wore baggy khaki cargo pants and a flowing green top. Her laugh lines were deeper and her hair a bit grayer, but otherwise Melinda looked just as Annie remembered.

Annie squeezed back, careful to keep her arms at her sides. Sometime during the bumpy van ride from the cow pasture airport to the office, the humidity won a hard fought battle against her deodorant. "Thank you so much for letting me come along."

"Of course." Melinda turned to her son. "'Lipe, take Annie's bags to Marisol's room, *por favor.*"

With an audible exhale, he loaded himself down like a pack mule and hiked up the stairs. Marisol was at his heels, leaving Annie alone with their mother.

"Your father tells me you're headed to our old alma mater next year?"

Annie stared at the ground and shrugged. She couldn't explain the pull that Brown University's campus had on her. The looming brick buildings and all the wide-open spaces. The leaves morphing from green to canary yellow in the New England fall. The first time Annie had visited, she was ten. Her dad had bought her a red and white Bears sweatshirt at the bookstore, and she wore it every night to bed, even in the summer, until the sleeves were so tattered and small that he ordered two replacements for her birthday.

But if her MCAT scores were any indication, she wouldn't be heading to Brown. The grueling medical school entrance exam was the reason she'd ended up here, in the middle-of-nowhere Nicaragua. This trip was a desperate, last ditch attempt to pad her resume. "We'll see," she said.

"Are you also considering the schools closer to home?" The tilt of Melinda's head and the frown lines near her mouth gave away her concern.

Annie nodded, but the unspoken question—whether her

father's heart failure meant she should stay close to St. Louis—soured her stomach. His condition was nothing new. His heart had been giving out for more than ten years. But now, his panting and swollen ankles were getting worse, not better, and he needed someone to take care of him. There was no way Annie could manage that from Rhode Island.

She had already given up on Brown once. When she was seventeen, her parents went through a cantankerous divorce. Annie was unsure her father could weather the shock of being abandoned by both the women in his life in such quick succession. That fall, she shredded her Brown application and applied to the pre-med program at St. Louis University.

"I'm sure you'll get a glowing letter of recommendation when this is all said and done. And from what your father tells me, any school will be lucky to have you." Melinda's gaze flicked to the ceiling. "I have to get to this grant request. But if you're thirsty, there's a cooler of water on the counter that's safe for drinking and brushing your teeth. Marisol's room is upstairs on the left."

"Thanks." Annie wondered what else her father had told the woman. He and Melinda had been friends for ages. They'd even been in practice together for a little while. Then Melinda picked up and moved to Nicaragua, where she started *Ahora* with her life savings and a tattered visa. Somewhere along the way, she adopted Marisol and Felipe.

Annie climbed the creaking wooden stairs. Her bags lay in a heap at the top, and she dragged them behind her into Marisol's empty room. A medley of photos stuck to the walls, their corners curling in the sticky air.

She ran her fingers along the edges of each one as she took in the smiling faces. Marisol and Melinda. Marisol surrounded by a group of smiling children. Marisol and Felipe making faces at each other. Marisol getting what Annie assumed was her nursing degree. Another, blowing out the candles on her cake, while Annie stood to the left, smiling at her friend. Her fifteenth birthday. In the corner of the shot, Felipe's brooding figure watched Annie watching Marisol.

She walked to the small window, trying to forget her father's illness and medical school and Mike. Trying to ignore the nagging pull of embarrassment that plagued her every time she saw Felipe's face—even in those old photos. On the street below, a slight, stooped woman carried two chickens by the feet, letting them dangle upside down. Their wings were motionless and splayed wide.

Twenty-eight days, Annie told herself, pulling out her phone. *You can stick anything out for four weeks.* She stared at the screen, willing the arcs in the upper left corner to connect her to the world. Her world—the one with air conditioning and Internet and water you could drink straight from the tap. After another minute of searching for a signal, she gave up and powered down the useless hunk of plastic.

Annie leaned her forehead against the bars lining the window. She'd called her dad from the hotel the night before but was only able to leave a message. *What if he's sick?* The thought hit her like lightning. *What if he's sick and no one can reach me?*

She pushed the power button again.

"That will probably not work on this side of the country." Felipe stood in the doorway, shaking his head. Annie jumped at his voice and the phone spilled from her hands, clattering to the wooden floor. "I have told my mother to tell the Americans, but she always forgets. It will probably not work on the trip either. You should leave it here."

She ducked her head and crouched to pick up the phone. "Okay. Thanks."

"Do you need to call someone?"

"My dad. Do you have a phone?"

The edges of his mouth turned down, and he crinkled his forehead. Annie's throat went dry. That look of pure concentration was as horrifyingly gorgeous as his smile. "My mother has a phone she loans to the foreigners."

"Really?"

Felipe laughed, and the dimple emerged. "Come."

Downstairs, the office was empty. He pulled a long, black block with an extendable antenna from Melinda's cluttered desk. It looked like something from a NASA museum. "You must dial the country code first," he said.

Annie nodded. "Thank you." Her voice trembled, and Felipe rushed toward the front door, as if he couldn't stand being in the same space with her for one second longer.

She dialed, and a long pause filled the phone's speaker between rings.

"Yellow, London residence."

"Dad?"

Silence.

"Dad? Can you—"

"Annie!" His voice overlapped hers, and they began talking simultaneously, stopping and starting again. "Are you having a good time?" he asked. "Making a good impression?"

She turned toward the wall of crooked photos, her eyes too blurred with tears to make out any of the faces. "I don't know. I—" She sagged against the wall. "I don't think this is a good idea. I need to come home. What if something happens?"

"What's going to happen? You'll be fine."

A whimper escaped Annie's chest. "No, what if something happens to *you*? I'll be all the way over here." She waited for her plea to cross the gulf and hit her father's ear.

"Listen, Ann. I'm fine. You're not putting your dreams on hold again because your dad's getting old." His voice was a mash of sternness and warmth. The same one he had used when someone stole her bike in elementary school. When her beloved pet guinea pig died. When her appendix ruptured junior year of high school.

"You're really feeling okay? Tell me the truth. Are you remembering your meds? Weighing yourself?"

"Yes. Every day."

"I still think I should come home."

"Why?"

"The doctor, Marisol's brother, I don't think he likes me very much."

"Felipe? Why would you think that?" He coughed, and Annie's heart cracked.

"Just a feeling." She straightened, and a drop of sweat rolled down her chest. "I need a great letter of recommendation. It's dumb to spend an entire month here if I can't get it."

"Annie," he sighed, "it's *dumb* to turn down the opportunity of a lifetime."

"I think I already blew it." Static cut through their connection.

"What was that? Annie? You there?" Concern climbed her father's voice.

"I'm here." She sighed through the words.

"If you want to get into Brown, you have to stand out. Learn everything you can. Observe every procedure. Ask questions and write down all the answers. When you get home and work on your essays, you'll have it all right there in front of you. Brown'll be knocking on our door, begging for you."

"Learn everything. Write it down." She fiddled with the end of the antenna.

"Exactly. And, Annie?" She waited through the beat of silence until he spoke again. "I'm proud of you. You'll be glad you did this. I promise."

* * *

Felipe stood on the sparse front lawn, unfolding the last leg of *Ahora's* long banquet table. A giant, pale hand appeared in front of his face. "Let me give you a hand with that, bro." The voice stretched the words, running the vowels together in a way that made Felipe's brain ache.

The American poster boy looked like a life-sized replica of the Ken doll Marisol was so attached to as a kid. Some tourist had given it to her, a hand-me-down from a box of toys their own child had outgrown. When she was eleven, she took it everywhere.

"You must be Phillip." Felipe put on his most formal English.

"Did you recognize me? You must have recognized me. Even

all the way out here. The Internet age, man. The Internet age!" His hyper-white teeth glowed.

Felipe assumed his ability to understand was being impeded by the man's drawling accent. "Can you lift that side?" He pointed to the opposite end of the table.

"I got it." The blond man flipped the creaky table upright, its legs digging into the dirt, not a trace of effort in his features. "What's your name? I mean, *cómo te llamas?*"

"Felipe."

"Wow, man. Phillip and Felipe. It's like you're the Nicaraguan version of me. Have you ever been on a reality show? Because that would be too much."

"No, I do not think so." He frowned. "You are the American dentist, yes?"

"Dental student, actually. On a short hiatus," Phillip said as the third member of *Ahora's* regular crew stepped outside.

Juan was a dentist from Managua and the oldest of them, fast approaching his sixties. The years of sun and stress had etched deep wrinkles into the corners of his eyes. His thick greying mustache obscured his upper lip and some of his words. But the ones he offered today were bubbling with wry humor. "I see you have met our celebrity."

"*Sí,*" Felipe said.

"Your mother says to play nicely with the Americans." Juan's Spanish was a harsh stage whisper, and Felipe turned his gaze toward Phillip. He simply looked at them, clueless and grinning.

"What's with that guy?" Phillip asked as Juan stepped inside. "He barely said anything the entire drive here yesterday. I—" His mouth fell open. "Whoa."

Felipe followed the man's stare to the front door. Where Juan had entered the house, Marisol exited.

"Who's that? Because, damn." Phillip shook out his hand like it was on fire.

Marisol sashayed her way across the yard with Annie at her heels.

"*¡Hola!* Are you Phillip?" Marisol embraced the guy and kissed his cheek. Phillip's eyes flicked to her chest as she pressed against his upper arm. "I am Marisol, the nurse."

"It's a pleasure to meet you." He flashed his teeth, and Felipe tried not to roll his eyes as Marisol practically melted under the intensity.

"Hi, I'm Annie." She gave a quick wave but hung back, her forehead crinkled. "You look so familiar."

She knows this *guy, but when you pick her up from the airport she has no idea who you are?* Felipe's gaze landed on a handful of defiant curls that had escaped her ponytail, wild with the humidity and the wind. Last night, one had brushed his cheek as she leaned in, and he could still feel it against his skin.

"Did you see *Barnyard Boyfriend?*" Phillip cocked his chin and tilted his forehead in what Felipe recognized as a well-practiced move. "Phillip from Arkansas."

Annie's face lit up. "Yes!"

"You are a celebrity?" Marisol practically preened now, standing straighter and flipping her hair over one shoulder.

"No," Annie said.

"Kind of," Phillip added. "I was on a reality TV show last year. It was pretty popular in America. That's why I'm on a break from school. Had to take some time off for filming."

"*¿Verdad?*" Marisol asked. "What did you do? Are you a ninja?"

Felipe shook his head. His sister had been obsessed with ninjas since they were kids, and she was on a perpetual hunt for a ninja warrior to claim as her own.

"Sorry, Mari. He's not a ninja," Annie said. "They put a bunch of farmers together in a fancy barn to fight over this one girl. And the guys had to do all these different farm chores for the chance to be her boyfriend."

"Well, not exactly," Phillip said. "I mean, it was more complicated than that."

"Did you win?" Marisol asked, her eyes alight.

"No, thank God. That chick was crazy."

DAY THREE

Annie stared at the musty, frayed backpack in Marisol's hands. "This is it?" The bag was bigger than a standard school kid backpack, and a metal frame ran through its well-worn edges. A *real* backpack—the kind Annie expected to see on an unshaven man walking down the highway or on a new army recruit, fresh-faced and ready to be launched into enemy territory. Annie was neither of those things, and she needed more stuff than would fit in this contraption.

"*Sí.*" Marisol gave her a tiny smile. "I will help you."

"No!" Annie's voice rose, and she threw her hands over her mouth. "I'm sorry. I like to pack my own stuff. So I know where everything is."

Marisol sat on the bed and tucked her legs under her body. "Oh, I forgot about your anal problem." She laughed, and a dimple appeared in her left cheek. Even though Annie had seen that pixie grin hundreds of times, this was the first time she saw Felipe's smile reflected back at her.

"Mari," Annie begged, "please, *please* do not tell anyone I have an anal problem."

"But they will see, no? It is not so easy to hide these things when you are on a trip like this."

With a steadying breath, Annie explained the difference between an "anal problem" and being a teensy bit anal retentive. Marisol stared at her for a beat, then collapsed into a fit of giggles.

"Is everything okay?" Melinda appeared in the doorway, a bemused smile on her lips.

Annie nodded. "Marisol is helping me pack."

"Good." Melinda glanced at Annie's bags. "You'll have to

cut your things by at least half. But I'm sure the two of you will figure it out."

By half? Any lingering amusement shriveled inside her as Annie contemplated an entire month with less than half of her belongings. "Okay," she told Melinda, her voice stilted and cracking.

Annie started with her rolling carry-on bag, grouping the items together by function and placing each set in its own pile. She moved on to her suitcase, propping the lid against the bed as she pulled out armfuls of shirts, skirts, shorts, and underwear. Finally, she emptied her cross-shoulder bag, making a careful spread of her smallest but most valuable items. Money. Her passport. Medications. Baby wipes. Chapstick. The small photo album she put together before she left. When she finished, her belongings formed a twisted obstacle course. She stared at it, shifting a present from Mike between her palms.

The Pink Stringer—a stun gun, disguised as two flamingo-pink tampons and held together in the center by a mish-mash of buttons and wires. Just over two weeks ago, Mike had shown up at her apartment, presented her with this monstrosity of a going away present, and dumped her without explanation. As soon as the door slammed shut behind him, Annie threw the tampon gun in the garbage, but the next morning she fished it out and added it to her growing packing list. *It* is *the jungle. Safety first and all that.*

"I really think I need all of this, Mari." She stared at the piles and lines. A month was a long time, and she couldn't understand how she was supposed to fit everything into a single bag. "And my itinerary. Your mom said I would get an itinerary for the trip before we leave."

Trapped on the bed, Marisol shook her head. "You have a copy of your passport, yes?"

Annie nodded.

"Take the copy. Your real passport stays here." She gestured toward the dark blue booklet, and Annie handed it over. Marisol dangled over the edge of the mattress and pointed toward Annie's supply of sunscreen and bug spray. "You can share these things with me. And you do not need this." She grabbed Annie's homemade first aid kit—a mix of ibuprofen, neon Band-Aids, a thermometer, and alcohol wipes. "I am a nurse. Felipe is a doctor. We have many medical supplies."

Annie's hands clenched at her sides, but the oblong box took up a lot of space, so she nodded and handed it over. This went on, Marisol dictating what Annie should keep and what she should leave behind. In the end, she found room for four shirts, a pair of pants, two pairs of shorts, and a handful of underwear. She was allowed to take her own shampoo and body wash, but Marisol insisted she put some in travel-sized bottles and leave the rest behind.

"But this won't last a month," Annie insisted.

Marisol pried a king-sized bottle of shampoo from her hands. "You do not want to carry this many heavy things."

Annie squeezed her photo album, journal, and the electrified tampons into the front pocket of the pack, not giving Marisol time to object. "And this stuff? I really need it for my class." She held up a drawstring bag. Inside was a model of the female reproductive system, complete with removable ovaries. She'd begged it off of a doctor in her dad's building. The bag also held the flashcards she'd made to help her learn the proper Spanish terms for the body parts inside.

Marisol pulled the model out and stared, her mouth falling open.

"What?" Annie stuffed it into the bag. "You're a nurse. You've seen vaginas before!"

Marisol laughed. "*Mi Anita.* You are thinking too advanced for this class. You need to explain the birds and the bears to them. That you get a baby from sex, not from *Dios.*"

A prickle of anxiety rose in Annie's throat. She pushed it down, reminding herself of the hours she had spent preparing for the sex ed class. "Birds and the *bees,*" she corrected.

"Birds, bears, bees, vaginas, condoms. All of it. But we will put your plastic woman in the medical supplies, okay?"

Annie shook her head, anxiety still swarming. "I have to practice my lecture. I need it." She filled the last of her space with the model and a swimsuit. Everything else, more than half of what she originally packed, would stay in Marisol's room.

"And the itinerary?"

"What is that?"

"A schedule."

Marisol shook her head, her hair rippling around her shoulders. "Here." She pointed to her temple.

"Really? Don't you think you need—"

"It will be like this: clinic, boat, clinic, boat. Then a rest in the middle, where we will drink lots of *cervezas* and get new supplies. Then boat, clinic, boat, clinic. Until we are home."

"A rest in the middle?" This was news to Annie. "Where? For how long?" She couldn't imagine where or how they would find a place to relax in the middle of the rainforest.

"Sahsa," Marisol said. "I am so excited for you to see." She grinned and stretched across the bed, her brown legs crossed at the ankles. "It is where Felipe and I were born."

A twinge of excitement settled in Annie's stomach as she stuffed her "extra" belongings into her suitcase. Marisol's past had always fascinated her—so much drama, travel, and upheaval in such a short span of time.

Footsteps came from the hallway, the wood floor groaning with each step. Felipe ambled by the open door and down the stairs. Even though she'd been deep in a drunken haze at El Bar, Annie remembered exactly what he smelled like. The sweet citrus of the shots lingering with a hint of something spicy.

"…I think so, yes? Annie?" Marisol's voice brought Annie back to herself.

"Sure," she answered, not knowing what she was agreeing to. "Hey, why didn't you come get me at the airport?" She forced her voice into a calm, everything-is-perfectly-fine nonchalance.

Marisol sat up tall. "Felipe said he would do it. I think—"

"Mari, I was expecting *you*." Annie blinked and looked at her friend. Anger and shame burned in her voice, cutting through her detached ruse.

"I gave Felipe my phone. You made it to the hotel safely. What is wrong, *mi Anita?*" Marisol twisted the bracelet dangling from her right wrist. From a distance, it looked like an assortment of shiny red and purple beads. Up close, the diabetes alert tag was obvious.

"He really didn't tell you?"

"No. Tell me what?"

"Never mind." Annie stood and pulled the zipper closed on her suitcase, sealing off the belongings that would stay behind.

Marisol caught her arm. Her eyes narrowed to slits, but mischief oozed from her features. "Sit. Tell." She pointed at the bed.

Annie flopped onto the mattress. Her face scorched as she spilled the entire story.

It was three minutes before Marisol stopped giggling long enough to get out a response. "He probably liked it."

"He didn't. Trust me."

"He had a big crush on you before, when we lived in Missouri." Marisol bit down on the "ss" sound, making Annie's home state sound far more exotic than it was. Of course, it had been Marisol's home state too, once upon a time. During that year she had been in and out of the hospital, being trained and retrained on the use of her shiny, new insulin pump. "He probably thought his dreams were coming true."

"It was horrible. I can't even look at him."

"It is fine." Marisol patted her arm. "He has had much worse from the Americans."

"Really?" Annie stared at the ceiling. "Worse than getting drunk and mauling him in public?"

"*Sí.* In the last group, one of the American doctors told him he is not a real doctor because he did not go to medical school for enough years. The time before that, someone refused to eat anything but peanut butter."

"So?"

"Felipe is allergic to peanuts." She shook her head. "He is always trying to tell our mother she should stop with the poverty tours. But she says we need the donations."

"We're here to help. Why wouldn't he want help?"

Marisol shrugged and picked at an invisible thread on her plain green bedspread. "I thought you were here for a letter of recommendation?"

Annie looked at her hands and guilt sneaked its way up her chest. "It's complicated."

* * *

The door stood open, but Felipe knocked on the frame anyway. Annie lay sprawled across the bed, open mouthed and unmoving on top of the covers. "*Buenas*," he tried before raising his voice. "Annie? Are you awake?" He took a step into the room and called her name again.

She shot up, blinking and rubbing her eyes. "I'm awake. I'm awake." She whipped her head around the room.

"Do you know where you are?"

A fleeting moment of silence passed, and she frowned before answering. "Nicaragua?"

"*Sí.* Is everything okay? You have been asleep for a long time."

A tangled knot of curls sat on top of her head, twisting in every direction around her face. Her t-shirt rumpled up, exposing her stomach. He knew he should look away, but his eyes wouldn't budge.

"Did I miss something important?" she asked.

"Lunch. And dinner."

"Oh." Her brown eyes were still foggy with sleep. "I have some granola bars. I'll be okay."

Marisol's voice trickled in from the hallway. "'Lipe, take her to Alma's with you. She needs real food."

He rubbed his temple. "Come." He gestured toward the stairs. "There is no arguing with my sister." And even if there were, Felipe wasn't sure he could bring himself to try. Not with that sliver of Annie's skin staring back at him.

Ten minutes later, they walked along the red dirt road in silence. The thin, finger-like leaves of mango trees stirred around them, tossed by the wind wafting in from the ocean. The town was quiet at this time of day—too late for dinner, too early for parties. But Felipe knew soon it would bustle with activity as the locals and a handful of tourists took to the bars lining the main street.

Within a few minutes, he and Annie arrived at a small restaurant down the block. Felipe took a deep breath as he pulled out her chair, hoping to relax into the smell of garlic and searing hot cooking oil. It seeped from every corner of the narrow dining room. Always had.

He'd been coming here since he first moved to Puerto as a gangly ten-year-old, still acclimating to his recent adoption, still mourning his biological mother. Even then, Alma always found an extra bottle of Coca-Cola to spare, placing it in front of her sullen young neighbor in exchange for a smile. After the first year or two, the smiles came without prompting, and for a short stint as a teenager he had worked in the back of the restaurant, washing dishes and plucking the feathers from recently decapitated chickens.

Felipe stared at the painting jutting from the wall above Annie's head, a formal portrait of Daniel Ortega raising a fist in front of a fading red star. It was the first new painting to dot the walls in years. Across the table, Annie confronted the tattered paper menu, and her forehead creased as if the restaurant had fifty gourmet items instead of three semi-palatable options.

"Do you need help?" he asked.

"No, I can read Spanish better than I can speak it." Her face reddened when she finally looked at him. "I wanted to say I'm sorry about the other night. I drank too much." Her voice faded out as she stared at her hands. "I didn't recognize you. Obviously."

Felipe released a deep, unsteady breath. His eyes moved between the menu in his hands and the bow of Annie's lips. His mind jumped to that moment he'd nearly let his mouth sink into hers. "We will forget it."

She nodded.

Silence.

"What's this?" Annie pointed at a line on the menu.

"You do not want that."

"But what does it say?"

"I think you call it a guinea pork." His muscles tensed in anticipation of a tantrum. He'd been down this road with a few Americans before.

Her eyes narrowed. "Guinea pig?"

His embarrassment flared again, but he pushed it away. "Guinea pig." He watched her from the corner of his eye. Waiting.

"You're right. I don't want that." Her words lifted at the ends with muffled laughter.

He let out a breath, eager to change the subject. "Where did you learn Spanish?"

"High school. I took three classes, but I guess they weren't great. I can't understand anything." Her voice held a tinge of desperation, and Felipe understood. Even after living in a bilingual household and spending an entire year in the States, English escaped him now and again.

"By the end of the trip, you will understand more." He almost believed the words as they left his lips. Most of the Americans gave up after their first couple of days. Instead, they spoke slower and louder to the people who didn't understand.

Alma interrupted with a nod and a smile that left crinkles in every nook of her weather-worn face. He stood and hugged her.

"Who is the pretty *Americana*?" the old woman whispered against his cheek.

Felipe shook his head, suddenly aware that he'd never brought anyone but family on a visit to this place. "She is here for the brigade," he said. He kissed Alma's cheeks and placed his usual order, ignoring the questions in the woman's raised eyebrows.

They both turned to Annie, and she made an earnest attempt to order, rubbing her forehead between words. It wasn't perfect, but she managed to ask for the chicken soup.

"Good choice," he said as Alma shuffled into the kitchen.

Annie covered her face with her hands. "I can't believe how horrible I sound."

Felipe chuckled, and she slouched further in her chair. "You are trying." He reached across the table and pulled her hands away.

His voice softened as his fingers tangled with hers. "That is better than most."

Her eyes darted away from him, and Felipe dropped her hands, his throat dry. He stood and scrambled behind the counter, desperate for something to soothe his nerves. He poked his head into the dim hallway. "*Doña, dos Modelos,*" he called out as he shoved aside the smudged glass doors of the refrigerator and plucked two amber beers from inside.

Annie's eyes were wide. "Is it okay? I mean, I don't want to end up in Nicaraguan jail. Especially if it's anything like Mexican jail." She didn't touch the beer he sat in front of her.

Felipe took several long swigs of the fizzy liquid. "You have been in Mexican jail?"

Annie's cheeks pinked. "No, but you hear stuff sometimes."

"You know someone who has been in Mexican jail?"

Now her cheeks were aflame, and from a distance it would be difficult to tell where her hair ended and her face began. "No, I guess I heard about it on TV."

Felipe pushed her beer closer to her tightly laced fingers. "A joke, Annie. You will not go to jail. Mexican or Nicaraguan. The owner is a friend."

"Oh." She smiled. "Can I have a Coke instead? I don't think I can handle alcohol right now."

He grabbed a soda from the cooler and shoved the unopened bottle inside the frigid air.

"So you're a doctor now?" she asked as he returned to his seat.

"It does not take so long to become a doctor here," he told her, cutting off the inevitable questions.

"Do you like it?"

Most everyone assumed he enjoyed being a doctor. And he did. But this wasn't the job he wanted long-term, working under his mother's direction, always scraping for funding and waiting on government grants. Ever since he first applied to medical school, Felipe had pictured himself in charge of *Ahora*. He wanted to turn their small, family-run practice into the most renowned rural medicine organization in the Western Hemisphere. He wanted to sit on advisory boards, directing funding and resources to the right places. He wanted to make *Ahora* self-sufficient, scrapping the need for American donations and their many attached strings. But his mother refused to turn over the reins to him, insisting he needed more experience and a public health degree to qualify for the job. And after the last brigade, she'd threatened to shut him out altogether if he couldn't find a way to make peace with the poverty tourists and their crazy demands.

The beer hadn't loosened his lips enough to give voice to his dreams. "It has good moments and bad. More good." He took another long swallow as their food arrived. "How do you feel about *monos?*"

"Monkeys?" Annie held her spoon halfway to her lips, and gold broth dribbled from the edges. "I don't think I want to eat one," she said.

He turned and jogged to the back, returning with a new distraction—a small, furry guest on a leash. The monkey sat in the chair between them, its face turned toward Annie.

She looked between Felipe and the animal with wide eyes. "What's his name?" she asked. "Is he friendly?"

"Don Juan, and he is very friendly. Probably too friendly." He held out a finger, and Don Juan grabbed on, offering a formal monkey handshake. Annie let out a full, throaty laugh that made Felipe's pulse throb, and held her own finger out to the monkey. He shook it gingerly, then swiped a carrot right out of her bowl.

Broth splashed everywhere, leaving a slosh of yellow across her shirt. A tense moment of silence crept by, but then Annie's face flashed from shock to laughter. She pulled the last vegetables out of her bowl and offered them to the monkey. The furry beast gobbled the offering down in two bites and climbed straight into her lap, as if the two of them owned the place.

Felipe leaned back in his chair and laughed. "Last year, *Doña* Alma took him from some kids across the street. They were tormenting him."

"Oh, you poor baby," she cooed, stroking the animal's head.

"Did they hurt you?"

"He had a broken leg. We set it," he said. "But please do not tell my mother. She will be angry if she knows I used supplies on a *mono*."

Annie looked up from the monkey and smiled. "Our secret."

. . .

As they exited the tiny restaurant, Annie didn't feel the acute, empty pang of homesickness. She felt more relaxed than she had in days, maybe even weeks. For the first time since stepping off the plane, she thought she might actually survive this. Might actually enjoy this.

Under the glow of a single dull street lamp, they walked toward *Ahora*, the ocean crashing against rocks in the distance. Muffled voices drifted from the barred windows of the buildings lining the street, and Annie squinted, trying to understand the rolling, rapid Spanish.

"Thanks for dinner." She stole glances at Felipe's outline as she fell into step beside him.

"*De nada.*"

One house away from *Ahora*, the bellows of a heavy-lidded, gape-mouthed man broke the sound of the waves. "AMERICA!" He bumbled toward them like a zombie on steroids. "I LOVE WHITE WOMEN!"

Annie froze, then continued walking straight ahead. She wouldn't acknowledge him. Travel tips like this were listed in the yellow booklet they gave her at the student health center—on one of her five vaccination visits.

Felipe pulled her close and yanked them both onto the front stoop. His hand paused against her shoulder as the man stumbled on past them "I am sorry. He was…"

Under the dim porch light, she could see him searching for the right English word. A hint of his warm, spicy cologne drifted in the air. "*¿Borracho?*" she asked.

"Ah! Your Spanish is already getting better." He smiled, and

Annie's heart ended up somewhere between her tonsils and her collarbone. His fingers slid to her elbow, lingering there.

The thudding in Annie's ears made her own words seem far away. "I learned that one the other night." She looked at her flip-flopped feet then at him. He still smiled at her, and her body moved forward another inch.

"Annie!" Phillip's voice popped the bubble around them as the door opened wide. "I'm so glad you're back. I was going to give you the inside scoop on next season's *Barnyard*."

DAY FOUR

Every time Felipe closed his eyes, the American man made another observation about their surroundings. By observation number three, he had no trouble understanding Phillip's loose accent, with its long vowels and the extra r's inserted into his words.

"Isn't this the rainy season?"

"*Sí.*"

"It hasn't rained at all since I've been here."

"It will." Felipe closed his eyes again, his limbs numb from the constant vibration of the truck bed. He never rode inside the cab—the bumps and curves of the dirt road combined with the recycled air inside turned his stomach to churning lead. Today, the nausea of the cab was beginning to seem like a viable alternative to Phillip's company.

"What will we do with the supplies if it rains?"

"When it rains."

"Okay, but what do we do? My equipment can't get wet."

Felipe opened one eye. Only a shred of blue showed through the green ceiling of leaves. This time of year, spoonfuls of water pouring from the sky were usually the first sign of rain. "The packs are waterproof."

"Oh."

They hit a dip in the road, and Felipe's body left the ridged bed. He came down hard on his tailbone and thumped on the window in protest.

The glass slid open, and Marisol's head poked out. "What?"

"Remind Juan there are people back here, *por favor.*"

She rolled her eyes and closed the window, disappearing behind the mud-speckled glass.

"She's a fox. She always go on these trips with you, bro? I wish—" Felipe's glare cut him off. "Uh, sorry, man. Is that your girl? 'Cause, nicely done. Nicely done."

"Marisol is my sister."

"Really? You don't look anything alike."

Felipe closed his eyes again.

"So, is she single?"

He shrugged. Marisol had a string of admirers lined up in Managua, and she moved from one to the next without much fanfare. Occasionally, she brought someone to the house they shared, but Felipe never saw the same guy twice. He didn't ask. Some things were better left in the dark. Like his sister's sex life. It belonged in the deep, unable-to-see-a-hand-in-front-of-your-face kind of dark.

"Maybe she can nurse *me* back to health."

Felipe kept his eyes closed. "Are you sick?"

"No, man. It's like this thing in America. Sexy nurses are like a *thing.*"

Felipe knew all about sexy nurses. The last was a willowy one named Slema. Things had fizzled out between them after a few dates, and they pretended not to know each other during the workday. It was awkward, but soon Felipe left for this brigade. Conveniently, he was always on the cusp of leaving for a brigade.

When he returned, there would be a new crop of nurses at the *Ahora* clinic. They never stayed long, lured away by the promise of more money at the private hospitals. His clinic offered little in the way of money and a lot in the way of uncertainty and burn-out— one of the many things he wanted to change.

"Uh, oh," Phillip said.

This got him to open an eye. A few dark spots dotted Phillip's shoulders. A single drop hit Felipe's face. Another his arm. The giant drops of a midday flash storm. Short, but bone-soaking.

He pulled two thin, clear plastic ponchos from one of the many bags between them. "Here." He tossed one to Phillip as the truck continued on, bumping and jerking across the uneven road.

"I've got it." The American tossed it back and dug in his own backpack.

Felipe shrugged and pulled his head through the hole of his poncho as the drops grew heavier. When he looked up again, Phillip was covered from head to toe in thick, fluorescent yellow plastic. He'd even tugged on a pair of matching knee-high boots, transforming himself into a waterproof, human plantain.

• • •

Annie's eyes popped open, shocked into consciousness by the echoes of a slamming door. She sat alone in the unmoving truck, the glorious air conditioning long gone. Outside, rain came down, turning the world hazy and unfinished. She ran a hand along one cheek, checking for the telltale signs of drool, when a flash of yellow appeared at the driver's side. She crawled across the sticky bench seat, narrowly avoiding the gear shift, and cracked the window.

"We're stuck." Phillip's voice was nearly smothered by the pounding rain. He pushed a folded rectangle of plastic through the window. "You have to get out."

"What? Why?" Annie stared at the plastic—a clear poncho, the kind you bought at the dollar store. The ones that barely kept you dry in a light drizzle.

"Less weight. Juan's going to drive, and Felipe and I will push us out."

Annie turned the handle until the window closed, then pulled the rumpled plastic over her head. Through the foggy passenger side glass, the others waited under an overhang of trees, each covered in a layer of protective plastic.

She scooted to her side of the cab. The numbers and letters on the gear shift were smudged and worn, probably from years of use. It was the only part of the truck's interior that wasn't immaculate. The pebble gray dash shined, dust free. Freshly vacuumed mats spread across the floor, and there wasn't a single piece of trash to be found. It was a far cry from Annie's car. No matter how often she cleaned, she always found at least two stray French fries stuffed in between the seats.

Phillip pounded on the driver's side, waving at her through the drops streaking the window. "Okay, okay. I'm coming," she muttered, not bothering to roll the window down again. With a deep breath, she straightened her poncho and flung open the passenger door.

Warm water pelted her body through the thin plastic, and the sound of rain smacking the earth rose up, deafening her. She swung her right leg out of the truck, ready to sprint toward the rest of the group. But her foot disappeared into a pool of cold muck, and the mud kept climbing, sucking her further into the pit. She slipped and slid along the edge of the vehicle as the rain pelted her eyes and cheeks.

After a solid thirty seconds of cursing and tugging and sliding deeper into the sludge, Annie managed to steady herself, but the weight of the mud and the strange angle of her body kept her stuck—half in, half out of the truck and floundering in the raging monsoon. From across the mud pit, the others shouted at her, but she couldn't understand them over the drumming of the rain and the thudding of her own heart.

With a grunt, she yanked her leg upward, using the handle of the truck for leverage. The brown goop gave a little, and her foot came loose. With a second pull, it dangled free. The rain slowed, leaving her hanging from the open door. She stood perched on the doorframe, afraid to go inside. Afraid to coat the pristine truck interior with the thick, red-brown goop.

"I tried to tell you to come out the driver's side," Phillip said. He stood at the edge of the mud hole, arms outstretched. "Jump. I'll catch you. On *Barnyard Boyfriend* I won the bale toss. You know. You saw that episode, right?" He winked as he said it, and the memory of the episode flashed through her mind. Phillip caught twenty bales of hay in the span of thirty seconds, and when his potential girlfriend jumped from the loft, he caught her too.

Beyond him, the others stayed in their line, watching in silence. Juan stared past her to the inside of his truck, and his expression became more pained with each glob of mud that fell from her clothes. *Here goes nothing.*

She leapt, pushing herself off the ledge with every bit of force she could gather. It was only after both feet left the safety of the truck that Annie realized she hadn't told Phillip she was about to jump. His hands slid past her waist as her chest slammed into his. She ricocheted off his body and flopped onto her back in the mud. His banana jacket covered her eyes and mouth as he fell on top of her, and his weight pushed her deeper into the slop.

I'm going to drown in a mud hole in Nicaragua.

Annie flailed her arms, searching for something solid. Fingers grabbed her slimy wrist, and Phillip rolled off her. Through mud-soaked eyelashes, she saw a shock of short, dark hair. She reached her other hand out; Felipe wrapped his fingers around her wrist and pulled.

"Are you okay?" He stood in the overgrown puddle, mud climbing to his mid-calves.

Annie started to say yes, or maybe no, but the taste of dirt filled her mouth. She shrugged.

"I am going to pull and you stand, yes?"

She nodded then clasped her fingers around his forearms. He yanked, and she stumbled straight into his chest. "Sorry." She gripped the front of his poncho for balance and glanced up to find her lips an inch from his.

"It is okay." He put a hand on her low back, grazing the bare skin exposed by her tangled, muddy mess of a shirt.

To her left, Phillip struggled like a turtle on its back. "Guys? I think I need some help over here."

Marisol waded into the pit after him, and Annie bit back her laughter. "Is this really happening?"

"*Sí.* Now, push through the mud," Felipe said. "Do not lift your feet. Like this." He let go of her and shuffled one hand against the other.

It worked. Annie scooted the two feet, and he pulled her onto solid ground. Her clothes and hair hung heavy with mud, and the chaos left her poncho shredded.

Felipe smiled and pulled at a tattered edge of the plastic. "You are trouble, *Americana*." Even in her mud-soaked state, she couldn't resist grinning at him.

"You ride here now, yes?" Juan scooted between them and patted the truck bed. He marched to the driver's side without waiting for her response.

"What?" Annie looked to Felipe for translation.

"Juan keeps the truck very clean." He scraped the mud from his pants. "It is his obsession. Now you will have to ride with me."

Annie's stomach curled in on itself. Growing up in the Midwest, she'd heard enough horror stories about people being thrown from the beds of pickup trucks to last two lifetimes. Maybe three. She knew she should protest and insist on riding somewhere with a seatbelt, but as she watched Felipe shove the truck out of the mud, a hint of his triceps peeked out from the sleeves of his shirt, and she forgot all her concerns.

"We will go slowly." Felipe pulled the latch on the gate and held out his hand. She took it, and he launched her into the damp truck bed. Mud squished between her toes, but when he sat beside her, Annie nearly forgot about the missing seatbelt and her inadvertent mud bath. With every bump in the road, the truck heaved, and Felipe's shoulder pressed into hers. Her mind refused to focus on anything else.

* * *

As they approached the village, the spiked pochote trees thinned enough for Felipe to make out the shapes of houses along the riverbank, gnarled and leggy on their stilts. The sun reflected off metal roofs, and mud dried in a thick crust over his blue scrub pants. Annie sat next to him, slowly morphing into a mummified version of herself. Her hair was a clumpy, brown mat on her head, and she pulled hunks of caked, drying mud from her shirt. Phillip was in better shape. His banana suit offered some protection, and his clothes were only brown at the edges.

The three of them rode in choppy silence for the final leg of the drive, and each time they hit a bump Felipe's mind wandered to a new question. *Bump.* How many people would show up for the clinic? *Bump.* How many would it take to convince his mother he was ready to run *Ahora*? *Bump.* Would they have enough supplies? *Bump.* Why was he still thinking about the way Annie had looked up at him on the porch the night before? By the time they rolled to a stop in the makeshift town square, his head was overflowing.

At least thirty people waited. Some were familiar. Many were strangers. Some would have been waiting for days by the time *Ahora* arrived. Others would have walked miles with children on their backs and at their sides. The rest would have popped out of their houses and down the well-worn path to the one-room church where the clinic would take place.

"*¡Buenas!*" Felipe threaded his arms through his backpack and hopped from the truck. He stood taller as the villagers returned his greeting, grinning at him like he was a dear friend.

"A good turnout, no?" Marisol asked.

"*Muy,*" he said. "I will count them. *Madre* will want to know." Getting the people in this miniscule town to trust *Ahora* had taken Melinda years. And in the short time since he'd taken over the brigades, the turnout had doubled. *Maybe this will convince her you are ready.*

Two teenage boys escorted Annie from the truck, and Phillip hopped out behind her. A few curious stares flickered their way. This group was used to seeing the stray Americans *Ahora* towed along, but most weren't encased in mud.

"The clinic is in the church. First we see the children. Women and men second," Felipe told the Americans, handing out backpacks and bags of medical supplies.

A needle-thin man with a patchy black beard led their group to the church. Wide slats of wood formed the walls, and strips of electric blue paint peeled away from the exterior, revealing a rotting gray. The two teen boys followed closely behind, toting bags of medical supplies between them.

Inside the musty building, Felipe took a bag from the boys and set it on the first of the three pews. "Annie, you will do the mosquito nets this time."

"What about the sex ed class?" she asked.

"Yes, she brought a plastic vagina," Marisol said.

"What?" Felipe squeezed his eyes shut. "Never mind. You will do the classes after Sahsa. Those are the villages for sexual education. These are not ready. The people need more time. Marisol did not tell you?"

"No," his sister answered. "I thought you would maybe have a change of mind."

Of course she did. Marisol was always pushing, pushing, pushing.

"So what am I supposed to do instead?" Annie slouched into the pew next to the teenage helpers as Marsiol slipped away.

"Every child should take home a mosquito net." Felipe opened the black garbage bag at Annie's feet to show her the fine, baby blue netting inside.

"Okay." She gave him a half-hearted smile and picked at a clump of dirt clinging to her shirt. "But I'll still get to do the class?"

He nodded. "After the rest days. First, you need time to see how the clinics work. Do you know how to ask how old someone is in Spanish?"

"*¿Quantos años tienes?*"

"Good. If they are over eighteen, no net. We do not have enough for adults."

She nodded.

"*Bien.*"

The afternoon was flooded with the tears of babies being vaccinated, the ailments of the elderly, and even a few serious injuries. One man's pinky finger dangled at on odd angle, creating an awkward, constant wave. Felipe splinted it and gave him a shot of steroids while the man told him about his two-day hike to the clinic.

His patient disappeared into the crowd, and Felipe walked a lap around the room, checking in on Juan and Phillip as they cleaned teeth, then on his sister as she stuck needles into the thick thighs of infants. When he arrived at Annie's table full of mosquito nets, a group of children hovered to her left, their cheeks and bare feet smudged with dirt.

"Everything is okay?" he asked.

"Sure. Just not sure what to do now. Everyone got a net."

"Put the extras away and come to the exam area. You can observe, yes?"

"Really?" She scrambled to shove the nets into the bag.

Felipe ignored the flicker of hesitation sparking inside his chest and handed her the last of the nets. So far, Annie hadn't complained about travel conditions or made jokes under her breath about the dozens of unsupervised children running through the clinic space. But it was early still. "Come."

A girl of about fifteen waited in silence. Her feet scratched at the floor, leaving patterns and lines in the dirt. Her eyes were glassy with fear, and she didn't wait for him to ask any of his usual exam questions. "I think I am pregnant," she said in a swift mix of Spanish and indigenous Miskito.

He nodded, careful to keep his expression blank. "Why do you think you are pregnant?"

The girl pulled in her lips and shook her head. Felipe wasn't sure if she was afraid to tell him or if she truly didn't know. Neither option would surprise him. *There is one way to find out.* He handed her a cup and pointed her in the direction of the outhouse.

Annie nudged him with her elbow, the scratch of her pen audible even through the chaos of the clinic. "So what's going on?"

"She thinks she is pregnant."

"Oh." She glanced at him for half a second, eyes wide, then went back to writing. "She's young."

He nodded. "What are you doing?"

"Taking notes."

"And you are writing about what a good doctor I am, yes?"

Her cheeks turned pink, and when their patient returned, he had to push the smile from his face.

The three of them waited in silence, staring at the white stick bobbing in the cup of urine. *Negative.* The girl flopped back on the pew, as if the news left her muscles unable to hold tension. Felipe peered around the exam curtain. Almost everyone from the village was gone, so he slipped his patient a sleeve of condoms. She stuffed them in her pocket and darted off with a muffled thanks.

"What are you doing? You said we couldn't—"

He laid a hand on Annie's forearm. "Secret."

She nodded and gave him a small smile. "Seems like I'm keeping a lot of your secrets lately."

"Now you owe me a secret." He began stuffing his supplies into the nearest duffle bag.

"I owe you?"

"*Sí.* You know two of my secrets, and I know zero of yours."

She tapped on her bottom lip with one finger and rolled her eyes to the ceiling. "Okay." She handed him a plastic bag full of tongue depressors. "When I was five, I had an imaginary friend. Her name was Brandy."

"Everyone had an imaginary friend as a child. I do not think this counts as a true secret."

"Yeah, but Brandy was mean. And we fought *all* the time. My dad even banned her from the house once because she made me cry."

He raised an eyebrow. "You were a disturbed child, I think."

"I know, right?"

The two teen boys from the morning reappeared in the doorway. They called out to Annie and waved their hands high above their heads, trying to grab her attention.

"I think you have some admirers." Felipe nodded at the boys. "Maybe they want to talk to you?"

"I do not think they are calling *me* the beautiful *gringa*."

"Oh." Her eyes widened. "They're harmless, right?"

"*Sí.* But do not break their hearts."

Her laughter trailed behind her as she wandered over to the boys and slid out the door behind them.

Once he finished securing his supplies, Felipe stepped outside. The bright afternoon sun stretched into early evening, and his stomach rumbled for dinner. In the church lawn, he expected to find a single villager with a kettle of rice and beans for the group to share. Instead, a horde of children surrounded Annie. To her left, the rest of his group watched, passing a black pot around the circle and ladling their plates high with food.

His stomach growled again, but he stood under the last rays of daylight and watched her fold sheet after sheet of notebook paper into miniature diamonds.

"What do you call this thing?" he asked, cutting through the crowd.

She shrugged. "A fortune teller, I guess. Want to try?"

"Okay." He took the paper. "How do I make this fortune teller?"

"Watch." Her fingers moved in an intricate dance, tearing off a strip from the bottom and folding the remaining square into points. Children buzzed around them, tugging on her and stumbling into one another, but Annie's movements stayed smooth and steady.

Felipe tried to mimic them, but his fortune teller came out crumpled and torn at the edges. One side lay flat, while the other was deeply bowed. "I do not think mine will tell fortunes."

She took one look at his disfigured paper and grinned. "It takes practice. The next one will be better."

At their feet, a small girl toddled in the dirt, naked from the waist down. Her tiny upturned nose was a smidge too small for her face, and her thin, dark hair stood on end. Annie finished another paper contraption, and three more sheets of paper appeared.

"Okay, watch." She handed him one of the pages and began folding again. He tried to focus on her technique instead of the way the beads of sweat collected at her hairline or the way she pulled in her bottom lip as she worked. He was so lost in her nearness and the folding that he didn't connect the resounding escape of gas with the tiny, half-naked girl in front of them. The children screamed and jumped back as the girl left an enormous pile of poop in front of Annie's flip-flopped feet.

"Oh my god." She drew a hand over her nose and mouth, stumbling into him. "Is there something we should do?"

Before he could respond, there was an awful squealing, accompanied by the squish of hooves on the damp ground. Round balls of pink, splashed with brown and white, charged toward them. Felipe wrapped his arms around Annie's waist and yanked her out of the pigs' trajectory. The swine shoved and snarled at one another as they cleaned up the mess.

"Bacon is never going to be good again." She laughed and twisted to face him.

Felipe stared at her lips, momentarily wishing he knew how they'd feel against his. "Come." He clasped her hand. "I want to see Phillip's face when you tell him about the pigs. I think nothing like this happened on his American television show."

A surge traveled up his fingers as she squeezed his hand. "Definitely not."

DAY FIVE

Before she climbed into the boat, Annie downed two Dramamine and said a small prayer for steady waters. Last year, on a spring break trip to Cancun, she and her roommates took an excursion that involved a small boat, choppy ocean waves, and a bottle of tequila. Annie's breakfast came up before they stopped at the first snorkeling location, and she spent the rest of the afternoon on the floor of the boat, hoping for death.

But today it seemed that her prayers were working. The group's first boat ride was smooth and slow, and the breeze was cool enough to feel like air conditioning.

The siblings shot Spanish back and forth over her head, too quick for Annie to catch more than one word every few seconds. She stared out over the riverbank as the drum of the engine filled her ears. In some areas, the stream narrowed, leaving barely enough space for their boat to make its way through. Branches, leaves, and vines stretched from one bank to the other, creating a dense tunnel that blocked most of the sun's rays. The darkness was cool and quiet, and it made her eyelids heavy.

"*¿Dónde quieres ir a la escuela de medicina?*"

"What?" Annie squinted and turned toward her friend.

"Where do you want to go to medical school?" Marisol asked.

She shrugged as if it didn't matter, but her heart tore in half with the weight of how much it mattered. "Brown. But I'm keeping my options open." There were other schools on her list, but Brown had been *the one* for so many years, she didn't know how to seriously consider someplace else.

"I am also keeping my options open." Marisol giggled and

nodded toward Phillip as their boat left the tunnel. He sat alone at the tip of the boat, squinting like a mole. Every so often he would turn and smile at them, pointing at something along the shore. It was impossible to hear him over the din of the motor, but Annie and Marisol nodded and pretended to understand. Felipe stayed silent.

"What is he saying?" Annie whispered.

"Who cares? Look at him."

Annie laughed. "Why do I feel like you've done this before?"

"Done what before?"

"Seduced one of the American guys who come through here."

"Also one Spanish." Marisol's grin was contagious. "He is cute, no?"

"Sure."

They fell silent. Marisol drifted off into her own world, which apparently involved undressing Phillip with her eyes. Annie stared out at the trees. The sun scorched her cheeks and the part in her hair as she searched for signs of wildlife.

"What are you looking for?" Felipe asked.

"Monkeys." She smiled, keeping her eyes on the greenery. "Or sloths. Pretty much anything cute and furry that doesn't want to eat me."

"So you like the rainforest?" he asked.

"Yeah. I don't really have anything to compare it to, though. Before this I'd never even been camping."

"What do you mean?"

"Camping. Like sleeping outside and stuff. This is my first time."

"¿*Verdad?*" He wrinkled his forehead.

"*Verdad.*" She paused. "Okay, *no verdad*. Once I went to Girl Scout Camp. I was eight. We slept in cabins though, not outside. So I don't think that counts."

"Girl Scouts? The ones with the cookies?"

"Yes! In fact," she sat up tall, "I sold the most cookies in my troop every year."

"How many years was that?"

"One."

He grinned. "Why one? If you were the top seller."

"My dad said I could only do one after-school activity at a time. The next year I wanted violin lessons."

"You play the violin?"

She shook her head. "I was horrible. After the first round of lessons, the teacher sent me home with a note that he couldn't keep taking my dad's money."

"*Pobrecita.*" His full bottom lip stuck out. Felipe's face cracked into that full, spectacular smile. Her stomach leapt.

"Do you still play the guitar?" She remembered the times she and Marisol had sneaked into his basement lair, searching for the phone or food. A beautiful acoustic guitar rested along his wall, and even though Annie never saw him play it, his smooth voice came up through the vents of the house.

"*Sí.*" His smile grew even wider as they made their way through another darkened tunnel.

That dimple.

* * *

Those freckles.

The three pinpricks of brown dancing across the bridge of Annie's nose begged for his attention. But the boat motored into another tunnel, and the freckles disappeared into the darkness.

"We need to work on your Spanish," he said. Even in the cool dimness, he saw the smile slide off her face.

"I know."

"You can speak it if you try." The words didn't sound as encouraging out in the world as they did inside his head. He grimaced. "That is not what I mean."

"I do try. It's not easy."

"I know. It is hard, but you are smart."

"When it comes to dissecting frogs, sure. When it comes to Spanish, no way."

"What words do you know?"

"I don't know."

"You do not know what words you know?" He regretted the question as soon as it came out.

She sighed.

"We must fix this." The darkness of the tunnel made him brave, and he laced her fingers through his. "I will say something in English and you say it to me in Spanish, yes?"

Annie glanced over her shoulder at Marisol, who had her face deep in a book. His sister smiled at the page, and Felipe knew she wasn't reading. There wasn't enough light. And no one smiled that wide while reading *To Kill a Mockingbird*.

"Okay," Annie said.

"Hello."

"*Hola.*" Her smile escaped at the tail end of the word.

"My name is Annie."

"*Me llamo Annie.*"

"You can also say *mi nombre es Annie.*"

She repeated the phrase, her lips turning deliberately around the strange words. He blinked hard and fast.

"Where is the bathroom?"

"*¿Dónde es el baño?*"

He shook his head. "*Está.* But in an emergency, that is okay."

"*¿Dónde está el baño?*" Her accent made the words sharp, but they were understandable.

"Now you are prepared for anything. I am a master teacher."

She pulled her hand away and tugged her hair into a rumpled ponytail as they emerged, blinking, into the sun. "Hardly."

"I think you know more than you are letting on."

"It's the verb tenses." She shook her head. "I can't keep them straight. Sometimes I think I'm saying 'I went to the store,' but I end up saying 'I wanted to have been at the store.' And then everyone looks at me like this." She cocked her head toward her shoulder, her lips puckered together.

"There are no stores here. I think you will be okay."

"That's not what—"

"*Broma, Annie. Broma.*"

She shook her head.

"Joke," he told her. "You are learning. Use present tense for everything. People will understand."

"But I'll sound stupid. Like a tourist."

"Everyone knows you are a tourist." Red hair running wild in the wind. Pale skin pinking and sprouting freckles in the sun. "It is okay."

She stared out at the shore then turned. "Okay. Teach me more words, and I will teach you to tell better jokes."

"What is wrong with my jokes?"

"Nothing. They're perfect."

He pressed one finger to her forearm. The light pressure made her sun-seared skin go white. "Sunburn," he said.

"No clue."

"*Quemada.*"

"I guess I shouldn't plan on going home with a great tan."

"I do not think so." She smiled, and he gave her a new word. "Freckles."

DAY SIX

The first time Annie went skinny dipping she was seventeen, full of teenage bravado and Natty Lite. The second time, she was with Mike one late night at the pool attached to her apartment complex. She didn't know if today counted or not, but in the interest of making her life seem more exciting than it really was, she decided yes. Definitely yes.

She also decided that later, when she told the story of her not-so-sexy skinny dipping trip in a foreign country, she would leave out the part about scrubbing her clothes with pruney fingers in the brown river and scanning the water for the telltale ripples of a snake in their midst.

She laid her now cleanish shirt on a sunny boulder and squirted a handful of shampoo into her palm. Beside her, Marisol leaned against the chain of rocks separating their side of the river from the men. Annie tried to work the lather through the tangles and crusted mud in her hair, but she stumbled on a submerged rock and floundered forward, catching her balance a second before she belly-flopped into the river.

"Shhh. Come here." Marisol's voice was low. She jerked her head toward the rocks.

"What are you doing?" Annie trudged through the water and squatted next to her friend.

Marisol shushed her again as she peered around the edge of the rock wall and pointed. "I want to know what I am working with."

Phillip stood on the other side of boulders. His back faced the girls, and he held a florescent blue bar of soap in one hand. He kept lifting his arms, sniffing his pits, then scrubbing them with the soap. He fit the pattern of all-American boy perfectly. Blond hair and tanned skin, perpetually bulging biceps. It was all there. *Except the sniffing his pits part.* If Marisol could look past that, he'd make the perfect summer fling.

Just like Mike. For a beat, Annie's heart threatened to crumple, thinking of her ex and whatever summer fling he might be having. But as quickly as the feeling came, it was gone, replaced by images of Mike and Phillip competing against each other *Barnyard Boyfriend* style. Obviously there would be an armpit sniffing competition. Perhaps a fake bedhead styling event. *Maybe I'm getting over this breakup after all. Or I'm totally losing it.*

Annie wagged a finger at her friend. "What if you see your brother instead? Or Juan?"

Marisol's dark hair dripped down her back, and suds clung to the crook of her ear. "I have seen them all before. You cannot go on these trips without seeing someone naked. Besides," she grinned, "don't you want to see my brother naked?"

Annie tried to deny it, but the words caught in her throat. Heat inched up her neck and settled into the tips of her ears.

Marisol shook her head. "You think I do not see the way you turn to a ball of kitten fur when my brother looks at you?"

"Kitten fur?"

"Yes, all soft and a little bit strange."

"Kitten fur isn't strange. What are you talking about?"

Marisol ignored her. "And you think I do not see the way he stares at you all the time when you are not looking? If you are not looking at him, he is looking at you, *amiga.*"

"It's just flirting, Mari," Annie said, as a streak of shampoo slid down her forehead.

Marisol waggled her eyebrows. "Think of me like the Cupid of Nicaragua."

"What? No."

"Why no? You like him. He has been waiting for years for you to like him. I saw you in the boat yesterday." Marisol crossed her arms against her chest.

Annie flushed at the memory of his warm fingers wound between hers. "What's the point? I'll be gone in a few weeks anyway." As she said the words, the weight of their truth pressed harder against her chest. "Besides, it's like my IQ drops ten points every time he looks at me."

"I do not understand."

Annie sighed and ducked to rinse the shampoo from her hair. "I keep saying stupid stuff. Doing stupid stuff. And our lives are so different. He's out here in the middle of the jungle saving people while I'm going to sorority formals. It makes me feel so..." she swallowed hard, searching for the right word. "So insignificant, you know?"

"Leave it all to me. A girl has got the needs, no?"

Annie smiled despite herself. "Well, yes."

Marisol tugged her arm, pulling her to the edge of the rocks. "Here comes Juan. *Un hombre grande*, if you know what I mean."

Annie stared for a moment, trying to string the Spanish together. But when Marisol ducked her chin and held her index fingers two feet apart, it all came together. She threw her hands over her mouth, droplets of river water hitting her lips. "He's old."

"Shhh!" Marisol shoved her forward. "Here."

She braced herself for the train wreck, but Juan was nowhere in sight. Felipe stood underwater to his hips, and the perfection of his brown skin drove all thoughts of Juan and sorority formals straight from her mind. His shoulders rippled as he rubbed shampoo through his dark hair and lathered up his face to shave, and her eyes followed the trail of white suds down his sinewy back to the curve of his ass, barely submerged in the river. *I'm a total creeper.* But she didn't look away, thinking about tracing that line of soap with her fingertips.

"Did you see Juan yet?"

Annie took a deep breath and turned, praying her expression didn't give away the extent of her dirty thoughts. Marisol held her hands an unfathomable distance apart.

She shuddered. "God, no."

• • •

Felipe lay on his hammock with a book in his hand. The coarse fabric scratched the backs of his legs, and his brain refused to comprehend the words in front of him. His gaze strayed across the cramped church, following the line of wet clothes dripping onto the dirt floor. At the end, Annie sat on a purple mat, scribbling in her journal.

"You did not bring a hammock," he said. "Why?"

"Momentary insanity, I guess. I didn't think I would be able to sleep in one." She kept writing, her hand moving faster with every passing second.

"Do you want to sleep in my hammock?" he asked.

She jerked her head up, eyebrows raised to her hairline. "What?"

"Not with me, I mean." He fumbled for words. "I can sleep on your purple thing."

"Really?"

"*Sí.*"

"But the yoga mat is kind of horrible." She scrunched her nose. "That wouldn't be fair."

"I will live."

"How about we switch back and forth? Then I won't feel as bad."

Near the center of the room, Marisol stood and pulled a sandwich bag of cards from a backpack. "UNO!" She threw the cards at him, knocking the book from his hands.

"*No, gracias.*" Felipe tossed them back.

His sister rolled her eyes. "Annie? You still love UNO, *sí?*"

Annie looked up from her journal. "Sure."

"So you will play, yes?"

Her gaze flicked to Felipe, and her wide, round eyes locked on his. "Maybe another time."

"Annie Sue, it will be like the olden times."

Felipe corrected her. "Old days."

"Maybe tomorrow, Mari." Annie returned to writing.

Marisol put a hand on her hip. "You cannot even spare a few minutes for your oldest, dearest friends? Even though 'Lipe brought this UNO game along just for you?"

"Mari—" His face warmed.

"Look what I found." Marisol lowered her voice in a horrid impression of her brother. "Remember how Annie was so good at UNO?"

"You brought it?" Annie's eyes shifted from the journal to Felipe.

"*Sí.*"

"I will deal." Marisol smirked and skipped outside, leaving him alone with Annie.

She uncrossed her legs and stood, tucking the journal into the front pocket of her pack. "Remember how you always tried to cheat?"

"I did not." He had. Every game.

"Doesn't matter. You never won." Her lips broke into a small smile. "Except once. But your mom told me and Marisol to let you win."

"That did not happen." Felipe stood and brushed a wet curl from her face, letting his finger trace the outline of her cheekbone. The distance between their lips was so tiny, and his desperation to kiss her grew stronger every time her warm breath hit his skin.

"It did," she insisted. "She said it was…" Her face fell.

"Said it was what?"

She shook her head. "I don't remember. It doesn't matter." Her lips lifted, but the smile was stiff and forced.

At once it hit him. He remembered that game—literally the only time he ever won. It happened on the tenth anniversary of his biological mother's death. He knew Melinda had arranged that win. She always took extra care with him on those days. The birthdays and anniversaries. Marisol's grief passed quietly, noticeable only to a select few. But those days always ripped him wide open, putting his pain on full display.

"That was not as difficult as I thought it would be." Marisol's voice drew them apart, but Felipe didn't look at his sister. His gaze stayed steady on Annie's face, flickering between her strawberry red lips and the freckles on her nose.

"Go away, Mari," he said.

"So I guess this means you aren't going to play UNO?"

"Oh we are. Felipe actually thinks he can win." She followed Marisol into the night, and he stared, wondering how this American had gotten so deep under his skin.

Outside, the sun was setting into a wash of pinks, blues, and yellows. At the edge of a small bonfire, Juan turned a stick full of impaled fish, and Marisol plopped down next to Phillip, who shuffled and reshuffled the tattered deck of cards. Behind them, the night moved in, bringing in its thousands of white flickering stars.

Annie picked a spot across from Marisol, and Felipe slid in next to her, ignoring the looks Juan gave him as he passed out their dinner.

"I've gotten better with age, you know." Annie picked up her cards.

Felipe grinned but kept back the words he wanted to say. He feared his agreement would lead to her laughter, which would lead to his inability to do anything but kiss her. In front of everyone.

Juan threw down a blue three. "We are going to play or flirt?" He dropped a lump of fish in his mouth and stared at the rest of them, eyes gleaming.

"UNO is Juan's other obsession," Felipe said.

"*Otra* obsession? I do not have obsessions." His protests were undermined by the way he picked up the front half of his fish and moved its mouth to the words.

"*Sí*," Marisol chimed in. "You are obsessed with washing the truck. You are obsessed with winning at UNO. You are obsessed with your mustache. You are obsessed with playing with your food." She ticked each one off on her fingers.

"If you had a mustache as beautiful as mine, you would have an obsession too."

DAY SEVEN

After the last boat ride, Annie convinced herself that Dramamine was more of an option than a necessity. Not to mention that after a night of tossing and turning in Felipe's hammock, the effort of digging through her backpack for the tiny bottle of pills had seemed too great. But this time the river was swollen with rain, and it pushed and pulled the boat against its waves. Twenty minutes into the ride, her eyelids begged for sleep, but nausea kept her wide awake.

The boat slowed as its bottom hit earth, and she pried her head from her knees. Ahead, a slender stretch of sand narrowed to a rocky path. It gave way to a cliff face, charcoal gray jutting against the deep greens and browns.

They came to a stop, and Annie stood on wobbly legs. The movement sent her insides twisting, and she slid into something like a sitting position on the shore. The others unloaded the boat around her, bag after bag of supplies whizzing by her head. Behind the opaque curtain of nausea, Annie knew it was rude and selfish to sit watching while everyone else worked. But sickness and frustration tethered her to the sand.

The commotion around her came to a halt, and she lifted her head. Felipe squatted next to her. "Are you ready, *Americana?*" he asked.

She nodded and used his elbow for leverage as she stood.

"You can carry this up the hill, yes?" He held out her backpack and dropped a duffle of medical supplies at her feet. Damp sand kicked up around the bag, pelting her bare legs.

"That hill?" She nodded at the cliff in front of her. She started to ask more questions, like how, exactly, he planned to scale this steep bluff. But her breakfast came out.

Felipe jumped back, but he couldn't escape the vomit geyser. Half-digested rice and beans clung to his shoes and his scrub pants, and she couldn't bring herself to look him in the face. "I'm so sorry," she mumbled. Acid burned her throat, but the blazing heat of her humiliation was far more painful.

"Are you okay?" He didn't even look at the vomit covering his pants, but Annie couldn't stop staring at it. She stepped away, terrified she would retch all over him again. Between the puking and the way she'd shoved her foot in her mouth the night before—*great job bringing up his dead mom, Annie*—she couldn't win. Like a kid taking the same math test again and again but failing for a new reason each time.

Felipe stripped off his shirt and walked into the river. Almost everyone else turned away, giving her the privacy to gag and heave without being examined in the process. She wondered if they would also give her the privacy to quietly drown herself in the river.

"*¿Todo bien?*" Marisol pulled Annie's hair from her face and rubbed a tiny hand across her back.

Annie nodded and took a water bottle from her friend's outstretched hand. With the taste of vomit sufficiently deadened, she dug in her pack for her toothbrush. Around her, the others shuffled their feet as Felipe returned to the group in fresh clothes, but she still couldn't look at him. It was too horrifying, and her stomach still churned. After a quick brushing, she reached for the duffle of medical supplies, but both Felipe and Phillip grabbed it at the same time.

"I'll get it."

"*No es necesario.*"

She reached between the men and took the bag, hiking it over her shoulder alongside her own pack. It weighed nothing, and she realized Felipe must have given her the bag full of gauze and Band-Aids. "I've got it. Let's go."

Juan took them up a winding, narrow path hidden in the cliff's face by spindly branches and lush leaves growing between the cracks.

Annie's shoulders ached with the weight of her backpack, the straps rubbing and chafing her sweat-laden skin. As they ascended, she fought the urge to look down, certain the sight of the water rushing below would fling her straight into another puking catastrophe. She focused on Juan's steady steps ahead of her. His right arm moved rhythmically as he chopped brush with a machete, leaving a trail of severed branches behind him.

They reached the top, and Annie took two solid strides onto the flat field and peered over the edge. From there, the river was a trickling creek. Their boat, left tied to an adolescent tree, was a child's bath toy. For all the tall, jagged rocks and thick leaves on the river, the field in front of them was open and barren. Waist-high grasses slapped against their legs. Only a single twisted and gnarled tree grew out of the earth. Its branches were gray and bare, long dead and full of decay. Blackened tree stumps dotted the landscape, partially hidden lumps in the swaying grass. As they walked, the stumps grew closer and closer together, and Annie weaved in and out of the remains.

"What is this?" she asked.

"Logging," Felipe said.

Her stomach still sloshed as though she were in the boat, and the effort to speak exhausted her energy stores. But she swallowed back her nausea and pressed on. "I'm sorry about earlier. The puking thing."

"It is fine. I am a doctor. Getting vomited on is only another Tuesday." He plucked a stray bit of grass from her shirt. "You will see."

The field gave way to hard-beaten earth and to a trio of small, giggly girls who blocked their path. Their dresses were made of thin fabrics; faded patterns of apples, cherries, and unicorns left the impression of a fruit here or a mythical creature there. The girls fell silent and looked right past Juan and his giant knife to Annie. Their wide, caramel eyes blinked again and again.

"*Hola.*" Felipe waved to them.

"*Hola,*" the tallest girl replied, never letting her stare fall from Annie's face.

Annie cleared her throat and squatted. "*Hola. Me llamo Annie.*"

The two smaller girls ducked behind their leader as Annie held out her hand. A sluggish moment of silence passed, and the child sized her up, pursing her pint-sized lips and backing away.

"*¡Su pelo!*" the girl screeched, turning to her minions. "*¡Es rojo como una bruja! ¡Una bruja!*"

The other two shrieked, and all three darted off. Their bare feet pounded the ground, dust flying behind them. The tall one limped to the right as she ran, falling behind her friends.

"What did she say about my hair?" Annie asked. Juan shrugged, and no one spoke up. "*¿Bruja?*" She mimicked the little girl's scream.

"She is surprised you have red hair. She has probably never seen it before." Marisol took her elbow, pushing them forward.

Ahead, a cluster of houses sprung up out of the dirt. Thatched roofs topped walls made of thin, warped logs, giving each of the homes an unsteady appearance. Between them, a handful of people stared in their direction. Cows meandered through the open space.

Annie patted her messy topknot and followed the rest of her group into a single-room hut. Strips of sunshine poked through the gaps in the walls, making it difficult for her eyes to adjust. There were no windows, and the stagnant air trapped the sweat against her skin. In one corner, two flat wooden benches formed an L. In another, a lumpy pile of blankets created a nest. No indoor plumbing. No electricity.

"Welcome to your new home," Marisol said.

Annie pushed back a groan. "How long are we staying here?"

"Two nights."

A stout woman followed them inside. Her black sapphire hair ended abruptly at her ears, which perked up with a wide smile. Annie tried to smile back. Her arms dangled at her sides while the woman kissed her cheek. The sour smell of body odor filled her nostrils, and she swallowed hard, trying not to gag.

Marisol launched into a string of Spanish and kissed the woman's cheek, rescuing Annie.

"This way." She grabbed Annie's hand and pulled her outside.

Dusk crept up around them, and the air outside cooled. Annie gulped it in.

"I told her you needed to use the *baño*. Everyone knows Americans have weak stomachs."

Annie let out a note of shaky laughter. In most circumstances, she'd be horrified to have someone discuss her bathroom habits with a complete stranger. *Desperate times.* "Thank you. I mean, *gracias.* I'm sorry, it's so hot in there, and my stomach's still upset from the river."

Marisol laughed. "And *Doña* Lynda smells bad."

"I probably smell bad too."

"By the time we are done, we will smell like ten *Doña* Lyndas."

A rustle came from behind them, and they both turned. Near the door, Felipe was bent over at the waist, in deep conversation with the screecher. Annie caught the girl sneaking glances at her over his head.

"Her name is Chowmey," Marisol said, following Annie's gaze. "Last time we were here, she had dengue. Her fever was so high, Felipe thought she might die. She could not walk. He made us stay at this village for two extra days until she was better."

Annie nodded, still watching Felipe and the girl. He smiled, his dimple on full display while the child waved her hands in every direction. She reminded Annie of a miniature Marisol.

Marisol tugged her arm. "Come. Breathe through your mouth."

Inside, the hut bristled with energy. *Doña* Lynda shot between the house and the yard, bringing in plate after plate of food. Felipe came in and sat next to Juan, eating and playing a game of peek-a-boo with a pants-less toddler. Phillip sat next to Annie and Marisol and droned on about a reality show full of obese virgins.

"It's called *Losing It.* Anyway, I had some other offers," he said, "but I would've had to drop out of dental school."

"Now you are done with dental school, you could go back to television, no?" Marisol fluttered her dark lashes, and Annie had to hold back her laughter.

This guy is never going to know what hit him.

Phillip shook his head. "I'm not done. Just on a break. Besides, I think my fifteen minutes are up."

"Fifteen minutes?" Marisol's expression went cloudy.

"He means no one's interested in him anymore." The words were out before Annie could stop them. "Sorry, that's not what I meant. I'm tired." She stared at her hands, willing her body to disappear into the thin reeds covering the walls.

Chowmey's silhouette appeared in the doorway, and Annie's spine stiffened. The girl shuffled forward until she stood within arm's reach. Up close, Annie saw the tuft of baby hairs escaping her pony tail. The girl wound her arms tightly behind her back and shifted her weight from one bare foot to the other.

Annie made no move. The shrieking would be worse at this distance.

Silently, the girl held out a single green orb.

She reached for it, careful not to touch the child's fingers. "*Gracias.*"

Chowmey backed away, stumbling over the feet of the adults and her little brother, until she huddled next to Felipe. He put down his plate and whispered in her ear. The girl ran the few steps to Annie, stopping a foot away. "*De nada.*" She tore out of the house.

"What is this?" Annie rubbed her fingers along the hard piece of fruit. A few rough brown lines cut though its apple green skin.

"Coconut." Felipe held out his hands. She stood and dropped it in his palm. With a small pocket knife, he bore an oblong hole in the top. "Drink the milk," he said. She started to protest, but he cut her off. "It will help your stomach. I promise."

Annie nodded and turned to the opposite bench. Phillip stretched across her former spot, inching closer to Marisol. "Remember that band Good Charlotte?" he asked.

Marisol shook her head.

"No? Well, the lead singer is married to..."

It's like he's reading from the pages of an Us *Magazine. From 2002.*

"Sit here." Felipe scooted toward the wall.

She squeezed onto the bench beside him. "Thanks." She brought the coconut to her lips and took a small pull. The milk had a sweet, tangy flavor, but it wasn't horrible. She took another swallow and another. By the time she sucked it dry, her stomach felt nearly normal—except the butterflies going mad inside every time Felipe looked at her.

"Better, yes?"

"Thank you." Annie's eyes locked on his before she dragged them to the empty fruit in her hand.

Doña Lynda appeared, a full plate in one hand and a black pot in the other. With ballerina grace, the woman took the dry coconut and replaced it with Annie's dinner. She plopped another ladle of rice onto Felipe's empty plate and scurried away.

Annie's mouth watered. It was rice and beans—the same thing she'd eaten for every meal since the night with the soup and the monkey and the drunk man who loved white women. But a small hunk of meat in a red sauce sat in the center of the plate. The smoky, spicy smell reminded Annie of her father's brisket. She dug in, using the sauce to add flavor to her mushy pile of gray rice.

After dinner, they set up for the night, scrunching into every corner of the room. A host of nails were forced into the bones of the house, and the others strung their hammocks from one end to the other. She unrolled her bedding in a small nook between Marisol's hammock and the wall.

"Are you sure you do not want the hammock?" Felipe asked.

"Yep," she lied. "It's your turn." She sat on the yoga mat and tried not to let her thoughts of climbing in next to him show.

Doña Lynda and her kids clucked around the room, chatting with the other Nicaraguans in quick Spanish Annie couldn't follow. Her best guess was a village dispute over the color of chickens.

"*Doña* Lynda asked if you enjoyed dinner," Felipe said.

"Oh!" She stopped fussing with her sheets and turned toward their host. "*Sí. Muy bueno.*"

The woman asked another question.

"She wants to know if you have ever had this meat before."

Marisol sat next to Annie, stretching her legs out in front of her.

"Beef?" Annie cocked her head. "*¿Vaca?*"

"No, no." The woman went outside, and the group was silent as she rustled in the backyard cooking space. A moment later, she returned, carrying an oblong, dappled shell in one hand and a long scaly, gray tail in the other.

Annie's hands flew to her mouth as a gasp escaped her lips.

"I think you also call this armadillo, no?" Marisol asked.

DAY EIGHT

Felipe ducked into the house in search of Chowmey. He was tempted to stay outside with the others, relaxing and watching the chaos unfold as Annie and Phillip tried to ask *Doña* Lynda about the best way to hunt armadillo, but the way the girl had favored her leg as she tore away from Annie the day before sparked his concern.

Inside, the scent of baby powder and lavender overpowered his senses, and it took Felipe a moment to realize the smell came from a line of crumpled baby wipes littering the floor. The trail started at Annie's backpack and led to his hammock, where Chowmey lay. She hummed to herself, one scrawny leg dangling over the edge of the rough fabric and an empty, clear bag between her fingers. The sheen on her face and arms told him exactly what had happened to the wipes.

"Chowmey?"

The hammock froze. The girl scrambled down, stuffing wipes, even the smudged, ripped ones, into the bag. Around her, the rest of Annie's things lay strewn haphazardly on the floor.

"What's going on?" Annie appeared at his side.

His shoulders tensed. On the last brigade, one of the children pulled a jar of peanut butter out of an American's bag and ate half of it before smearing the rest on the walls. Felipe had clutched an EpiPen for half an hour as he tried to convince the middle-aged man he could actually survive on rice and beans. "Chowmey was curious about your things."

Annie's upper body slumped, and she lowered herself to the floor, picking up the rest of her belongings.

"Sorry." He squatted beside her.

"It's not your fault." She stood, her hands full of stray toiletries and half-used wipes. "Here." She motioned for him to stand, and when he did, she rubbed a spot on his neck, right below his ear, with one of the wipes. "That's been bugging me since yesterday."

"*Gracias.*" His feet stayed rooted to the dirt floor. "Annie, I—"

Chowmey put two small hands on his hip and pushed. The force sent him stumbling. She ducked behind his legs, and he caught a flash of purple in the front pocket of her dress.

"What is this?" He pointed. Chowmey's eyes lowered to the floor, and she took out a small photo album. "Yours?" he asked Annie.

She nodded. "*¿Quieres*...How do I ask if she wants to see?"

"*¿Quieres ver?*" He asked Chowmey.

The girl nodded, her eyes wide. Annie sat and patted the floor next to her, but Chowmey didn't move. Felipe stretched out beside Annie instead, letting his arm rest behind her back. The girl followed, gingerly crossing her legs without looking the American in the face.

The first picture was of Annie and an older, round gentleman. They stood in front of a looming brick house, and a layer of thick white snow covered the ground behind them.

"My father and my house." Annie pointed at the figures, her mouth working deliberately over the basic Spanish words.

"*¿Qué es?*" Chowmey whispered, lifting a finger to the snow.

He started to tell Annie the word for snow, but she tugged in her bottom lip, and Felipe's mind flashed to the airport bar. To the way he'd wanted to pull that lip between his while her hands trailed up his thighs.

"*Nieve.*" She turned the page in slow motion. The next picture was a close up of a black and white cat licking its salmon pink nose.

"*¡Gato!*"

"*Sí.*" Annie smiled as the girl slunk closer.

Felipe found himself grinning too. "What is your cat's name?"

She glanced at him, and this time it was the curve of her top lip that sent his pulse careening into breakneck territory. "*Hombre* Flowers," she said.

Chowmey threw her fingers to her mouth and laughed. She scooted closer.

So did he.

Annie turned the page again. In this photo, she wore a tight black dress with a deep V in the front. His mouth fell open. Her shoulders were bare, and her hair hung loose and shiny, the out of control curls tamed into submission. And her smile was bursting, as if she were on the verge of laughter. He could almost hear it just by looking at the image.

"*Púchica*," he muttered. "I mean, you look very pretty."

Annie smiled and glanced at him. "Thanks."

"You are a princess?" Chowmey asked, her Spanish slow with awe. The girl was practically in Annie's lap now, any trace of suspicion long gone.

"No." She laughed and shook her head.

The other half of the picture held a tall, broad-shouldered college boy, outfitted in a tailored suit that matched the pitch black of Annie's dress. He stood with his arm looped around her waist, a smug, lazy smile on his face. Other well-dressed couples mingled in the background, and sparkling bottles of wine lined a bar behind them.

"Can I turn it?" Annie asked.

"*Sí, sí.*" He pulled away from her and turned to Chowmey. A stony lump of disappointment and indignation grew in his stomach as he examined the girl's damaged leg. *Of course she has a boyfriend.*

Chowmey and Annie went through the rest of the book. Each time they turned a page, he fought to keep his focus on the atrophied muscles along the girl's calf. He stayed silent, swallowing the bitterness that threatened to come out with his words.

"What are you doing?" Annie tucked the album into her bag and replaced it with her notebook.

"You can keep going with the pictures. It is not a problem."

"She's seen them all."

"I am checking her muscle strength."

"Why?" There was the scratch of her pen on the paper.

"She contracted dengue," he said. "It is a mosquito-borne illness. Very common here." More scratching. "She had a high fever and could not walk for many days."

"But she can walk now."

"*Sí.* But this one is still weak." He pushed the girl's legs side by side, to demonstrate the difference in muscle mass.

There was more scratching and a few quick strokes of her hand. Next to him, Chowmey squirmed, and he made a series of ridiculous faces at her, keeping the girl still long enough to complete the exam. When he finished, he sent her off with a pat on the head, and she scurried outside with the smell of lavender wafting behind her.

"So, what's wrong with her? Does she still have dengue fever?"

"I am not sure what is wrong with her." He took a deep breath, defeat filling his lungs. He had no way to see what was going on—no X-ray machines, no way to test her blood, nothing. It was a guessing game, and he was certain someone whose everyday life was as bright and shiny as Annie's could never understand.

"What about—"

He stood and brushed off his pants. "The clinic will be at noon, outside in the open area. You will do the nets again." He didn't look at her as he slipped out the door.

• • •

Annie sat alone under the thick layer of dried banana leaves protruding from the roof. The bit of shade they created let her hold on to the last breaths of cool morning air.

What day is this again? She looked at the journal in her hands. *Eight. Two days since I've bathed.* She would have to figure something out soon. Chowmey's foray into the world of wet wipes left Annie defenseless against her own body odor.

She flipped through the morning's entry, thinking about the girl's symptoms—her too-small leg and the way her hip joint seemed locked into place. Annie wished she could scoop her up, take her to St. Louis, and have the best doctors run a battery of all the best tests on her.

She does have a pretty good doctor here. She smiled, thinking of the way Felipe hunched next to the girl, making the exam a game instead of something to be feared. She scribbled this down. On the next line she jotted his words. *You look very pretty.*

Four minutes later, she'd filled an entire page with observations about him. The way he transformed from good-looking to gorgeous when he smiled. The cowlick behind his ear that grew a little more prominent every day. How he went cold and distant as she went through her photo album.

Insignificant. The word had hovered close to Annie's heart ever since she let herself say it aloud to Marisol. And the way Felipe grew bored and disinterested in the details of her life made the word pound louder in her chest—everything she'd accomplished in the last twenty-one years was small and stupid in comparison to Felipe's life here. Helping people. Preventing disease. Saving beautiful, mischievous little girls from dengue fever.

A pair of shadows blocked the slanted rays of the sun, and Annie tore herself from her thoughts. One shadow belonged to Chowmey. The other to a tall, lanky man with a hint of a mustache and small, shifting eyes. He carried a yellow backpack over his left shoulder and began talking in a clipped mix of English and Spanish. It was neither English nor Spanish enough for her to follow.

"I'm sorry. I don't understand." Annie held her palms out to the man. "I mean, *no entiendo.*" She wiped the sweat from her forehead and stood to find someone to translate.

His hand jerked forward, and he grabbed her forearm. "*Mira, mira,*" he said, letting go before she could pull away. He pried open the zipper of the backpack and held the open bag out to her.

A black blob shuffled inside.

Annie leapt back, her breath stalling in her chest.

"Fruit loops. Fruit loops."

She squinted into the bag again, and at last his words made sense. Nestled inside was a tiny toucan, the mascot of her favorite childhood breakfast cereal—still her favorite really. But she always forced herself to buy the high fiber, fifty grain, cardboard stuff instead. Less sugar. More adult. No taste.

"Fruity loops is nice," said the man.

Annie knew squat about birds, but this one had to be miserable. Its frayed feathers piled at the bottom of the bag. "Is sick?" She tried to remember the word for sick but fell short. *I really should have made more flash cards.*

"Is nice. Very nice."

Maybe he wants to see a doctor. I doubt there are any vets all the way out here. "Doctor? *¿Medico?"* She nodded at Chowmey, who stared silently.

"Usted." He nudged the bird toward her.

Looking at the animal nearly cracked Annie's heart. She lowered a finger into the bag, stroking the feathers on top of the toucan's head. They were greasier than she expected. The thing was all crumpled and sad, and she reached in further to pet the patch of lighter feathers on its chest.

A barb of white-hot pain hit her index finger, and she yanked her hand from the bag. Both a squeal and a squawk competed for airspace, and Annie realized the former must have come from her mouth. Brick-red blood streaked her hand and pooled in her palm as the skinny man zipped the bird away and slipped into the thick layer of trees behind the house.

Chowmey darted toward the door while Annie stared at the wound. The tear at the tip of her finger wasn't large, but her heart pounded in her chest as if she'd narrowly escaped a fatal stabbing.

"Fucking Fruit Loops." She suddenly felt less nostalgic for the bright, sugary rings.

"Raise your arm. Over your head." Felipe appeared in front of her, one hand hanging on to Chowmey and the other jerking over his head in demonstration. He still hadn't shaved, and his eyes seemed darker somehow. "Annie! *¡Levanté!"* A deep crease formed between his eyebrows, and she stared at him, unmoving. He grabbed her wrist and held it high.

Blood trickled to her elbow, leaving curling red ribbons along her forearm. Chowmey's small hand found her intact fingers and squeezed.

"I'm okay." She took a deep breath and loosened her locked knees.

Felipe turned to Chowmey, keeping hold of Annie's arm. "*Tráeme una silla.*" The girl took off toward the house. "Fruit loops?" Felipe's eyebrows crept up his forehead.

"Huh?" Her eyes darted to the shadow of dark stubble along his jawline, and she thought about feeling its roughness against her skin. *Get it together.* She pulled her gaze to the ground. "A bird. It bit me, I mean. A toucan. This guy kept showing it to me, and it looked sick. Then it bit me."

The low drag of plastic on dirt told her the chair had arrived. As soon as Chowmey put it behind her, Annie fell into it, not trusting her knees to remain steady.

Marisol ran toward them, a bag in one hand. "Chowmey said you needed this. *¿Qué pasó?*"

"I got bit," Annie said.

"Fruit loops," Felipe interjected, as if this explained everything.

Marisol pulled her chin to her chest, eyebrows raised.

"This guy showed up with a toucan in a backpack." Annie left out the part about Chowmey bringing the man to her. "He kept saying, 'Is nice, is nice.' But the stupid bird looked sick, so I thought maybe he was bringing it to you guys. Ouch!" She tried to jerk her hand away, but Felipe held tightly as he dumped saline solution into her wound.

Marisol and Felipe cocked their heads in identical expressions of skepticism. Chowmey slipped her little hand into Annie's.

"What? It's not like there are vets out here, right?"

"You are lucky you still have a finger." Felipe shook his head. "And you need a stitch."

"He was trying to sell the bird to you," Marisol said.

"Sell it? What would I do with a toucan?" She whipped her head toward Felipe. "I need a stitch? Only one? How do you know?" She managed to slip his grip and bring her hand to eye level.

With a sigh, he grabbed her palm and pulled it skyward once

more. "I think, yes. If you hold still, I will have a better idea."

She froze at the sharpness edging his voice.

"The fingers move and stretch," he said. "It is harder for a wound like this to close on its own. It is deep." He stooped to look her in the eye, and for a moment she expected that full, send-the-sky-spinning smile. But his lips held a tight line. "Is that sufficient for your medical reports?" he asked, tilting his head in the direction of her journal, forgotten and wide open in the dirt at Marisol's feet. The last page—all about him—was practically public domain.

Annie's chest tightened. She shifted in her seat and gripped her knee with her free hand, blurting out the first idea that came to her. "I want to watch. The stitches, I mean." She tried to keep her voice even, as if the needle he threaded wasn't about to sew her up like a ripped doll.

Marisol picked up the journal, her eyes sparkling as they flicked over the open page. "I will go get ready for the clinic." She dropped the closed notebook next to Annie with a wink and left, pulling Chowmey behind her.

"Are you sure?" Felipe asked.

"What?"

"You want to see the stitches?"

"Oh. Sure." She swallowed. "Learning opportunity and everything."

"Okay," he said. "Can you stand?"

She shot up, her arm still extended. Lightheaded, she swayed, then lurched straight into his chest. "Sorry."

His right hand clasped her waist, steadying her. The throbbing in her finger became a faded memory. "You are going to sit," he said.

She eased herself back into the plastic chair.

Felipe squatted in front of her. "I am going to numb your finger, yes?"

Annie squeezed her eyes shut and held out the mangled hand. The needle pierced her skin, and her fingertip went fat and numb. Hit with the weight of sudden guilt, her eyes flew open. "You shouldn't use the supplies on me. What if we run out and you won't have enough thread or whatever for someone who needs it?"

"You need it." He pressed a finger against her fingernail. "Can you feel this?"

She shook her head.

"Ready?"

She muttered her assent, and he picked up the threaded needle. His eyelashes were thick and dark, and a single drop of sweat rolled from his temple to his cheek. He squinted a bit as he worked, bringing out those tiny lines around his eyes.

"Finished." He rolled back on his heels and looked at her. "Did you watch?"

"No."

He sighed. "No more touching strange animals, yes?"

She nodded, but panic swarmed her. "Do you think I need a rabies shot? I got the two pre-bite shots at the student health center, but I think you're supposed to get more if you get bit by something." *What are the symptoms of rabies? Fear of water.* She pictured the river, rolling waves of brown and green. *Not afraid…yet.*

"No, you do not need a rabies shot."

"Are you sure?"

"Yes. You get rabies from mammals."

"You're positive?"

He packed up the supplies, separating the used gauze and needle from the others. "*Sí.*" He handed her a thin purple surgical glove. "Keep your finger covered today and tomorrow. Maybe the day after too. Chowmey can help you with the mosquito nets."

"Okay." A stray curl clung to her forehead, and she blew at it to no avail.

Felipe reached forward as if to brush it away. But he pulled his hand back with a start, leaving the clump of hair glued to her face. "Please do not be late for the clinic."

DAY NINE

Every step toward the next village took more of Felipe's energy than the last. They were half an hour into the two-hour hike, and already his body begged for a break. But it wasn't because of the sun searing his neck or the ninety-something percent humidity or the weight of the medical supplies on his back. It was the way Annie's t-shirt hung off one shoulder. How the fine sheen of sweat made her skin reflect the sun.

He'd managed to avoid her for most of the last day, dodging her attempts at small talk and an invitation to play UNO. And last night, he'd curled up on the stupid, lumpy yoga mat and closed his eyes, pretending to be asleep when she came by to keep up the routine they'd started.

"Are you sure?" one of them would ask, one leg already in the hammock.

"*Sí*," the other would insist, stretching out on the yoga mat, as if it were a luxurious king-sized mattress filled with the softest down imaginable.

But last night, he'd closed his eyes. And when she nudged him with her toe, he rolled toward the wall and waved her off. "It is fine."

He peeled his stare away from Annie's bare shoulder as Phillip's booming voice exploded behind him. "Hey man, do you know?"

Felipe jumped. "What?"

"Why does everyone have the decorative gold tooth caps here? I mean, for a place that has so little dental care, there are a lot of people walking around with gold hearts on their incisors."

The same reason it is impossible to look directly at your teeth, Barnyard Man. Vanity. As they side-stepped down the steep winding path,

Felipe ducked under a clump of branches and searched for a diplomatic answer—one that wouldn't piss off his mother and tank future *Ahora* donations from Phillip Jones, D.D.S.

"I think—" He looked over his shoulder at the blond man as he walked. But Felipe stumbled, groping for balance as his chest smacked into something solid.

Annie.

"*Lo siento.* I mean, sorry."

"It's okay, I—"

"Silence!" Juan had one arm raised—his machete arm—and the shiny metal glinted with sun and bits of decapitated plants.

Felipe's muscles went rigid as muffled voices crept up the hill.

"What's up man?" Phillip asked, his voice half a decibel lower than usual.

There was no time to answer or to shush the American man. Not before the gunshot rang out, echoing through the air and shaking every leaf and branch with the force of the sound.

Felipe flew to the ground, pushing Annie beneath him. Mud and damp grass clung to his mouth and cheeks, and sweat stung his eyes. Beneath him, she groaned.

"Are you okay?" he whispered against her ear. Her head bobbed once, and he shifted his weight to give her room to breathe. On his other side, Marisol lay belly to the dirt, her eyes darting. Phillip too. The entire group lay on the ground, except for Juan, who stood, his machete ready for action.

"Okay?" Felipe mouthed to his sister. She nodded, but her eyes were wide and brimming with fear.

Six bare feet appeared in Felipe's line of vision as a band of ragged youths wearing discarded American rags moved toward their group. The leader stood tall and skinny with sharp elbows and knees. A long, shiny, slender rifle hung over his shoulder. He wore a pointed sneer and a red Nike t-shirt. Under the white logo, it proclaimed, "I Run Like a Girl."

"*Millonarios.*" The boy's smirk grew, consuming his entire face and showing off a jagged chip in his front tooth. He shoved around his friends and stepped close to Felipe. "You must pay to pass. *Mucho.*"

Felipe stood slowly, stepping in front of Annie and Marisol. "We do not have anything. We are doctors." He took care to make his voice flat, as if he hadn't noticed the firearm or the wild-eyed, drug-deprived expression the boy wore.

"If you are doctors, you have *drogas.*" The leader licked his lips as he turned to Juan. "Drop the knife."

Felipe kept his face blank, but his mind raced through the supplies, trying to remember what drugs they had left and who carried them.

Annie.

When they had hiked out that morning, she'd carried the duffle with the pain killers. But now it lay strewn on the ground next to her backpack, an arm's length away. Felipe sized the teens up, wondering if it was worth the risk to try to pass off a handful of antibiotics as narcotics, when Phillip pushed his way forward. Felipe pivoted, ready to shove the American man to the ground. The last thing they needed was some cowboy antagonizing a group of teenage junkies with firearms. But as Phillip's yellow hair reflected the sun, recognition rushed the teenagers' faces.

"*Barnyard Boyfriend!*" one of them called out. It sounded more like Barn Fiend.

"Uh, yeah. I mean *sí.* How about I give you guys an autograph and we call it a deal?" Phillip flashed them a brilliant smile. For a moment, Felipe hoped the teens would be blinded and the group could make their getaway.

The leader stared at Phillip, one eyebrow cocked and the other furrowed. He couldn't have been older than sixteen, and the way his forehead crinkled made him look even younger. He could tell the boy didn't understand Phillip's offer, and Felipe started to translate as the American reached for his bag.

The cocking of the rifle cut him off.

"Do not move," the boy ordered in Spanish, spittle clinging to his chin.

Felipe translated, and Phillip dropped his bag and drew both hands into the air. "Sorry, man. Sorry."

The boy turned, bringing the barrel of the gun to rest against Felipe's midsection. He forced his lungs to inflate even though the air tasted rotten in his mouth. "I will give you the drugs." He kept his eyes trained on the boy's face, afraid that looking at the rifle would mean losing his composure.

The kid pressed the weapon harder into Felipe's gut. "Where are they?"

He shrugged. "I need to look for them. I am going to search the bags, yes?"

The boy looked to his cronies, but both stared blankly. "No," he said. "I will look." He pulled the gun away, and relief surged from Felipe's neck to his fingertips.

Until the kid squatted next to Annie and jerked the end of the rifle in her direction. "*Mira* pretty *Americana.*"

* * *

Annie's fingers shook as the boy sneered at her. He crouched close enough for her to make out the fine red lines in his eyes and the hint of a mustache shadowing his upper lip. At this distance, it was harder to conceal the Pink Stringer, but it would also be easier for her to strike. She clutched the fake pink tampon hard enough to make the veins in her hand strain against her skin.

"You want to be my barn fiend?" The boy pulled at the end of one of her frayed curls, then turned away to toss her backpack to one of his mute friends. The kid fumbled and dropped the bag, and the contents spilled everywhere. Bras, shirts, a few toiletries. Across the tiny clearing, the other boy picked up a supply pack and dumped it. Vials of vaccines clattered against one another as they fell to the ground, and every head turned toward the commotion.

Except Annie's. She took a deep, shaky breath and jammed the electric gun into the leader's side. Her thumb jammed against the black switch.

Nothing happened.

For a split second the world went too white, and the acrid taste of vomit climbed her throat as the boy turned to leer at her.

From her left, there was a shuffling and shifting on the ground, and then a clatter as Felipe launched himself on top of the kid. The rifle slid off the boy's shoulder as they fell into a pile of limbs and dirt and angry Spanish.

Annie grabbed the gun as Juan held the other boys back with the machete. "Get out of here." She could barely bring her voice above a whisper, and the weapon was heavier than she'd imagined. Rougher. The end of it kept sinking toward the ground as she stood. "Get out of here!" She found her voice this time, waving the gun wildly in the air. She'd never even shot a BB gun before, always too scared she would blind herself or slaughter an innocent squirrel. But now, here she stood, in the middle of nowhere, aiming a giant gun at a trio of teenagers like she was the last defender of the Alamo.

The two smaller boys took off into the trees, their bare feet smacking hard against the grass. Next to her, the boy in the Nike t-shirt scrambled away from Felipe, bloody and spitting. He glared at Annie one last time, then grabbed a handful of the things strewn on the ground before he followed his friends into the forest.

They're gone.

She slid to the ground, and the rifle tumbled from her hands. Her vision narrowed, the edges of it turning a deep blue-black. Her entire existence felt precarious, and all of her muscles seemed too loose, like they were only attached to her body by the thin cover of her skin. There were words, but she couldn't understand them. They were too muffled by the thumping of her heart in her ears and the rush of adrenaline leaving her body.

She tried to stand but couldn't. She was being squeezed. Trapped. *Back. They're back.* The words cartwheeled through her brain, even though a tiny, faraway voice told her the boys weren't coming back. They'd be stupid to come back. *But they are stupid.* She pulled away, trying to breathe, but her arms stayed pinned to her sides by her attacker. She squirmed and fumbled until her fingers grasped the end of the Pink Stringer, and she found the nerve to jam it into her assailant's thigh. She pushed the switch again, shoving it with every ounce of strength and desperation she could find.

Please work. Please work.

He stumbled and collapsed, freeing her arms and legs. Annie tore away, rushing up the hill, toward the boat, to safety.

The footsteps behind her grew louder, overtaking her before she could make it out of sight. *"Mira, muchacha. Mira. Es Juan."*

She froze, her body soaked with sweat and her breath coming in shallow, raspy bursts. Juan came around to face her, his hands next to his face, palms to the sky. He spoke again, but his words were very fast and very Spanish. Annie looked over her shoulder. Marisol and Phillip squatted next to a flattened Felipe, making half-hearted attempts to tug him to his feet. The teens were nowhere in sight.

Juan moved to her side. "You are okay?" He kept his hands high.

She rubbed her eyes, blinking back dirt and fear. "They're gone?"

"Sí." He took a step toward the group and motioned for her to walk ahead.

Annie slid a hand under her shirt and pulled it away from her skin. The shrink of her sweaty clothes against her body made it harder to breathe. As they walked closer, Felipe sat up, both hands clamped on his left thigh. The Pink Stringer sat an arm's length away, half-buried in the mud.

Shit.

Felipe stood. *"¿Qué diablos, Annie?"* he asked through clenched teeth, his arms swept wide. "What were you thinking?"

"I'm sorry. I'm so, so sorry." The weight of what she'd done was still sinking in. "Are you okay? I panicked. I couldn't see. I don't—"

He shook his head and walked away, picking up the rifle from the ground.

"I think this one is yours." Marisol held out a mud-soaked bra with one trembling hand.

Annie grabbed her friend and hugged her, squeezing as tightly as she could and sobbing into Marisol's shoulder.

"Are you okay?" Annie asked.

Marisol nodded. "This has not happened in a long time."

"It's happened before?" Annie wiped her nose on her shirt sleeve as a flint of anger sparked inside her.

"Sometimes the people hear we are coming and set traps to steal drugs or money. It was in the papers you received. With the packing list." Marisol's voice wobbled and her features were all strained and tense, as if she expected Annie to lash out at her.

"I thought it was one of those things that never really happens. And I hate that you have to go through this. You're doing so much good, risking so much, and people take advantage."

"Yes, but it is only a few people. And this is the first time they carried a gun." Marisol held her arms out again, and Annie wrapped her friend in a tight hug.

"Is your brother okay?" she asked when Marisol's sniffles dried up.

Marisol clamped her lips together, but a small laugh still escaped between her tears. "I did not know your tampons were electric. Those were not on the packing list."

The corners of Annie's mouth tugged up, despite the terror and embarrassment still swirling inside her. "But you don't think he's really hurt or anything, right? Should I go check on him?"

"Only his pride, *mi Anita*. Give him some time to recover."

Over her friend's shoulder, Felipe stood motionless, his arms crossed tightly against his chest and the rifle slung over his shoulder. Everything about him screamed stay away.

Around them, Phillip and Juan repacked bags, plucking gauze pads and vials from the dirt. Annie took a deep breath and squatted next to her things, dividing them into four piles. Then two long lines. She merged them all into one and reached for her backpack.

"What are you doing?" Marisol raised an eyebrow.

"Packing," Annie said. "It makes me feel better."

"Oh yes. Your anal probl—"

"*¿Vamos?*" Juan's voice was quiet.

Annie moved faster, trying to keep her mind and her belongings in order. "Will we take the boat all the way to the truck?" she asked, trying to shake torn blades of grass off a shirt. Even now, fifteen minutes after the boys had disappeared into the woods, her hands still trembled.

"What do you mean?" Marisol asked.

"We're going back, right? So we can make a police report or something?" *And maybe I can call my dad about an emergency flight home.*

Her friend shook her head and looped an arm around Annie's shoulders. "We will keep going. It will be fine. You will see."

DAY TEN

The midwife fluttered around Felipe in a panic, pelting him with detail after detail about her patient's progressing labor. Her face grew redder with every syllable, and she ran her sausage fingers up and down her stomach as she spoke. Around them, waiting patients stirred and mumbled, staring at the dirt beneath their feet. Felipe knew they were only pretending not to listen.

He put a hand on the woman's fleshy forearm. "I will come as soon as I can get my things together," he said. "You stay with her."

She scurried out of the clinic, glancing over her shoulder every few steps, as if to be sure Felipe was packing up his things to follow her. She paused in the doorway and turned to face him. "It is my daughter." Both her eyes and the pitch of her Spanish pleaded with him. "Please hurry."

Felipe gave her a single nod and scoped out the line of patients. Four people waited, none of them bleeding, broken, or teetering on the brink of death. "I am very sorry, but there is an emergency. If you leave your names here, I will come to your homes tonight."

He paused, anticipating an outcry. He knew some of these people had been waiting for days to see him, maybe even months— since the last time his team visited. But they all nodded and patted him on the back as he passed by. One man even promised to say a prayer for the baby's safe delivery, and gratitude filled Felipe's chest.

"Where is Marisol?" He dropped his supply bag on the bench next to Annie. She'd taken up residence there during the clinic, first as she handed out nets and then to entertain the children who came to stare and ask her questions. The kids froze and stared at him with scowls and narrowed eyes.

"Can you move that please?" Annie asked.

He lifted the bag over his shoulder. A smattering of scuffed metal jacks and a blue rubber ball clunked to the floor with the movement. "Sorry," he said to the children. "It is important. Where is she?"

Annie cleared her throat and looked pointedly toward the door. "I think she and Phillip went off somewhere…"

Of course. "I need help. Do you want to see a childbirth?"

She was on her feet and at his side in half a second, leaving the kids alone to their game of jacks. "Obviously. Also, about yesterday—"

He waved her off. There was no time. "This will be a complicated birth. I am not sure what will happen." A flash of doubt ran through him. The mother, or the baby, or maybe both could die. And Annie would be forced to watch. "If you do not want—"

"I want." She flipped open the notebook and held her pen over a blank page. "Tell me what's going on."

As they zipped along the path between the houses, Felipe told her everything he knew—the patient was young and pregnant for the first time. She wasn't due for another four weeks, but her water broke that morning. And the midwife was certain the baby was breech. He told Annie how he would first try to turn the baby inside the mother's womb and what he would do if the baby refused to move.

He didn't tell her he'd never delivered a baby outside of a hospital.

"How do you know the baby's breech?" she asked.

"The midwife told me."

"Yeah, but how does she know? I'm assuming there aren't any ultrasound machines out here."

"It is possible to tell. I will show you."

Her face lit with excitement, but the smile slid from Annie's face as they stopped in front of the midwife's house. Ten people gathered on the overgrown front lawn, their hushed voices unable to drown out the screams coming from within.

"*Buenas*," he said.

The crowd descended on him like a flock of vultures on a carcass.

"She is in much pain," one woman whispered to him in a mix of Miskito and Spanish.

A man with a scraggly beard shook his head. "This sounds very bad."

The voices followed Felipe to the house, and by the time he and Annie reached the entrance, his heart thumped so hard he could feel his pulse in his toes.

"*Buenas.*" He pushed back the length of fabric over the door frame. A scream slashed through the air, and beside him Annie's eyes widened. "Are you sure you want to stay?" he asked.

• • •

"Yes." The word came out in a squeak, but Annie lifted her chin and tried to slow her breathing. "I want to stay."

"Okay. Come."

She followed him into the house. A rotund man with hound dog jowls greeted them in the front room. He clapped Felipe on the back and ushered them in. A barrage of hushed Spanish passed between the men, and Annie didn't even try to follow. She shifted her weight and clicked her pen as the screams echoed off the thin walls. Each cry wound her insides further, and by the time Felipe pried himself away from the man, Annie's whole body was a rubber band, pulled tightly enough to snap in half with the next scream.

"Okay?" Felipe asked.

"Sure." She pushed a breath out between her teeth and followed him to a second room, separated from the rest of the house by thin plywood walls. A single, narrow window provided the only source of light, and the air inside the tiny room was at least fifteen degrees hotter than the rest of the house. Beads of sweat sprung up on every inch of Annie's skin, rolling over the preexisting layer of perspiration and dirt.

On the floor, a girl about her age panted, her face screwed up in pain. Sweat plastered her thick black hair to her forehead. Beside her, a woman twice as round as the man in the front room stared at Annie as if she were an alien species.

"Felipe? Are you sure it's okay that I'm here?"

"It is fine. This is the midwife of the village. And this—" he nodded toward the girl on the floor, "is her daughter, Angela. So there is some extra nervousness." He turned to the woman and rattled off more Spanish. She stood, wrapping him in a hug. He squeezed the woman, then knelt next to her pregnant daughter.

"What do you want me to do?" Annie asked, kneeling beside him.

He took her hands in his and placed them on Angela's stomach. "Here." He pressed her fingers into the girl's abdomen until they hit something hard and smooth. "This is the baby's head."

"Wow." Annie kept pressing, even after he let go, searching for more body parts. She found what she suspected was an elbow, and her stomach jumped into her throat. "This is so cool. You're going to flip the baby over?"

"We will try. But first you must stop pushing her stomach." For the first time in days, he gave her one of those grins, the ones that brought out his dimple and turned her insides to mush.

"Sorry."

Three hours, dozens of contractions, and two buckets of sweat later, Angela was fully dilated, and all Felipe's attempts to turn the baby had failed. Resignation hung from the midwife's, and even Annie's earlier excitement was melting amid the humidity and failure.

"What now?" she asked.

"We will prepare for the breech birth." He sighed and peeled off his gloves. "Go to the front room and ask the man to give you blankets."

"How do you say blankets?" She pulled the neck of her t-shirt from her sticky skin and licked her dry lips. Salt lingered on her tongue, making her even thirstier.

Felipe glanced up from his supply bag, his features creased and heavy with worry. "*Mantas.*"

Stepping into the main part of the house felt like slipping into a cool bath. She'd forgotten how much hotter it was in that tiny bedroom. But the man was gone. Even the plastic chair where he'd sat earlier was missing. Her eyes darted around the room, taking in the hammock hanging in one corner and a single framed photograph sitting on a cracked table near the front door.

The girl in the photo was around ten with bright, playful eyes and a smile that stretched from ear to ear. It was miles from the pained grimaces Annie had seen in the back room, but the crooked nose told her it was Angela.

Angela. Blankets.

Annie jolted, shaking her head clear. It'd been hours since she'd had anything to eat or drink, and fog muddled her brain. "*¿Hola?*" she called out, her tongue tacky and dry in her mouth. She stuck her head outside the door, letting the fresh air cool the sweat on her cheeks.

"*Hola,*" the man said, eyes wide and hopeful. He sat outside among the crowd, which had doubled in size since they'd arrived. "*¿Bebé?*"

"Uh, no." Annie shook her head. "No baby. I need *mantas?*"

The man turned to the crowd. "*Mantas.*" The people rushed from the yard, and Annie stared after them, her stomach knotting. *Where are they going? Maybe I said the wrong word. Shit. Did I tell them the baby died? Shit, shit, shit.*

But two minutes later, the blankets rolled in. One after another, the villagers returned, their arms loaded with cloth. When Annie had a pile so high she could barely see around it, she stumbled into the house.

"*Espera.*"

She turned, shifting her weight to keep the blankets from tumbling to the ground. "I think this is enough." She hoped her expression and the massive stack in her arms would make her meaning clear.

The man slapped a damp cloth on her neck and stuffed a piece of sweet, ripe mango in her mouth. The juice ran down her chin, and she closed her eyes, savoring the liquid on her tongue as she chewed. "*Gracias.*"

He gave her a smile and shuffled outside as the sugar roared through Annie's system and cleared her head. She jogged to the room with her mound of blankets and tore back the curtain. "Here. It took a little while because—"

The coppery scent of blood mixed with the harsh odor of antiseptic, and Annie froze in horror. Felipe knelt in front of Angela, slicing her open with a shiny scalpel. He'd told her this was what he'd have to do. And she'd heard of episiotomies before, but seeing it in person was not the same. At all.

Her knees wobbled, and a blanket fell off the top of the pile. From across the room, the midwife glowered at her, then barked at Felipe in Spanish.

He didn't look up from his work. "Annie, are you okay? If you need to go, it is fine."

She swallowed her fear and set the blankets beside him. "I'm good."

"Okay." He dropped the scalpel next to a giant syringe and nodded toward Angela. The girl's cheeks and nose blazed red, and her eyes were swollen and bloodshot. Silent tears rolled down her cheeks. "I need her to squat. Stand behind her and hold her up."

Annie rushed to the girl as Felipe translated the request. She hooked her arms under Angela's armpits, and both of them groaned as she struggled to move. It took three attempts and one hefty push from Angela's mother, but Annie planted her feet and heaved the girl into a squat.

"What now?" Annie panted and wiped her forehead on her sleeve, still supporting Angela from behind.

"Now we push." Felipe looked at her. Blood and sweat stained the front of his shirt. "On the next contraction, Angela will push. You will have to hold her steady. Yes?"

She nodded. He spoke to Angela in a hushed voice, and the girl whimpered and squirmed. Annie's fingers slid and slipped as she tried to keep hold of her sweat-laden skin.

"*Empuje, empuje,*" Felipe and the midwife chanted.

The world erupted.

Angela grunted and groaned. Her body weight shifted as she pushed, throwing Annie off balance. Her foot skidded in something wet as she scrambled for leverage, but she refused to let herself look down. *Don't want to know.* Annie jerked the girl upright and joined in the chant, adrenaline surging through her.

And for a minute, the world calmed again.

"We have one leg." Felipe said. "On the next contraction, I will try to bring down the other."

Annie peered over Angela's shoulder. One tiny, bloody foot dangled from between her legs. "Wow." The girl's sobs shook Annie's body. "Hey," she whispered. "It's okay. It's okay." She couldn't find the right Spanish words to soothe the girl's tears, but she hoped her tone would be enough to offer some comfort.

"Ready?"

It took Annie a beat to realize Felipe was speaking to her. "Yeah. How do I say good job?"

"*Bien hecho.*"

Angela writhed and grumbled, sliding dangerously close to the floor. The midwife's shouts echoed off the bare, unfinished walls as Annie tugged her upright. Plopping down could mean crushing that tiny little foot.

She wrangled the girl into the squat and the chanting began again. "*Empuja, empuja.*"

"*Bien hecho,*" Annie said between pushes, but she doubted Angela could hear anything over her own pants and curses and screams. Each shout reverberated through Annie's chest, sharpening the fear growing inside her. And as Felipe delivered the baby's other leg, for the first time, the full weight of what was happening hit her squarely in the chest.

This girl could die. In my arms.

Panic boiled inside her, but Annie blew at the hairs clinging to her forehead and pushed it away. Angela's body tensed against her, and soon the room was caught in the midst of another contraction, leaving no room for anything but focus.

Three pushes later, Felipe managed to deliver the baby's arms. The girl's mother squatted between Angela's legs and wrapped the half-born infant in one of the many blankets Annie had procured from the neighbors. Angela leaned over and rested her weight against her mother, giving Annie a brief reprieve.

She shook out her arms and legs, long numbed by the constant tension in her muscles and the pressure—both physical and emotional—of supporting Angela's weight. Her back ached, and the metallic taste of blood invaded her nose and mouth.

Angela leaned into Annie's arms, ready to push again.

And again.

The girl strained and cried out, and it took everything Annie had to keep her upright. Felipe and the midwife swapped positions with every contraction, taking turns at easing the infant into the world. But with every push, Felipe's face darkened and the midwife's voice grew shriller as she half cried, half encouraged her daughter.

Annie had no idea how long it had been since they'd arrived in this dim hut, but every second that passed with those legs and arms dangling outside the womb made her heart ache.

In a rare moment between contractions, Felipe and the midwife began arguing. They pointed and stomped and shook their hands as the words flew between them.

Angela sagged in Annie's arms, pale and sweaty.

"What's going on?" Annie asked.

For a moment, the arguing stopped and they both stared silently at Annie.

The girl's mother pointed and nodded at her, shrieking in Spanish, but Annie didn't understand a word of it.

Felipe held up a hand. "We are having some trouble delivering the baby's head."

The midwife yelled and pointed again, and before Annie could ask what she was saying, the woman stood and nudged her out of the way with her rotund mid-section. She looped her arms through Angela's and took the girl's weight.

Annie stumbled, her muscles too tired to change position. She squeaked to something that resembled standing, but her back refused to straighten. Felipe looked at her, eyes flashing with fear.

"We need you to deliver the baby," he said.

* * *

Felipe watched the redness seep out of Annie's cheeks.

"What? Why?" she demanded.

As he rewrapped the infant's lower half in a fresh blanket, fear overtook him. Everything could go wrong. In one fell swoop, he could lose the mother and the baby, and Annie. "Your hands are thinner than mine. Thinner than hers." He nodded at the midwife. The woman was right. There was no other option.

Annie's mouth fell open, and her body shifted as if she were ready to charge through the door and never return.

"Please," he said. "I will tell you exactly what to do. I think—"

She knelt beside him. "What do I do?"

Above them Angela squirmed, and her mother shushed the girl, rocking her from side to side. "Rest for a minute," she whispered in low, mournful Spanish.

"Get some gloves out of the bag."

Annie darted to the supplies, and she pulled on the latex. He gave her the quickest, most basic explanation he could find, but amid the exhaustion and strain of the moment, his words were half English, half Spanish.

"Sorry," he said. "I am not making sense."

Annie crouched beside him. "Tell me what to do as I go, okay?" He nodded.

She reached into the birth canal without an ounce of fear in her features. "I feel the neck, I think. Yes, definitely the neck."

"Good. Reach further."

"And the chin…I think."

"Find the baby's nose. You will have to reach past the cervix."

"Its nose?" Her lips set in a thin, harsh line, and her eyelids snapped shut. "What will it feel like?"

He racked his brain, but everything was so damn foggy. "Like a nose."

She opened her eyes to scowl at him, nostrils flaring. "Okay, thanks."

"No, I did not mean…It will be on the underside. See how the baby's toes are pointing at the ground?" He pulled back the blankets to show her.

She nodded and closed her eyes again. A handful of seconds passed in silence except for Angela's intermittent moans, and his heart hammered against his ribs.

"Got it. I think." Annie twisted her shoulder, reaching a bit further as Angela let out a wail. "Definitely. I feel the nose."

Relief washed through him, neither he nor the midwife had been able to squeeze past the infant's chin. "I am going to have her push. Keep your fingers around the nose so the head does not move."

"But don't we want it to move?"

"I mean, do not let it turn to the side. Keep it straight, yes?" She nodded, and he went on. "Guide the face down with your hand. I will work on the rest of the body."

Angela whimpered. Felipe looked into her slack face and then into her mother's tear-streaked one. He'd never seen a midwife cry. They were steely, solid, unshakable. They had to be, dealing with this kind of work every day. But this wasn't everyday work.

"One more push," he said. "Angela," he waited until the girl opened her eyes and stared at him, "push with everything you have."

She let out a deep, guttural moan. Annie must have realized what was happening, because he didn't have to translate for her. Her eyes snapped shut, and the infant's body moved downward a fraction of an inch.

Angela slumped against her mother, taking a portion of the progress they'd made with her. Both he and the midwife began talking at once, throwing ideas and fearful, barbed words at one another.

Annie's knee brushed his as she stood. Her jaw set and her

gloved fingers squeezed into balls. "Stop it," she shouted over them. "I can't think." Everyone fell into silence, and she squatted next to Angela, dipping her head low to force the girl to meet her eyes. "Tell her I felt the baby's face."

"What?"

"Just do it."

He did.

"Tell her that her baby has fat little cheeks."

He did.

"Tell her it's a boy."

Felipe glanced at the infant between his hands. She was right. He'd hadn't stopped to look. "*Es un niño,*" he said.

"Now tell her we need her to push one more time. Tell her she can do it. For her baby boy."

He translated the words. Angela's features stayed slack and loose, but she gave an almost imperceptible nod.

"Okay." Annie lowered herself to the ground beneath the girl's legs. "I've got the nose," she said a few seconds later. "Let's do this."

Angela groaned and grunted as her mother chanted in her ear. Annie's eyes clamped shut, the freckles across her cheeks and nose scrunching in concentration.

One minute later, the baby boy let out his first cry.

DAY ELEVEN

The sun sizzled Annie's already-sunburned neck, and the constant whir of the boat motor and the distant call of birds lulled her to the edge of sleep. But Phillip pelted her with question after question about yesterday's events, and the memory of delivering that baby kept Annie awake, her body buzzing as if she'd downed three espresso shots and chased them with one of those chalky energy drinks.

"Man. I can't believe you got to deliver a baby," he said.

"It was *the* coolest thing I've ever done." She'd replayed the labor and delivery dozens of times since yesterday, first mentally, then to Marisol, and then to her journal—pouring every last detail into the pages. And as she lay in the hammock, too keyed up to sleep, she went over it again, her breath still catching as she remembered the moment the baby began to move.

"It'd be hard to top that," Phillip said. "I mean, I've had my hands in a few honeypots, and it's pretty awesome."

"Honeypots?" Annie scrunched her forehead, unsure if she'd heard him correctly. "What? No. Honeypots? Who says that?" The laughter bubbled over. "Honeypots. I think you just ruined Winnie the Pooh for me. Forever."

After three long hours in the boat, they arrived in the same village where they'd put on their first clinic, and the sights brought a rush of memories—the strange looks, being overwhelmed with the language, the mud pit, Felipe's bad jokes. It all stared back at her in the winding dirt road and the smattering of houses. She shouldered her pack and followed the group to the edge of the village. On their way, people waved from windows and stilted front porches. The truck sat untouched, still encased in a crust of mud.

Air conditioning. Giddiness bubbled inside her, and she closed her eyes, imagining her face in front of the vent. "Can I ride inside with you?" she asked Juan. He frowned. "Um, *puedo paseo* inside?" She pointed at the front passenger seat.

"*Sí, sí.*"

Annie scrambled into the cab. Juan opened the driver's door, and Marisol squeezed between them. He jammed the key in the ignition, and Annie waited, ready for the roar of the engine and the blast of hot air that signaled the air conditioner coming to life. But the truck only hacked and sputtered before it gave up altogether.

Juan turned the key again, and this time there was nothing. Not even a sickly cough from the engine. He popped the hood, muttering and smacking his palm on the wheel. She didn't need advanced Spanish to get the gist of it. Juan got out, and Annie opened her door to let in fresh air, her legs sticking to the seat as she moved.

"So…" Marisol raised one side of her mouth in a lopsided, trouble-making smile.

"So, what? I guess the truck is broken?"

"So you and Felipe have made up, yes?" The other corner of her mouth lifted, and Marisol's grin consumed half her face.

"Uh, yeah. I guess. I tried to apologize, but…" She shrugged. He didn't seem angry about the Pink Stringer incident anymore, but there was still a wall there. One that hadn't been there a few days before.

"You are blushing." Marisol made the last word a song, drawing it out over several unbearable moments.

The heat simmering below the surface of Annie's skin caught, and fire burned in her face. "It's…I just…He…"

"Spit it."

The inside of the truck seemed to grow even hotter, and Annie poked her head out of the open door and gulped in the ever-so-slightly cooler air. "I thought there was something there, you know? But—"

Marisol threw her hands to her mouth, and a deep cackle escaped between her fingers. "I knew it!"

"Knew what?"

Marisol sat up as tall as her tiny frame would let her. "That you would not be able to stay away from each other. I knew it since the day I told him you were coming to Nicaragua."

Annie's heart ping-ponged through her chest, shooting between elation and dread, once in a while hitting a little bit of fear on its way.

"What is wrong?" Marisol fanned herself. "You look like…Oh no. Are you going to be sick again? It is very hot in this—"

"No. It's nothing. I'm fine."

Her friend raised both eyebrows and tucked her chin toward her chest. Trying to sneak a lie past Marisol had always been like trying to sneak past a bloodhound while wearing a ball gown made from sirloin steaks.

Annie sighed. "I don't know if it's a good idea. My boyfriend and I broke up a few weeks ago, and…" she sighed. *I'm not ready for this*, is what she wanted to tell her friend. *Definitely not ready.* But the words wouldn't come.

"You did not tell me this."

"I didn't want to talk about it. It was easier to try to forget." And she *had* managed to forget. Not Mike necessarily, but in the midst of everything that had happened, she'd forgotten to be sad. Worrying about who her ex was hooking up with in her absence didn't even make it into her top ten list of problems—not when she was dealing with things like helping a woman give birth or staring down the barrel of a rifle. Or the way her world shifted when Felipe smiled at her. "It doesn't matter. I obviously misinterpreted things. Besides, I'm leaving soon anyway."

"*Mi Anita*, you will be here for," Marisol counted on her fingers, "seventeen more days."

"Exactly."

"Seventeen days is enough to make some *very* good memories. Trust me. I am the Cupid of Nicaragua."

"*Vamos.*" Juan stood at the door, waving them out of the truck.

Annie slid out and smoothed her sticky clothes, grateful to be out from under Marisol's microscope. "What's going on?"

"*Muerto*," Juan said.

"Dead?"

"What do we do?" Phillip asked. He stood with his head ducked under the hood and his hands behind his back, like a child afraid of breaking his mother's fine china.

Annie felt Felipe's presence behind her even before he spoke. It made her legs restless and her mouth dry.

"We will get a ride," he said.

"From who?" she asked. Other than their truck, there wasn't a single motor vehicle in sight.

"Someone will come."

"You mean hitchhike?" Her mind flew to the hold-up—those angry boys with their guns and threats. She wouldn't do that again. Couldn't.

"*Sí.*"

Marisol patted her arm and gave a small nod. "It is okay, not like in the States."

"I think it's better if we don't." Phillip slammed the hood.

Juan shot him a glare before turning to Annie. "You still have your electric gun, no?" He made a buzzing sound before jerking his limbs in every direction.

She smiled despite the tightness in her chest. "No. *Muerto.*"

Marisol looped an arm through Annie's and led the group down the dirt path to the rutted, unpaved highway. Tiny gnats swarmed their faces, and the road curved far into the distance—empty and barren.

The five of them sat, then stood, then sat some more. Marisol dug a paperback out of her bag and leaned against Phillip, devouring the pages. Annie had forgotten how much her friend loved to read. When they were in high school, Marisol read every piece of fiction in Annie's house—including the box of musty Babysitter's Club books they'd unearthed in the basement.

She turned away from them and closed her eyes, letting the breeze rush across her sweaty skin. The grass tickled her arms and legs as she forced her attention to the most pressing of her problems:

hitchhiking. Cold fear settled into her belly as she composed a mental list of every self-defense move she'd ever read about, learned, or seen on television. It stalled out around number four.

"What are you doing?" Felipe sat next to her, resting his elbows on his knees.

Annie looked at her hands. At some point in her self-defense review, she'd straightened her fingers into firm lines, Karate Kid style. "Nothing." She stuffed her hands underneath her legs.

"Annie, yesterday I—"

"Thank you. For yesterday. For trusting me."

He shook his head. "I am the one saying thank you. You saved them."

"How about this?" She took a stab at knocking down that wall. "You forgive me for the whole electrocution thing, and we'll call it even?"

"Deal." He rolled forward as if to stand, the wall still clearly intact.

"What do you do when you aren't on these trips? Do you work at a hospital?" The words ran from her mouth, quick and nearly unintelligible.

"*Ahora* has a clinic outside of Managua," he said, sitting back down. "I work there. Marisol too."

"Juan?"

"No, he is a *voluntario*." They both looked over. Juan lay on his back with his hands folded across his chest, eyes closed. "Do not tell him you know," Felipe said. "His head gets big."

Annie smiled. "I won't."

Something rumbled, and she tensed, waiting for a vehicle to come tearing down the road.

"Thunder."

"Do you think it's going to rain?" The sky was a thin gray blue, but there were no clouds.

"Maybe."

She took a deep breath and let the exhale rush through her teeth. "Tell me something else about you."

"Like what?" He looked at the grass then at her.

"What do you do when you aren't working?"

"Baseball," he said, the dimple coming out. "I coach a team. They are terrible."

"They can't be that bad."

"They are." He rolled onto his back. "But they are five and six years old, so no one minds very much. You?" he asked.

She lay beside him, letting the grass tickle the back of her neck. "I don't play baseball."

"No, what do you do? Besides school and spending time with your boyfriend."

For a fleeting moment, she considered making something up. Something that would put her in the same league as a gorgeous doctor who hikes out into the rainforest to save people *and* spends his free time coaching pee-wee baseball. "No boyfriend. I'm in a sorority. Treasurer. I handle all the money." *So basically nothing.*

"But your photo album."

"What about it?" There was nothing exciting in there. Random photos of her dad and her cat. A sorority formal or two.

A lumpy, foreign sound hummed among the buzz of insects and muted conversation. In the distance, a dirty canvas-covered flatbed truck rumbled along, and two women and a man already hung from the steel poles tenting the fabric. The mud-coated monstrosity lumbered toward them, and she jolted up, not giving Felipe a chance to confirm the paltriness of her accomplishments.

• • •

The vehicle rolled toward them in a cloud of dust. After a nod from the portly driver, Felipe stepped onto the rail and pulled Annie up next to him. *No boyfriend.* "Come on, *Americana.*"

She gripped a pole with both hands, and her fingers slid in the mix of grime and sweat. She wiped them on her shorts and tried again.

"*¿Bien?*" He put a hand above hers.

She squeezed her eyes shut. "I think so."

Phillip and Marisol managed to squeeze in the bed, perched on a tower of hay. Juan grabbed a free spot on the other side of the truck bed.

The driver hit the gas, and Annie wound both arms around the pole, pulling her body and face close to the dirty metal.

Felipe tried not to laugh. "If you relax your muscles, it will be easier."

She shook her head, plastering herself to the pole.

"Annie?" He leaned in closer, struggling to be heard over the purr of the engine. "This is going to be a very long ride. Do you want me to ask someone to trade places with you?"

She stared straight ahead, and even her lips barely moved. "No."

She will deliver a baby without blinking but cannot ride on the back of a truck. He shifted into his own space, but Annie's hand darted behind her and grabbed his. With one stilted movement, she wrapped his free arm around her waist, turning him into a human seatbelt.

The truck picked up speed, and the air made her hair whip against his face. He shuffled forward and slid his body behind hers. Annie's heart pounded so hard, he could feel it in his chest, and the pace of it nearly met his own—although it wasn't the hitchhiking that made his blood race.

One glorious hour later, they arrived in Sahsa. Felipe peeled himself from the curve of her hip and the softness of her hair.

"Where are we going? Is there, like, a hotel here?" Phillip ran a hand through his windblown hair as they crossed the road.

"We will stay here." Felipe pointed to the building in front of them. A two-room building made of cinder blocks and topped with tin. Sahsa, the town where both he and Marisol had been born, had a few stores, one clinic staffed by a rotation of three local nurses, and a handful of bars. But no hotels.

"This is the *casa materna*. No one uses it," Marisol said, unlocking the door. "Except us."

"*Casa de materna*? Who's Materna?" Phillip asked.

Beside him, Annie laughed. "It's like a maternity home," she said.

A rush of hot, stale air hit Felipe's face as he stepped into the building. A layer of grit coated the thin, plastic mattresses in the front room, all the beds clearly unused since the last time they'd stayed. He walked through the narrow space between the beds and pulled back the threadbare white sheet separating the two rooms.

Sweat rolled down his back. "Open the windows," he said as he turned and collided with Annie.

Her pink cheeks glistened with sweat. "So this is where we're staying for the next few nights?" She stared at a cracked porcelain sink along the wall. "And there's running water? What if someone wants to use the home while we're here?"

Felipe could practically see her salivating.

"Would we get to help?" she asked.

"Relax, *Doctora*," Marisol called out. "No one is due this week."

"Good." Phillip plopped down on the mattress closest to the door. "I can't wait to sleep in a real bed."

"I did not know you did much sleeping." Juan's mustache twitched.

"Careful, old man." Marisol wagged a finger at him. "If you are not nice, I will set a swarm of horseflies loose under your sheets."

Felipe turned to the corner, where an oblong table brimmed with boxes and other supplies. He dug through them as Juan and Marisol threw harmless threats at one another. "Your supplies." He handed a box to Annie.

Outside, the sun was setting. The light filtering in from the open window turned her hair a soft shade of pink. "Supplies?"

"*Sí.* For your sexual education classes." His stomach growled, and he reached for the opportunity to get her alone. Perhaps to find out a little more about this no-boyfriend situation. "Are you hungry? There is a restaurant—"

All the color leached from her face, leaving her freckles stark against her skin. "My vagina!"

Felipe took a step back. "I am sorry. What?"

"My flashcards. Oh my God. I can't—" Her hands fluttered around her face, pushing back her hair, lacing in and out of themselves.

"Annie?"

"Flashcards. I made flashcards so I could learn all the proper names for…things." She waved a hand over her midsection.

"That is good, no?"

"They're gone. I haven't seen them since…" She closed her eyes. "Shit. I can't believe this."

"Breathe. Where did they go?"

"Those boys. Out there." She waved toward the door. "The ones who stole from us. They took my vagina. Oh God, not *my* vagina. It was a model." She hung her head. "I can't believe I didn't realize until now."

"*Todo bien*, Annie. Maybe our *banditos* are studying them right now. We have a whole box of things here. *Útero.*" He pulled a stuffed toy from the tattered box, trying not to let his expression reflect the unease inching down his spine. Something always went wrong on the brigades. Usually multiple things. Someone would get sick. Or the supplies would run low. Or the rain would beat down so hard Juan couldn't maneuver the boat down the river, eating into their promised rest days. And more often than not, whatever went wrong at this point in the game would be the straw to break the American camel's back.

Annie took the plush uterus from his hands and turned it over between her fingers. "People like fuzzy, right?"

DAY TWELVE

As they marched to the clinic, Annie marveled at the tiny town. Hours of dense jungle separated them from the nearest actual city, but for the first time in two weeks, they passed a bar and a crowded convenience store, and a school painted in primary colors. Marisol and Juan pointed out the landmarks as they walked along the dirt road. The locals pointed at the Americans.

Twelve days, that's how long it takes to stop feeling like a zoo animal.

The sun perched over the treetops, sending its scorching rays to broil Annie's skin. She knew she probably smelled atrocious, but her stench was masked by the manure of farm animals wandering the main street of the town.

Marisol pointed to a tiny hut to their left. "We call her Tortilla Woman," she said. "I do not think anyone knows her real name, but everyone knows where to go to buy tortillas."

Annie nodded, barely hearing the words, and stepped around a pile of cow dung in her path. "Where's Felipe?" She tried to keep her voice breezy, but her friend's grin told her she'd been made.

"He went to visit our cousin." Marisol winked and guided their group into a square churchyard, where a flock of patients had already gathered. The crowd closed in around them as soon as the group set foot on the lawn, hugging and slapping Juan and Marisol on the back, waving to Annie and Phillip from a safer distance.

Inside the church, the wooden pulpit loomed over them, shiny and polished while the rest of the building languished under a coat of grime. The four of them moved seamlessly into their activities, and once Felipe walked through the doors, the patients streamed in behind him.

Annie enlisted a battalion of curious children to help with her job, and in the slow periods, she tried to recreate her sex ed lecture. But her mind wouldn't stop spinning, reliving her outburst the night before—*Who screams about their vagina like that?*—and then berating herself for forgetting the classes in the first place. Between teenage robbers and eating armadillo, she'd forgotten her one real responsibility during this trip.

You have *to get it together.*

"Do you want to watch my last exam?" Felipe stepped in front of her, looking exhausted but happy. Rumpled but perfect. Like he was born to do this kind of work.

"What's that?" Annie pointed at a tiny, dirty handprint gracing his scrub shirt just below his heart.

"I had to go to my cousin's house this morning. His daughter is a bit of a…trouble making girl?" He cocked his head to one side. "That is not the right words."

"Troublemaker," Annie said.

"Ah. I was not very far off then." He held out a hand. "Examinations? I think your helpers have this under control."

"I don't think I should. I'm trying to remake my sex ed lecture." She held up her journal, and he plucked the notebook from her fingers.

"Tonight we will work on the classes. Come." He tucked it in the back pocket of his pants.

"Can I have my journal?" In a blind panic, she followed him to the front of the church, imagining him cracking the pages to see her ridiculous schoolgirl crush laid out in the open. "To take notes."

Felipe waved his patient forward and unhooked the stethoscope from around his neck. He held the device out to her. "You cannot take notes and learn how to take blood pressure at the same time."

"Really?" She took the stethoscope.

He nodded and handed her a blood pressure cuff. The Velcro was worn to nubs, and dirt had worked its way into the crevices of the deep blue fabric. "And here is your patient."

The woman eased herself into the pew in front of them. A

shocking gray bun sat atop her head, dried and brittle from years in the sun. Felipe spoke to the woman in Spanish, frowning and nodding as he asked question after question and waited for her slowed responses.

"She has headaches, and she says that sometimes her feet swell," he translated. "She has some hypertension, but she managed it in the past by changing the foods she eats."

Annie nodded, itching to jot it all down.

"Also she wants to know if I am coming over for dinner tomorrow."

"Oh." Annie raised her eyebrows. "That's very nice."

"Not that nice." He grinned and the woman's return smile made something prickle in Annie's mind. *Something about the tilt of her chin.* "She is my aunt Barbara," Felipe said. "It is her duty to feed me."

The woman nodded, her bun shifting perilously atop her head. She spoke to Felipe once more, too fast and familiar for Annie to keep up. *Maybe something about a horse? Or hair?* She could never keep those two words straight.

Felipe shifted closer and placed two of Annie's fingers below his aunt's elbow. "First, you will have to find her pulse. Do you feel it?"

She pressed a bit harder, trying to ignore the thudding in her own veins. "Got it." She put the flat end of the stethoscope against the woman's skin.

Felipe took the cuff and wrapped it around his aunt's thick upper arm. He tucked the bulb between Annie's fingers. "You will squeeze this until you cannot hear her pulse any longer." He pointed to a small valve. "When it is silent, turn this very slowly."

Annie nodded.

He carried on with his explanation. But between her excitement and nerves, all his words ran together in a jumbled heap. Five tries and five different readings, all of them suggesting the woman was not actually alive.

"I'm sorry. I mean, *lo siento.*" Annie smiled at the woman.

Felipe's aunt waved her free hand and rambled on in Spanish.

"She says do not worry," he said. "She is used to being my test patient. I will not tell you the other things she said, because they are too embarrassing."

Annie kept her gaze on the woman's arm, trying not to think about how close he stood. "You won't embarrass me any more than I already am."

"No, no. Embarrassing for me. She says the first time I tried to take her blood pressure, I squeezed much too hard. She thought her arm would fall off."

Annie smiled as the tension drained from her shoulders. She stood. "What am I doing wrong? It's like the minute I turn the valve the needle falls all the way down."

"Maybe you are turning the valve too fast? Here." He spun her around. "Try again, and tell me when you cannot hear the pulse."

I delivered a baby the other day. Certainly I can figure out how to take someone's blood pressure. Annie took a breath, closed her eyes, and squeezed the bulb. "Okay," she said when the stethoscope fell silent.

Felipe covered his hand with hers—his thick fingers moving over her long ones, turning the valve a hair at a time. The needle inched down bit by bit.

"One sixty!" Annie jolted upright as soon as the woman's pulse flooded through the ear pieces. Felipe stumbled backwards. "Oh crap. Sorry."

He laughed. His aunt laughed. "You still have to take the bottom number," he said.

"Right." She shook her head and tried again—her body begging him to rest his chest against her back once more; her mind hoping he would let her do it on her own.

He stayed back.

"One sixty over eighty," she said.

When the exam ended, Felipe sent his aunt away with a prescription for blood pressure medication and a promise to come by for dinner soon. The clinic had ended sometime around Annie's third attempt with the cuff, and now they stood facing one another in the empty church.

"Now we will go fix your problem," he said.

"My problem?"

He held out her journal. "Your lectures."

"Oh!" Her eyes widened at the sight of the purple notebook. She snatched it from his fingers and stuffed it into her bag.

"Come."

She followed him out the door, and as they walked to the maternity house Felipe quizzed her again and again on how to take someone's blood pressure. By the time they stepped inside, Annie could recite the steps forward and backward.

In the narrow front room of the house, Juan lounged on his mattress, and light filtered in through the window to his face. He reminded Annie of a cat sprawled out in a patch of sun. Marisol had Phillip by the belt loop, pulling him out of the compact quarters.

"Everyone must stay here tonight," Felipe announced from the doorway.

"*¿Qué?*" Marisol asked. Annie could practically read you're-not-the-boss-of-me across her creased forehead.

"Annie needs help."

"What happened?" Marisol let go of Phillip.

"Those kids took my stuff. My flashcards and…stuff for the sex ed class."

Marisol shoved Juan's feet off the bed and sat. She drew her eyebrows together. "*Mi Anita.* You lost your vagina?" She was so earnest.

Annie nodded. "Now I have this." She held up the fuzzy uterus. "I think it has an STD."

"We will go to the store and get some drinks." Marisol stood and pulled Annie to her feet. "And food. *Vamos.*" Phillip rose, but Marisol put out a hand. "This is *chica* time."

Annie followed her out the door.

"I see you have made friends with my brother again." Marisol nudged her in the side.

"Sure."

"And maybe you have made more than friends with him?"

Annie shook her head. "I already told you—"

"He would not stay in for any old *Americana*," Marisol said. "Most times this is the night he spends drinking with our *primo*."

"Cousin? Oh, he said he went by there this morning—"

"Yes, to cancel. It is fine. You are much prettier than Carlos." Marisol winked and pulled her into the store. Annie swallowed the strange mix of guilt and elation that climbed her throat.

They returned to the house a few minutes later, arms loaded with bags. The lights sputtered on and the whirring of the fan filled the air.

"We have three hours of electric." Felipe took a soda from his sister's arms and sat on the bed, smiling. "Sit." His dimple made her dizzy, and Annie found herself squeezing in close enough to smell the mix of rubbing alcohol and fresh cut grass that always seemed to cling to him after a clinic. Medicine and sunshine.

"Thanks for staying here and helping," she said.

"It is nothing." He leaned in, resting his free hand behind her back. Her body buzzed, hyperaware of his every move.

The others climbed onto the bed facing hers—where Marisol supposedly slept.

"Teach us about sex," Marisol said.

Annie tried. She stumbled over the pronunciation of the proper words, and Juan tried to convince her to use several vulgar terms, arguing they were all easier to pronounce. She refused. They took turns pelting her with questions the villagers might ask, and for a little while, Marisol pretended to be a teenage boy who didn't understand why he woke with an erection every day. Annie never figured out how to explain that one.

Felipe was the only one to offer much in the way of actual advice. Repeating words and phrases again and again, writing down phonetic spellings, and clueing her in when Juan's suggestions took a tawdry turn.

"Pork sword. I think it will translate well to Spanish, no?"

Annie shook her head, and her cheeks ached with laughter. "Pork sword? Where do you learn this stuff?"

Juan shrugged as the electricity clicked off.

"You will do a good job." Felipe got up and pointed his flashlight at the ceiling.

"Thanks." She stood as Marisol slid by, pulling Phillip out the door with her. A moment later, footsteps shuffled along the ground, and by the moonlight, Annie watched Juan head toward the outhouse.

Beside her, Felipe pulled something from his bag. "Here. In case you are tired of eating *gallo pinto* all the time."

They were alone, and all her emotions tumbled around inside her chest. Flipping over and over again like a packed dryer set to high heat. She stepped closer, stopping when the heat radiating from his skin invaded her space. "What is it?"

"*Coco dulce.* Coconut candy."

A king-sized grin crept over her face, and she was helpless to stop it. "It smells amazing."

"Good night," he said.

"Felipe?"

"*¿Sí?*"

Annie swallowed, butterflies going mad in her stomach. "Thank you."

His flashlight clicked off.

"Annie?"

"Yeah?"

The silence stretched for eons. Finally, he stepped closer, barely visible in the darkness. "I really want to kiss you." His fingers brushed against the skin of her low back, firm but tentative. Gentle but wanting.

They eased the words right out of her. "Then kiss me."

She wrapped her arms around his neck, pulling him in until their mouths met. His lips were perfect against hers, mirroring the soft eagerness of his touch. And when he tugged her closer against him, a desperate whimper escaped her throat.

Too soon the shuffling footsteps returned. *Juan.*

She inched away, breathless and lightheaded.

Felipe took her stitched finger between his. "Tomorrow we will take out your stitches, *sí?*"

"Sure."

He brushed his lips against hers one more time, stealing a soft, quick kiss. "Good night."

DAY THIRTEEN

Felipe fell asleep dreaming about that kiss and woke up thinking about it. The way Annie pressed against him. The way her mouth fit against his. The way the soft skin on her back burst into goose bumps under his fingertips.

He made his way to the sink, brushing his teeth while his sister lay sprawled across her bed. Her mouth hung wide open and a string of drool stretched from her cheek to the pillow. A paperback with a cracked, worn spine sat perched open on the floor next to her. Across the narrow room, Annie was awake and staring at the replacement flashcards she made the night before. The morning sun filtered in through the window and danced off her hair. It was long and loose and tangled with sleep.

"Hi," she whispered, glancing at him.

"*Buenas.*" He smiled before realizing his mouth overflowed with minty foam. He cringed and fumbled with his water bottle, rinsing and wiping his lips.

He made his way toward her, and his feet echoed off the raised wooden floor. "Still practicing?"

Annie shrugged and pushed a curl out of her eyes. "We don't have anything else to do today, right?"

"*Sí.*"

She sighed, and her shoulders sagged. "That's fine. I need to brush up on this stuff anyway." Annie turned to the flashcards, but her eyes kept flicking up to meet his. A quiet blush crept into her cheeks, and he couldn't stop staring.

He'd never brought one of the tourists along to visit his family before, always eager to protect his loved ones from arrogance and looks of uneasy pity. "Do you want to come with me?"

"Where are you going?"

"I have to visit some family members."

"Your aunt? From yesterday?" Annie laughed. "I'm not sure I can face her after the blood pressure debacle."

"Well, she will be very disappointed when you do not come for dinner then. But this morning I am going to visit my cousin."

"The one with the troublemaker?"

"*Sí.*"

"Okay."

The town bristled with morning chores. People went in and out of the little store. Men herded cattle home after a wild night of grazing in the village. Children ran toward the school in stiff uniforms, their laughter and shouts trailing behind them.

"Are you hungry?" he asked as they walked through a crowd. Most of the people waved or clapped him on the back as he passed. A few stared at Annie and her long, pale legs. "Carlos, my cousin, makes very good breakfast."

"Breakfast." Annie's eyes rolled. "God, I am so hungry. Is it beans? Tell me it's not beans."

"You like eggs?"

"More than I like beans," she said.

He slipped his hand into hers. "Come."

They walked the rest of the way in silence, and he watched Annie take in the town. At first he was discreet, sneaking a glance or two her way as they moved. The closer they came to their destination, the longer his looks grew. Each time she smiled, he smiled in turn. But at the slightest hint of unhappiness—a frown here, a scrunched brow there—his pride drained. By the time they arrived at his cousin's home, he felt both unbalanced and elated, as though he'd just stepped off a roller coaster.

Carlos stood outside the wide, stilted home, splitting wood while his daughter collected eggs beneath a chicken roost nearby. "*¡Felipe!*" the girl called out, giggling.

Felipe lifted the five year old off the ground and tickled her sides.

She held tightly to the egg in her hands but squirmed enough to scare the chickens out of their tree. The girl folded over, protecting herself from his attack, but she straightened with a start when she noticed Annie. Felipe lowered her until her bare feet touched the ground.

"Eka, this is Annie. She is working with me. She is going to be a doctor one day," he told her in quiet Spanish.

The girl's eyes took up half her face as she looked at Annie.

"*Hola.*" Annie squatted and offered a wave. "What's her name?"

"Eka. Like Erica."

"*Hola, Eka.*" She waved again. "*¿Cuántos años tienes?*"

"*¡Cinco!*" Eka held up a handful of fingers.

"*¿Cinco? Dios mío.*"

Eka fell into giggles again. She handed Annie the egg cradled between her palms and pulled the American into the thick cover of trees along the back of the property.

"What is this?" His cousin's eyebrow arched so high it nearly touched his hairline.

Felipe shook his head, unsure how to explain. "*Nada.*"

"Looks like something, 'Lipe." He laughed at Felipe's glare. "Relax, *muchacho*. I will not embarrass you too much."

Felipe ducked away from the house, the mix of rainforest decay and heady flowers surrounding him as he searched for the girls. Under a thick cover of branches, Annie sat crossed-legged on the ground, eyes closed and hands folded around the half dozen or so eggs in her lap, while Eka combed and patted Annie's curls. The girl used a hair band to put it in one fluffy ponytail. She squinted, shook her head, and took it down. Then she put half of Annie's hair in a cockeyed pigtail. She stomped her foot and started again.

"I did not mention that Eka is a world-renowned hairstylist, did I?"

Annie's smile hit her face before her eyes opened. "You didn't."

"*Muy bien, Eka.*" He took the black elastic from the girl's fingers and handed it to Annie. "It is time for breakfast."

• • •

"Do you want to visit longer? I don't mind. I like Eka." Annie followed Felipe into the midmorning sun. Three women sat on the crooked front porch across the street, staring and pointing at Annie and Felipe. She assumed it was her hair. Eka's styling pursuits had turned it from frizzy mess to rat's nest of catastrophic proportions.

Felipe waved to the women. "No, I think you have heard enough of my embarrassing stories for today."

"I don't know. I still have some questions about that time you set all the worms free." She made air quotes around the last word. "Did you think they could swim?"

"I was four. I do not know what I was thinking." He shook his head, but a smile still played across his face. "I did not want to stab them with the hook."

The worm story was one of many Carlos told over their breakfast of plantains, eggs, and tortillas. Each tale made Felipe squirm further down in his seat at the oblong table. There had been the story about a seven-year-old Felipe trying to make tortillas and nearly burning down the entire house. And the time Carlos caught him in a tree playing doctor with a neighbor girl. And how, on Felipe's first visit to the town as a doctor, they tricked him into believing one of the elderly women in the village was eight months pregnant.

Annie laced her fingers between his. She expected the hysterical voice in her head to sound off, warning her that this was a horrible idea, but since the night before, it had been surprisingly silent. "Where now?"

"Shopping." He waved at a man carrying a basket of corn, husks brushing his beard as he walked.

"Are we going to buy a live chicken? Because I don't know—" She remembered the cages she saw the night before with Marisol, stacked one on top of the other behind the store's front counter.

"No. I have to buy something for Juan."

"What?"

"Underwear."

Annie's face went slack. "Underwear?" A laugh simmered inside her. "Why?"

Felipe grinned and tugged her along. "It is a long story."

"I have time."

As they walked along the winding road, dodging potholes and small children and a whole flock of chickens, Felipe told her the story of how they'd begun pranking each other years ago, when Felipe was a teenager and Juan was his mother's friend. How at fifteen, Felipe brought home his first girlfriend, and Juan had showed up dressed in suspenders and a red clown wig. He'd lurked around the house, as if there was nothing amiss about a middle-aged clown showing up everywhere they went. And how Felipe had repaid him by sneaking into his house and replacing every photo on the walls with drawings of penises. One exceptionally detailed drawing still hung in a frame in Juan's living room.

"Ever since then, it has been a thing. But I will need your help for this one." He squeezed her fingers.

In front of them, a tattered blue length of rope hung across the road. It drooped in the middle, hitting Annie below the knees. A hut the size of an outhouse stood to their right, and a uniformed police officer sat inside, watching. Felipe waved to the man before stepping over the string. Dust kicked up in the small space between them, grit and dirt clinging to the sweat on Annie's feet and legs.

"Are we supposed to—" She gestured toward the guard. She could feel his eyes on her.

"*Todo bien*. You can step over."

"Are you sure?" She chanced a look at the man. He watched them over his newspaper. A startling, sleek black rifle sat at his side.

"*Sí*." He tugged her hand, and Annie stepped over.

"What is that?" she asked, nodding over her shoulder at the string.

"They search trucks coming through. Make sure they are not bringing drugs from the coast into Nicaragua."

"And they think a piece of yarn is going to do it?" A drug dealer with a lead foot could take out the entire setup. *Or a pair of scissors.* "Must not take much to become a crime lord here."

Felipe's cheeks puffed out as he exhaled and let go of her hand.

Her stomach sank at his expression. "What?"

"The police are doing the best they can with the things they have."

"I didn't mean—" She stopped walking, realizing how dismissive and judgmental her comment must have sounded to him. "Sorry. I was trying to make a joke. It was stupid."

He held up a hand, shading his eyes as he squinted at Annie. "Okay."

"Okay as in you've already forgotten my stupid remark? Or okay as in you're going to toss me out of the boat on the way to the next village?"

The tension in her stomach uncoiled as he broke into a grin. "We will see." He pulled her along toward a rambling two-story building. The ground level was wide open, and two small, shirtless boys stood on the balcony above. People filtered in and out, arms loaded with baskets and plastic bags. It wasn't the same store she'd visited the night before with Marisol. This store was larger, and as far as she could tell, there were no caged chickens inside awaiting their certain doom.

"How many stores are there here?" she asked.

"In Sahsa? Three, I think. Unless someone has opened something new." He shuffled inside.

Annie followed. The inside of the store was dim and musty, but the smell of smoky chili peppers hung thick in the air. Racks and racks of goods crowded the space, erratic and disorganized without any type of aisles or reason. Three steps in, Annie knocked into a shelf full of lotions and rubber bands. But next to it, a display of snack-sized tortilla chips caught her attention. She rubbed her elbow while her mouth watered at the Doritos logo.

"Are you okay?" Felipe asked.

She nodded, biting her bottom lip. "I think I need these. I have some money." She picked up the bag and turned it. No price tag.

"Nacho?" He shook his head.

"I know we just ate, but junk food is kind of my thing. I mean—"

"Cool Ranch." He plucked the red bag from her fingers and replaced it with a blue one.

"Don't mess with a girl's Doritos." With a fake scowl, she put the blue bag down. She picked up the red one, then the blue bag too. "Because I'm a nice person."

Felipe rolled his eyes, but his dimple was showing. "Come. We need to find the largest pairs of underwear in all of Sahsa, and you need a *Rojita*." His lips brushed her forehead. The kiss was so easy. *Too easy.*

"*Rojita?*"

"*Rojita* is a soda. The best in Nicaragua."

"Will *Rojita* go with Doritos? Because…" She nodded at her haul.

"I think so." He picked up a wad of fabric. The fire hydrant red briefs had a thick white band at the top, and the leg holes were large enough to fit both of her legs. And maybe an arm.

Annie laughed harder each second Felipe held them to the window, inspecting the underwear as if they were a precious gem instead of the world's ugliest pair of men's granny panties. "What, exactly, do you intend to do with these?"

"Hide them in his things. He will reach into his backpack for his water bottle and find giant red underwear glued to it." He reached for another pair. These were blue and not quite as large as the others.

"Or," an idea took root in Annie's chest, "when he pulls out his dental instruments, ready to torture some poor unsuspecting soul, the world's largest pair falls out." She held out a green striped men's bikini brief. "And we write his name on all the bands, so when they fall out—"

"No one will believe they are not his."

"Exactly."

"You are a genius. I will buy your junk foods in exchange for your evil ideas." He took the chips and green briefs from her hands. "Ready?"

Annie nodded, but hung back. The lean, leggy girl at the counter was all wide eyes and flushed cheeks as Felipe pointed at the case behind her. She retrieved two bottles and tucked them inside a plastic bag, smiling and yammering in Spanish as she moved. Felipe's voice matched hers, moving at the speed of sound and leaving Annie unable to comprehend much of anything that passed between them.

On the way to the maternity home, she tried to ignore the prickle of jealousy hanging in the back of her throat. She'd never speak well enough to fall between English and Spanish mid-conversation the way Felipe did. And she'd never have the shared history that he had with all these people. Two more weeks was never going to give her that.

"Is that girl at the store your family too?" She knew the answer from the way the girl had looked at him.

"Nisha? No. Old friend." Felipe took her hand and pulled her along. "I am going to take your stitches out when we get back. Before you start eating chips." His laugh was deep, and the bags in his hand crinkled as he leaned in close to her ear. "And then we will set to work on our other project."

Flames raced through her as his breath eased across her cheek. "Other project?"

"Yes, this." He plucked the red underwear from the bag and waved them overhead like a pirate flag.

Once they arrived at the *casa materna*, Felipe tossed the bags on the ground and dug a pair of scissors from his supply pack. "Sit." He knelt on the ground beside her and flipped her hand palm up onto her knee. "Ready?"

She nodded, her face tired and sore from so much smiling. "Sure."

Felipe frowned as he worked, snipping and plucking the black thread from her finger. He lifted his head, and the crinkles near his eyes deepened as he grinned. "You are medically cleared to eat Doritos."

"You're done?"

"*Sí.*" He stepped back and grabbed one of the scuffed glass bottles out of the sack, popping the cap with his scissors. "In Nicaragua, you learn this in medical school."

Annie laughed and took the bottle from his hands. The warm,

red soda sloshed and fizzed, and a drawing of a girl in a feathered headband smiled back at her. "*Rojita.* Little red?" She scrunched her brow, and he nodded. "Well, that's not politically correct." She took a swig anyway, and the liquid was so sweet it burned her throat.

"Good?" Felipe sat next to her and the mattress shifted, forcing Annie's knee against his.

"Good." She ran her now stitch-free finger along his jawline, giving in to the need to feel his five o'clock shadow on her skin. She leaned in to him, keeping her lips a fingertip from his. "Really good."

He closed the distance, pulling Annie's face toward his with warm hands. He tasted like salt and the sugary red soda, and she pressed her mouth harder against his.

"Annie—" he started, but she leaned back, pulling him on top of her and easing her tongue between his parted lips.

Her hips strained into his as she intertwined their ankles. "Yeah?" she asked, gasping for breath.

Felipe pressed his forehead to hers. "I forgot." He kissed her again, driving her mad with the softness of his lips. She slipped her hands under his shirt, running her fingers along the smooth skin of his back and enjoying the way the muscles in his chest caught at her touch.

"*Hola.* Hello?" Juan's voice broke through their tangle of roaming hands and lips, and Felipe rolled off of her. "Do not mind me," Juan said. One hand covered his eyes, but he kept peeking out from behind parted fingers. "I only need a few things."

Annie stared at the ceiling, motionless, as all the blood moved from her more exciting parts into her face. Felipe groaned. "At least he's not dressed as a clown," he whispered in her ear.

On the other side of the room, Juan dug through his bag at fatally injured tortoise speed, glancing over his shoulder at them every few seconds.

"*Dios mío*, get out of here, old man." Felipe threw a pillow at Juan.

He caught it without ever turning around, tossed it back, and scurried out the door.

"How does he do that?" Annie asked.

"What?" Felipe leaned over her, tracing her cheekbone with one finger.

A shiver ran through her. "Never mind." She tugged him closer, her body anxious to pick up where they'd left off. "We'll get him back later."

DAY FOURTEEN

Felipe led them down the four steps of the maternity home into the bright morning sun. Annie looked at the plywood shacks with their rusty metal roofs and tried to picture a miniature Marisol running around outside, bossing everyone in sight. In her imagination, a tiny Felipe released a bucket of worms into the wild.

They reached a blue, two-story house. Sharp spears at the top of the iron fence glinted at eye-level. Inside the gate, Felipe's aunt waited for them in a frayed plastic lawn chair.

"*Buenas, buenas.*" She eased out of her chair and opened the gate, pulling Marisol into an embrace and kissing her cheek. She shook Phillip's hand, then Annie's, and as she did, her cedar scent hit Annie's nose.

She looked at Felipe before she turned to Annie. "*Carlos dijo—*"

"*Sí.*" Felipe took Annie's elbow and steered her to the backyard.

"What did she say? I wasn't—" Her face crinkled as she tried to remember his aunt's words.

"She wanted to know your name." He smiled. "Here is the laundry sink."

"But she already knows my name, right? What was the thing about Carlos? I'm understanding more things now, but—"

He ducked his chin and kissed her, cutting off her words and her air supply. His mouth was soft and teasing against her lips, and when he pulled away she was left gasping for more of him. He handed her a crusty jar of white powder and planted a feathered kiss on her lips. "Here is the soap. I have to go be interrogated by my *tía* now."

Annie dumped her clothes into the boxy laundry sink and tossed a scoop of detergent inside. She filled the basin with tepid water to her elbows, and a thin film skimmed the surface. She dunked her things again and again, swishing and swirling them through the water in her best impression of a washing machine. Within seconds, the water turned a vile shade of gray.

As she worked, a group of children gathered in clumps of two or three at the iron fence until they made up a single knot of at least ten kids, the oldest as tall as Annie and the youngest riding on the hip of another. She recognized a few of the faces from the last clinic and waved at them. Dirty water dripped from her fingertips.

"You have a fan club." Felipe's voice floated over her shoulder.

"Annie-watch. Like the zoo," she said. "Now with more gingers."

He cocked his head.

"Never mind."

"Have you ever washed your clothes this way?"

"By hand?" she asked, self-consciousness creeping up her spine.

"*Sí.*" Felipe stepped in beside her, watching her amateur, improvised technique. "You must scrub. Here." He nudged her over with his hip and a smile. His body echoed against hers as she stood next to him, fingers wrinkled and dripping, sharing the square sink. He dunked his hands into the water and came up with the old, gray sorority tee Annie had worn the day before. He rubbed the sides of the shirt together, hard and brisk. His face crinkled with the effort, but he sang under his breath in time with the movement. It wasn't a tune Annie recognized, but soon Felipe raised his voice and swayed his hips in an excellent lounge singer impression. The kids on the other side of the fence giggled and some joined in, singing at the top of their lungs and mimicking his horrible dance moves.

Annie's laughter bubbled over. Her hips moved in time with the song as she took the clean shirt from him and hung it on the line. But they shuttered and halted when she realized what Felipe held in his hand. With the fervor of a hockey player, she hip-checked him and seized a bra from his hands. "I think I can take it from here."

He kept singing as he shook his hands dry, but between beats he leaned in behind her. "*Interesante.*" His breath cooled the sweat on her neck, and a chill rolled down her back.

Annie looked at the bra in her hands. A pink lacy thing she'd thrown in her luggage at the last minute, which now seemed like both her stupidest and best idea ever. Her stomach fluttered, and her skin flashed hot as she remembered the way his fingers had crept up her ribcage the day before. She glanced behind her to the throng of eager children watching their every move.

"I will distract them." He tossed a blue soccer ball over the fence and followed with his body, smiling at her over his shoulder. The kids fanned out, breaking themselves into teams as she scrubbed.

• • •

The kids protested and shook their tiny fists at him, but Felipe picked up his ball and declared the game a tie. He hopped over the fence and wiped the sweat from his face as the crowd dissipated.

Annie pulled clothes from the laundry line. "It sounds like they want to keep playing." She reached for a pair of shorts, and he ran a hand down her side.

"I promised them a rematch tomorrow." His mind zeroed in on the way her hips shifted beneath his hands. It reminded him of how they'd arched to press against him yesterday, and he wondered if anyone would notice if he snuck her back to their temporary living quarters to explore them some more.

"Annie! Annie!" Three lanky boys stood at the fence, still sweaty from the soccer game.

She waved to them as she stacked a pair of shorts on top of her other clothes.

"You have *novios*." Felipe chuckled.

Annie smiled and shook her head at him. The freckles on her nose scrunched with the movement, and he found himself following her to the fence, where the boys dangled their arms and legs through the gaps.

"Annie. I am Leonardo," the tallest one said. His hair fell over one eye, and he pushed it away every few seconds.

"*Hola, Leonardo.*" Annie shook the hand he stuck through the posts. "*¿Cuántos años tienes?*"

The boy told Annie he was sixteen, but Felipe knew Leonardo was thirteen. He raised an eyebrow but didn't out the kid. Annie's smile was wide and welcoming, and her shorts showed off her smooth legs. Felipe couldn't blame Leonardo for trying.

"Brothers?" Annie asked, pointing at the threesome. Their heads bobbed, quick and eager.

"You get brothers?" Leonardo asked. His gangly limbs hung through the slats in a comedic mix of awkwardness and machismo.

Annie shook her head. "How do I say I am an only child?"

Felipe told her, and when the boys overheard, their eyes bloomed. Hands fluttered and weaved in and out of the fence as their flurried words moved between broken English and fluid Spanish.

"That is unusual here," Felipe said.

Annie smiled. She stood with her hands wrapped around the fence posts, talking to the boys. They pelted her with questions, some in Spanish, some in their rudimentary English. Sometimes Annie understood and answered. Sometimes he translated, wishing they would leave so he could have her to himself. The boys wanted to know her parents' names. *John and Linda.* Her birthday. *February third.* Her favorite color. *Purple.* Whether she liked Shakira. *Who doesn't?* Felipe wanted to know all those things too, so he didn't send them away.

"*¿Me gusta melocotón?*" Leonardo asked.

She twisted her mouth in concentration. "*¿Melocotón?*"

"I think you call this star fruit."

"*No sé,*" she told Leonardo.

The boy scrambled up the fence. At the top, Leonardo's arms gave out, nearly impaling him on the sharp edges. He fell to the ground, brushed his pants leg off, and tried again. This time he made it over on wobbling arms. The boy pulled himself up tall, and Felipe and Annie parted to make room for his teenage ego.

"*¿Vamos? ¿El árbol de melocotón?*" The kid bounced on his toes.

"There is a star fruit tree near his house. He wants to take you there." Felipe translated, praying she would say no. The trip would leave him no time to pin her against the laundry sink and run his hands along every part of her.

"Is that okay? I mean, can I leave my clothes here?"

"*Sí*," he sighed. "We will be back. I promised my aunt we will stay for dinner." Leonardo watched them from beneath his shaggy hair. "*Vamos*," Felipe told the kid.

Leonardo looped Annie's arm through his, and Felipe fell in step behind them. The boy led them out of the gate, where his brothers waited. Together, they left the dirt road and headed into a maze of stilted houses, drawing a few stares as they went.

They arrived at the tall, slim tree, and Leonardo dropped Annie's arm. He circled the tree, and under his feet the grass was worn thin and brown. Around them, small shacks dotted the landscape, and the thin cover of the tree split the searing hot rays of sun. After two complete loops, the boy chose a spot and snaked up the trunk. His long legs and bare feet gripped the bark, and he yelled to Annie, asking if she could see him. She shielded her eyes as she watched, shouting encouragement in halting Spanish. The other boys called out, guiding Leonardo to the closest fruits.

"I think he is too young for you." Felipe elbowed Annie in the ribs.

She twisted her mouth in a perfect impression of his sister. "A girl has got the needs."

With a thud, Leonardo came down from the tree and walked toward them. His hands were raw from the climb, and he'd tucked the hem of his shirt into his collar, creating a pouch for his spoils.

"Look!" He untucked his shirt, revealing four of the yellow fruits. He handed the biggest, ripest one to Annie and the smallest to Felipe. His brothers swarmed, taking the last two and leaving him empty-handed. Leonardo yelled after them and waved his fist in the air, but they were already kicking up dirt on the way home.

"Here." Felipe handed his to the boy, who accepted the fruit with a nod.

Leonardo nudged Annie. "Try. Try."

"How do I eat it? Do we have to peel them?" Annie's glance darted between them, then to the angular fruit in her hand.

"No. They do not have this in the store where you are from?"

Annie shrugged. "Maybe. I'm more of berry kind of girl."

"Berry?"

"You know. Strawberries, blueberries, blackberries, mulberries. Pretty much anything you can put in a pie."

Leonardo coughed. "Try, try." He nudged Annie again, his features flashing from fascination to eagerness.

"Okay, okay." She laughed and took a large bite from the middle of the star fruit. Juice pooled in the corners of her mouth and ran down her chin. *"Muy bien. Muy, muy bien."*

Leonardo's eyes widened at the sight.

"We must go. Try not to break his heart," Felipe said.

Annie let out a stiff laugh, but her ears turned pink. She held out a hand to Leonardo—her intent to shake unmistakable. *"Adios, amigo. Gracias por la…"* she turned her face toward Felipe.

"Melocotón."

"Melocotón," she repeated.

Leonardo nodded, and his smile stretched the width of his face. He took Annie's arm and insisted on chaperoning their walk home, rambling the entire way in stunted English.

• • •

They watched as Leonardo slipped through the gate toward home, looking over his shoulder every third step. When the boy was out of sight, Felipe pulled Annie in for a deep kiss, and she came utterly undone.

"How long until dinner?" she asked, her breath shallow.

He shrugged, kissing her again. It was softer this time, and she raked her hands along his chest. "Come on, *Americana*. I will give you the tour."

Barbara bustled in her dark, boxy kitchen, buzzing between the refrigerator and table. Phillip darted around the tiny room with her, sporting a yellow apron over his t-shirt.

"What's up, guys?" He held a wooden spoon. "Your aunt made me the sous chef. Cool, right? And she has a refrigerator, even though the electric doesn't work all the time. She keeps it cold with ice. And I'm not allowed to open it. Marisol's extra insulin is in there."

"Where's Mari?" Annie asked, trying and failing to wrap her mind around Phillip dressed as June Cleaver. The scent of sweetness and cumin clung to the sticky air, growing stronger with every inhale. "What are you making? Smells fantastic."

"It's this giant banana thing."

A warm, solid hand pressed against Annie's back, the weight of its palm inching past the waistband of her shorts. Phillip's words fell into a blur.

"Cool. Good luck with that." She pulled Felipe out of the kitchen. He guided her toward a steep set of unfinished wooden stairs.

The top of the staircase opened to a balcony that looked down at the street. Homes climbed the rolling hills beyond the road, and on the horizon a single jagged tree climbed toward the setting sun.

"This is the porch." Felipe gestured toward the long, narrow perch. But his eyes never left her face, and he trailed a finger down the length of her neck.

Her eyelids fluttered closed, and when she opened them, her gaze fell on a photo in an old wooden frame. The colors were faded, but there was no mistaking Felipe's dimple, even with the toothless smile. Her feet halted and refused to move. "Is this your mother? Your biological mother, I mean?"

He nodded and ran his fingers along the frame.

She stepped closer. His mother was stunning. Her long, dark hair fell around her shoulders in shiny waves. She had Felipe's earth-shattering smile with a hint of Marisol's mischief. "She looks like you. Mari too."

"*Gracias.*"

Annie kept her eyes on the photo but laced her fingers between his. "What happened to her?"

"Malaria."

"I'm sorry." She squeezed his hand and looked at him, trying to gauge his reaction.

Felipe pulled her into a rope hammock that stretched along the corner of the balcony. "It was a long time ago."

Her breath caught at his expression, and the burn of tears washed up her throat.

"What is wrong?" he asked.

"Nothing," she leaned in to him, trying not to think of her own father's health. At least she'd had twenty-one years with him. Probably a few more, if she was lucky. Felipe only had eight before his world crumpled.

"It is not nothing. I can see." He pulled her toward him. The thick rope dug into her arms, and she settled in next to him. Her head fit snug against his shoulder, and the feather-thin cotton of his t-shirt caressed her cheek.

"My dad is sick," she said. "Heart failure."

"I am sorry." He wrapped his arms around her in a tight hug, and his shoulder muffled Annie's sniffling.

"Sorry," she muttered, pulling back. "I didn't mean to be such a Debbie Downer."

"Debbie who?" His eyes narrowed.

She laughed through her tears. "Never mind."

"Okay, Debbie. Do you want to see more on the grand tour?"

Annie shook her head and snuggled harder into his arms. "Later."

The sun sank lower in the sky, and the town's generator began humming seconds before the lights around them clicked on. Without a word, Felipe reached over Annie's head and flipped them off.

"When will you apply for medical school?" he asked.

A rush of anxiety slithered into her chest. "When I get home. If I can come up with a good essay. My MCAT scores haven't exactly been stellar."

Beneath her Felipe shifted, and Annie glanced into his face. His cowlick was made worse by the weave of the hammock pushing against his hair, and his dark eyebrows were askew. It gave him a rumpled, just out of bed look that made her toes tingle.

"I am applying to a Master's program. Public Health." Frustration seeped into his features. "Or I am supposed to. My mother says I must have the degree before she will put me in charge of *Ahora*."

"You want to be in charge?" She propped herself on her elbow to study him. To watch the way his full mouth worked around his words. To see which phrases brought out his full smile and which left him dimple-less.

Felipe nodded as fireflies flickered around them, lighting the sky. "But this is not what I want to discuss." His hands inched up the bottom of her shirt, grazing her hip.

Annie raised her eyebrows. "What do you want to discuss?" She slipped her fingers beneath his shirt to trace his collarbone. "This?" She traced an imaginary line from his shoulder to his jaw. "This?" She lowered her forehead and let her lips flutter against his. "This?"

He tugged her closer and pulled her bottom lip between his. "*Nada*."

DAY FIFTEEN

At first it was only Leonardo and his brothers begging her to play.

"Annie!" The boy's face had popped up in the open window of the maternity home the second she and Marisol returned. "Come outside. ¿Play *fútbol?*"

Every bone in her body ached with exhaustion. She'd spent the last eight hours following Marisol from house to house as her friend checked in on elderly patients and caught up on local gossip. But the boy's expression was too bright and eager for Annie to say no.

She left Marisol and wandered into the evening heat. The sky glowed pink and orange, giving her some reprieve from the sun's beating rays. Soon it would be dark, and the lights in the town would flick on for a few precious hours. Once ten o'clock rolled around, they'd all be plunged into darkness until morning.

The boys drew lines in the rutted dirt road and divided themselves into two teams—or rather, Leonardo claimed Annie as his teammate and forced his brothers together. But within minutes, five or six more kids jumped into the mix. Then a few more. Before long, it seemed every child in Sahsa had converged on the soccer game. The teams and the rules were informal, and after a half hour of playing Annie drooped under a layer of sweat.

Felipe appeared as a mass of laughing kids moved down the makeshift field, leaving her behind to guard the goal. "Who's winning?" he asked.

It was the first time she'd seen him all day, not that she hadn't spent half the day thinking about him. The kisses. The touches. The way his teeth nipped her earlobe as they'd swung in the hammock the night before. "I have no idea. I just stand here, and anytime the ball comes this way I kick it back the other way."

The children ran toward them, the ball flying in front. Felipe dove into the mix, stealing the ball and driving it toward the other end of the field. The younger kids squealed and laughed, but the older ones tore after him, intent on taking back their command of the game.

She watched from the goal, her legs too full of cement to chase after them. The game spanned the width of the road, blocking any would-be traffic from crossing one end of Sahsa to the other. But so far, no cars had come through.

"*Annie, mira.*" Leonardo's voice rang out over the sounds of the game, and he waved to her from across the street. It was the third time in the last ten minutes he'd insisted she watch him. Each time he sprinted down the street and made a desperate grab for the ball. The kid was all sharp angles and uncoordinated bouncing, and he never managed to connect his foot with the ball.

"At least he's persistent." She waved back, and he took off. Dust and flecks of mud flew up behind him, and Leonardo drew his foot back and kicked, completely missing the ball. Just like every other time. But this time, the crowd imploded as he hit the ground, taking out a handful of kids with him.

Annie ran toward them, expecting tear-streaked faces and bloody knees. But everyone seemed fine, laughing and shoving one another. Except Leonardo.

His lay on his side, knees curled into this chest, moaning. Felipe knelt beside him, talking in low Spanish she couldn't understand.

"Is he okay?" It was a dumb question. Clearly he wasn't okay. "I mean—"

"Help me get him inside," Felipe said.

Together, they unraveled the boy and got him to his feet. Even with a coat of dirt and sweat caking his shirt, it was obvious something wasn't right. His left shoulder was higher than the right, and he kept his arm plastered to his chest, unmoving.

"Do you think something's broken?" Annie asked as they made their way into the empty maternity home. She eased Leonardo onto the nearest bed.

Felipe rolled up the boy's shirt sleeve. "Dislocated."

Annie leaned in closer. Leonardo's face was covered in beads of sweat, and a dozen tiny scrapes marked his elbow. A deep rivet sank into his skin just below the shoulder. "What are you going to do?" she asked. She fought the urge to touch it, to press her finger against his skin and feel for the out-of-place bone she knew was missing from the space.

Leonardo and Felipe began talking then, so quickly that Annie's mind only translated every fifth word. Something about pain. Maybe corn?

"He said this happened before. Three months ago. His aunt pushed it back into place," Felipe translated. He wrapped a piece of tape around the boy's sleeve, keeping it rolled out of the way.

"Maybe it never got reset right?"

Felipe shrugged. "This happens one time, it happens many times. He will need to learn how to fix it himself."

"Fix it himself?" Annie's cheeks scrunched as she sat beside the boy. No one should have to reset their own dislocated shoulder. Especially a kid.

"*Sí.* Or his family can do it. But we will do it this time." He pulled a supply bag out from beneath one of the beds and began digging.

"Annie can fix, yes?" Leonardo looked at her with wide, pleading brown eyes.

She started to tell him no. That she was just a college student from the suburbs, and that his shoulder looked angrier than her drunk uncle on New Year's Eve.

"*Sí.* I mean yes, right?" She glanced at Felipe, trying to look brave. If this kid's aunt could do it, she could too—especially with a doctor's supervision. Plus, she'd delivered a baby a few days ago. What was a measly shoulder after that? Of course, that woman had done most of the work for the delivery. "Or, I can watch, if you—"

Felipe grinned. "Yes, you can do it." He held a bottle of clear liquid in one hand and a packaged syringe in the other. "But first I am going to inject him to make his ligaments loosen. Plus it will help with the pain." He unwrapped the syringe, and beside her Leonardo went stiff.

"No, no." The boy stood, still cradling his shoulder against his body. His gaze darted around the room before locking on the door.

Annie put a hand on his good arm. "*Todo bien.*" She flashed him a bright smile, feeling only slightly guilty about using his obvious crush on her to distract him from the syringe in Felipe's hand. It was still covered by the cap, but she could tell that was a Godzilla-sized needle under the plastic. "*Siéntese.*"

Leonardo sat, but his stare pinged back and forth between the syringe and the door. She leaned forward and forced him to look at her.

"*Todo bien,*" she said again, as if Felipe hadn't just uncapped the giant needle behind her. If Leonardo turned around and saw that, he'd be gone. "*¿Cuándo es tu cumpleaños?*" It was an Intro to Spanish level question—in fact her first Spanish oral exam had centered around birthday party vocabulary—but it was the first one she could remember.

"*Febrero.*"

"*Yo también.*" Annie feigned fake excitement, as she asked him more birthday details. *What day in February?* His was the twentieth, hers was the third. *Did he have a party?* Yes, with his brothers and some candy from the store down the street.

Felipe tossed her a baggie full of alcohol wipes. "Keep him talking, but clean his arm. Here." He pointed to a spot on his own arm, then began drawing liquid into the needle.

Annie pulled out a wipe and gently rubbed the spot on the boy's arm. It took six sets of alcohol pads, but finally she got his arm free of mud and sweat from his fall. She was running out of things to say about birthdays, but luckily Leonardo wasn't. Maybe it was nerves. Or maybe he was a birthday fanatic, but he had a lot to say on the topic.

"*Bien,*" Felipe said. He leaned in and spoke to the boy. There wasn't a hint of worry in Felipe's face, and if she didn't know better, she would have guessed they were talking about the weather instead of the gargantuan needle behind the doctor's back. "*Mira a Annie.*"

Leonardo's eyes locked on hers as he followed Felipe's orders. The boy gripped her hand with the strength of a hundred hulking body builders, but Annie held in her gasp. He flinched for half a second as the needle went in, and the liquid disappeared into his body. Felipe pulled the needle out and recapped it with the protective covering.

"Good job. *Bien hecho.*" Annie patted Leonardo's good arm, and the boy's chest puffed out as if he'd just slayed a dragon.

"Now we wait," Felipe said. He eased Leonardo onto his back and poked around on the groove in the boy's shoulder. "You still want to reset the arm, yes?"

She gulped but nodded. "Can I feel it?"

He made room for her hand, and with fingers like feathers, Annie touched the spot on Leonardo's arm. Where a normal shoulder would be hard, it was mushy.

"*¿Lista?*" Felipe asked.

"Yep." Her voice cracked on the end, but she smiled as if she wasn't twirling in a cyclone of excitement and terror.

"Put one hand around his wrist." Felipe took her hand and clamped it to the arm clutched to the boy's chest. "Put the other hand here." He wrapped her fingers around Leonardo's forearm, just above the elbow. "*Bien.* Keep this hand steady and move his wrist very slowly. So he makes a half circle. Like this." He demonstrated with his own arm. "But if there is too much resistance or he is in too much pain, stop. Do not force it."

Annie's pulse thudded in her ears. "How do I know if it's too much?"

"You will know."

She gulped back her nerves, trying to find that excitement that had rushed through her a few minutes ago. "Okay. You talk to him this time. I have to concentrate."

Before long, Leonardo was rambling about soccer teams. Her fingers were sweaty, and she prayed they wouldn't slip from his arm, making things worse for everyone involved. As if moving the thinnest piece of porcelain imaginable, she lifted his wrist.

"*Bien.* Keep going," Felipe said.

She did, until the boy's forearm stuck out at a ninety degree angle from his ribcage. "Now what?"

"Keep one hand on his bicep and lift like this." He raised his own arm above his head, keeping the elbow bent. "You will feel it move back into place."

She licked her dry lips. *No big deal.* "Okay." She inched the boy's arm upward, and almost instantly his entire arm jerked into place. The odd curve in his shoulder disappeared. "I did it!"

"Better!" Leonardo's face brightened, and he started to sit up.

Annie's hands were still wrapped around his arm, and the feel of the bone sliding back out of socket made her insides drop to her feet.

"Owwww." He collapsed back into the bed and wiggled in pain.

"It is okay," Felipe said. He put a hand on the boy's chest. "Try again."

"Maybe you should do it?"

"He moved too soon. It is fine. Try again. I will hold him still."

"Okay." The arm was harder to move this time, as if the shoulder had gone from mildly annoyed to full-on rage. Leonardo groaned and writhed on the bed, and she paused.

"*Bien.* Keep going. Go slow. Pull down a little on his elbow this time. Do not jerk."

Annie clamped her jaw shut. Tears filled Leonardo's eyes but didn't spill over, and she pressed down. The arm wouldn't budge. She released the pressure but held his arm still, and counted to five.

"Annie?" For the first time, worry tinged Felipe's voice, but she ignored him and tried again. Pressing on the elbow while lifting the forearm, she pictured the bone slipping back into the C-shaped joint. Just like in her anatomy books.

A dulled pop rang out and the pressure released.

"Better," Leonardo said, again. He tried to shoot up to sitting a second time.

"No! Stay still." Annie scrambled to keep him down.

Felipe pushed against the boy's chest with one hand. *"No te muevas."* He prodded the shoulder with the other. "Better. Feel."

Annie ran her hand along Leonardo's shoulder. Except from the pinprick of blood where the injection had gone in, everything looked perfectly normal. *Better. Holy shit, I made him better.*

"We will make him a sling and then walk him home, yes? I need to talk to his mother."

Annie shook her head, fighting back a weird rush of excitement so high it made her eyes sting. "I mean, yes. Where's the sling?" She moved toward the supply bag so they wouldn't see all her emotions bubbling to the surface. Wearing a grin the size of the Grand Canyon might seem inappropriate after practically torturing a child.

"We will make one from a shirt," Felipe said. More Spanish chatter rose up behind her. Felipe. Leonardo. Felipe again. "No, no."

She turned. "What?"

Leonardo gave Felipe a look that would cut glass.

"He wants to know if we can make it out of one of your shirts." Marisol entered the room with a beer in one hand and a deck of UNO cards in the other. "To remember you."

Annie laughed and pulled out her backpack. "Sure."

• • •

The breeze was a welcome relief from the humid air inside Leonardo's house. They'd spent the last hour packed into the living room, as Felipe showed the boy's mother techniques to force his shoulder into place. All the while, Leonardo glued himself to Annie's side and rambled on about how she was the best doctor he'd ever seen.

Felipe would have been upset if it wasn't so ridiculous. And maybe even true.

Night had closed in, and the only light on their path came from the windows of the houses along the main street.

"Thanks for letting me do that." She stopped and squeezed his hand. Shadows covered half her face, but her eyes were still bright. "I can still feel his bones sliding back into place."

"*De nada.* Although I am afraid Leonardo will be heartbroken tomorrow when he wakes up and you are gone."

"I'm sure he'll survive." She shrugged and smiled simultaneously. "I *was* hoping to leverage his crush to get a few more star fruit, though."

"Hmmm." Felipe reached for her hand and guided her up the footpath that curved away from the road. "Turn here." A few meters later, the sweet fragrance of the pink flowers and tart star fruit drifted on the breeze.

"Wha—"

He put both hands to her face and pulled her lips to his. "Stay here."

The boy and his brothers had picked over most of the tree, but near the middle, Felipe spotted two clumps of fruit within reach of the thin, sprawling trunk.

He hadn't climbed that particular tree since he was six or seven, but he inched his way up, pulling himself by the thickest limbs. The bark scratched and scraped his hands, and as he eased himself along the branch below the fruit, his shirt snagged and ripped, leaving a tattered square of blue cotton amongst the leaves.

"Is everything okay?"

"*Sí,*" he said, trying and failing to pull his gaze from the overhead shot of her cleavage. "I cannot let Leonardo have all of your affection."

He shifted an inch, and the soles of his worn tennis shoes slipped. Felipe grabbed the overhead limb with both hands as the entire left side of the tree quaked with the sudden shift of his weight. The distinct pop of a branch breaking away from the rest of the tree rang out from his right. Felipe's heart seized, waiting to plunge to into the mix of mud and grass below.

But his branch held steady.

"Are you—ooooof."

"Annie? Annie?" He shuffled toward the trunk as fast as he could manage. The rest of the way down was a blur of scraped hands and knees, the bark tearing through his pants. His pulse thudded against his temples as he pictured Annie on the ground, knocked unconscious by a fallen branch. "Annie—"

Her hysterical laughter cut off his words. "Seriously? I think Leonardo wins this one." She stood where he'd seen her last, but leaves protruded from her hair and stray star fruit lay scattered on the ground around her.

"You are okay?" He rushed toward her, squinting to see her pupils.

"I think I'll make it." She held a piece of fruit between her palms.

The breath rushed out of him, and he wrapped his arms around her shoulders.

"I think we're even now." She smiled, her entire face lifting with the movement.

"Even?" He plucked a leaf from the end of her braid.

"I electrocuted you, and you threw an entire bushel of fruit at me."

Even though his entire body flashed with shame, her laughter was contagious. "Come. I promise not to cause any more head injuries." He nodded to a tall, rolling hill to their right. From the top, silhouettes of a hulking boulder and a single crooked tree looked down on them, illuminated by the full moon.

"Hold on." Annie squatted to pick up a handful of fallen fruit. "I don't care if this stuff tried to kill me. It's so good."

He took what she couldn't carry, and they climbed the hillside without saying a word. Annie walked ahead of him, the clack of her flip-flops announcing her every step. As they crested the top of the hill, Felipe forgot the fruit, letting it fall to the ground a second time as his hands slid down her ribcage, turning her and pulling her in for a breathless kiss.

Annie's haul let out a series of small thumps as it hit the earth, her hands rushing and tugging his hair. Below, the fireflies were out in full force, flashing and glowing, lighting the distance between the small homes. "Annie," he muttered into her neck, pushing away her braid. She let a sharp breath escape, and Felipe covered her mouth with his. The kiss built until his tongue crashed into hers. Their lips and hands and hips met, pushing and pulling and kneading into one another.

She stepped back. He kissed the freckle below her left ear. He kissed the hollow of her neck. He kissed the bit of collarbone poking out from her shirt.

Annie bit his earlobe, and the breath fell out of him. He was so impatient to touch her, so thirsty to feel her bare skin against his.

"Hey," she said.

He kissed her again, lightly this time, letting his lips graze the soft skin at the edge of her mouth.

She slipped her hands under his shirt, and each time her fingers grazed a new patch of skin, Felipe let out a sound that was half whimper, half roar. He let his tongue explore hers as he exposed an inch of her back to the moonlight and hesitated for a breath, expecting her to pull away again. But she pressed harder against him, and her tongue flitted across the ridges of his ear.

Felipe lay on the grass and pulled Annie to him. She wrapped her legs around his waist, straddling him, pressing into him with the same hard urgency in her kiss.

He shifted his weight, and they rolled. Her back arched toward him, and his breath quickened, overcome by how much he wanted her. By how much he needed her. His other hand inched up her shirt, tracing a line from her naval to her breast.

"Felipe?"

"¿Sí?" He pulled back to look at her face, counting all those freckles across her nose—the ones that had been there that first night in the airport, and the ones she'd sprouted since.

"I'm a little, uh…" Her forehead creased. "Prude, I guess."

"What is wrong? Prude?" The words were familiar, but all his blood was far from his brain. The only image they brought to mind was of a piece of dried fruit. He shifted his weight to roll off of her and tugged at the end of her braid.

"I, uh, um…" She stared at the sky. "I don't know if I want to have sex with you. Wait, no. I mean, I want to have sex with you, but I don't know if it's the best idea. I think—" Her words raced faster from her mouth with every passing second, and he could barely hang on.

"Annie." He tilted her chin toward him. "We do not have to do anything you do not want."

She hooked one set of long, delicate fingers behind his head. "We don't have to stop *just* yet." Her hand trailed down his chest as she arched up and placed a delicate, questioning kiss on his lips.

Felipe covered her body with his. He kissed her mouth. Her neck. Her ear. Her mouth again.

She wrapped her legs around him, her hands exploring. Between his adolescent crush and the way she leaned against him that first night in the airport bar, he'd thought about her hands on him many, many times. But when Annie finally touched him, it was better than anything he could have imagined.

He unglued himself from her, and peeled off her shirt. His wasn't far behind. The sight of Annie on the grass, shining under the sky, made every muscle in his body tense. In the seconds he knelt there watching the rise and fall of her chest, she slid out from under him with a single deft move, and Felipe found himself staring at her. Her shoulders were cloaked in freckles, and they faded into the skin near her collarbone, except the single brown spot that escaped and migrated to the top of her right breast.

She laughed. "There was a rock in my back."

Felipe stared, taking in every inch of her. The way a single curl escaped her braid and hung across her cheek. The fine sheen of sweat clinging to her cleavage. He sighed, knowing there would never be enough time to memorize it all.

DAY SIXTEEN

While the clinic wound down outside the tiny one-room school, Annie dug through her supply box. Again. She'd pawed through the sex ed materials at least a dozen times since they'd arrived in this village, organizing then reorganizing the condoms, laminated charts, fuzzy uterus, and other birth control options. This was her chance to prove herself. To do something entirely her own. To leave her mark on this place that seemed to be marking her at every turn.

She plucked a pack of birth control pills from the box, so ancient its yellow plastic case was layered with months of grime. A deep crack ran through the middle, and a single piece of dirt-tinged tape held it together. *Only for demonstration.* She sat the pill pack on the makeshift teacher's desk.

Next, she pulled a diaphragm from the box, and turned the small silicone cup in her fingers. *I thought these went out with the first Bush administration.* She propped it next to the pills, hoping no one would ask how to use it.

The door swung open, its apple-red wood creaking and groaning. Marisol smirked as she dropped a yellow-green plantain on the table. It was monstrous, nearly as long as her forearm and just as wide. "I got the biggest one I could find."

"Mari! I can't use that. The condoms won't even fit." Her insides were slushy and nervous enough without having to stretch a condom over a giant, edible phallus.

"They will. Trust me." Marisol's eyes were bright under her bouncing eyebrows.

"You do it then."

"What do they say? Those who can do it, do it. Those that cannot do it, teach it." She tossed her hair over one shoulder. "Besides, this is the first time for this class. If I do it the first time, they will expect me to do it every time. I already have too many things to do at the clinic."

"Wait. What? First time? Are you serious?"

"*Sí.*"

"I barely speak enough Spanish to find the bathroom. You think it's a good idea for me to be the first person to do this?"

"Of course. If the people make a riot, we will say it was the *gringa's* idea."

Annie's mouth went slack, gaping wide enough for a train to pass through. Apparently, the mark she was hoping to leave was going to be even darker than she'd imagined. She felt like a skydiver, overcome by both excitement and second thoughts as her toes dangled over the edge of the plane.

"I am not serious," Marisol said. She picked up the mammoth plantain and wagged it at Annie. "You are the first because I told my *madre* you could do it. She has been wanting to do this for a very long time."

"Oh."

"But if there is a riot, I will be outside with Phillip. Giving my own *educación sexual.*"

Annie threw a condom at her, but Marisol ducked and walked through the red door.

Three deep breaths, one cold panic, and two pep talks later, Annie finished organizing her display of antique birth control methods. *It's going to be fine. It's going to be more than fine.* She dragged ten pint-sized chairs into a semi-circle in the front of the blackboard. On one side of the board she drew the female reproductive system. On the other, the male.

Shit.

She erased it and redrew. This time it was worse—a giant erection and balls floating on the expanse of the chalkboard. She erased it with the side of her hand and wiped the chalk dust on her shorts. She drew it a third time, and a snicker grabbed her attention from the back of the room.

"It needs more veins." Felipe grinned.

She sighed. "I give up."

"Ready?" He stepped to the front of the room.

She shrugged. Marisol's words echoed through her head. *First time*. Gringa. *Riots*.

He rested his hands on her shoulders, then gave them one quick squeeze. His stethoscope hung around his neck, the flat end ducking into the pocket of his scrub shirt. "You will do fine," he said. "And I will be there to translate if you need help."

Annie glanced over at the giant plantain. "Okay."

"I will be right back." The door swung closed behind him, and she wiped her forehead on the hem of her shirt, trying to stay focused. A second later he returned, a line of people following. Bearded men sat in the child-sized seats with their knees inching toward their ears, and women bounced babies on their laps. Two teenage boys stood in the back, pointing and whispering to one another between glances at Annie and her table-o-birth-control.

Annie flushed hot, and she couldn't remember if she had put on deodorant that morning. She suspected not, given the sweat stains forming on her gray shirt. Felipe stood and introduced her to the crowd, but his words were muffled by the thudding of her heart in her ears. She plastered on a stiff smile.

"*Hola*." She stepped forward and waved.

The people muttered a greeting.

"*Hablemos de sexo*." She raised her eyebrows, praying for a laugh or at least a nervous giggle from the audience. But her students stared at her, twelve silent, blank faces. Annie's toes went numb, and her dry, sticky throat made it hard to swallow.

"Read the paper," Felipe mouthed from his spot next to the teenage boys.

She picked up the notepad from the desk. Her hands quaked, leaving smudges of sweat along the edge of the yellow paper. With a shaky breath, she rammed through the first half of the lecture, reading too fast and barely stopping for air. Her Spanish tumbled out, harsh and angular, but the more she thought about smoothing it, the rougher it became.

A woman raised her hand wildly in the air, jolting out of her seat with the movement. Her purple dress shifted with each flail, and for a minute Annie feared the woman was about to give them all a firsthand view of the female reproductive system.

"She asks you to talk louder," Felipe said.

"Oh." Annie's voice sounded too loud to her own ear, but she pulled up from her diaphragm and increased her volume.

The expressions in the crowd never changed, twenty-four wide eyes blinking back at her. *Maybe I'm still not loud enough.* She raised her voice another decibel. The audience's reaction failed to improve. As she strained against her ugly Spanish, she resorted to simply yelling.

"*EL SEMEN ENTRA EN LA VAGINA.*" The words tore at her throat and the effort left her short of breath. But Annie kept going, tumbling toward the end of the lecture.

A man in a green t-shirt put his hands to his ears and screamed at her. Spit flew from his mouth, clinging to his syllables while Annie fell silent.

"Okay. It is okay." Felipe moved toward the man, speaking to him in hushed tones, slipping Spanish words in between the man's diatribe.

"What's going on?" Annie leaned against the desk, her knees threatening to give out.

Felipe waved her off, still talking to the man. The others in the room stared at Annie, the fervor of their collective gaze searing holes into her already shredded confidence.

"You can continue." Felipe gave her a quick nod as the man calmed.

Annie wanted to slip out of the school and hide in the boat until it was time to leave this village. Instead, she fumbled through the rest of the lecture. Her tongue still tripped over much of the terminology, but she kept her voice steady and slow, speaking louder than she wanted but not at sonic boom levels. She paused every few lines to catch her breath, tearing her eyes from the page to see if anyone walked out.

They stared at her, expressionless, but stayed planted in their seats. By the time she pulled out a condom and Marisol's monster plantain, Annie's pulse had slowed from just-ran-a-marathon pace to somewhere around out-for-a-light-jog.

"*¡Dios mío!*" The woman in the purple dress threw her hands in front of her face. The plantain slid from Annie's fingers, and she fumbled, catching it before it smacked the dirt floor.

The teenagers in the back snickered. Annie pretended not to notice, but her ears flamed. And it was impossible to ignore the boys once the room exploded into laughter. She tried to keep her chin up and her shoulders back, but they sagged. *Get through this.*

"What are you doing with that? Is it a real plantain?" Felipe asked. His face contorted as he tried to keep it hidden, but Annie saw the amusement flickering on his lips.

A bruise bloomed on the end of the fruit, right where she'd been clutching it between her nervous fingers—which barely wrapped around the width of it. "I asked Marisol to find one for me." She shook her head and a smile crossed her face, even with the horrible shame gnawing at her insides.

Felipe looked at the ground then at Annie, his shoulders shaking with pent-up laughter.

The woman in the purple dress shot from her chair and pried the plantain from Annie's hands, giggling and dropping her arms low, as if the fruit weighed fifty pounds.

"No, no. I need that," Annie said, but even she couldn't help but laugh at the woman's expression. "For the, uh, condom demonstration."

Felipe said something to the plantain thief, and she waved her hands in reply, nearly smacking Annie in the forehead with the penis substitute. The entire class erupted into laughter.

Before she could ask what was happening, one of the leering boys in the back sauntered to the front and plucked the plantain from the woman.

Annie turned to the kid, holding out one hand. "*Gracias.* I—" Her sentence was lost as the boy held the plantain to his crotch, rubbing against Annie and stroking it as if it were his own giant, yellow genitalia. "What? No. Come on." She grabbed the fruit from his hands. "Knock. It. Off."

The kid's smirk stayed plastered on his face, but he let go of the plantain, holding his palms up in surrender.

Felipe inserted himself between them. "You are okay?" He grabbed the collar of the boy's shirt, and the faded green fabric bunched around the kid's neck.

Annie nodded. "Let him go."

Felipe's face puckered. "I think I will take him outside."

Behind him the other students shuffled in their seats, muttering and whispering to one another, all eyes trained on the trio at the front of the room. *I'm losing them.*

"No. He stays. I need him. And I need you to translate." She shoved the half-burst plantain into the boy's fingers and tugged him to the center of the room. The voices dimmed as she cleared her throat. "We have a volunteer for our demonstration." She held up an unopened condom.

Felipe stared at her.

"Translate. Please."

He shook his head, and a small smile played at the corners of his lips. "*Tenemos un voluntario.*"

The room buzzed with nervous laughter, and Annie's plantain molester shook his head furiously. "*Sí,*" she said. "Oh, so much *sí.*" She kept her gaze steady and locked on his, hoping she looked sterner and scarier than she felt.

"First, you have to open the condom. Look for the little notch along the top." She held up the foil square and pointed to the notch as Felipe translated. "Now our *voluntario* will show us how much he loves this banana."

* * *

The last person filtered out of the classroom, and Felipe wrapped his arms around Annie's waist. She kept packing, her spine stiff and straight.

"What is the matter?" he asked.

Annie sighed, and Felipe felt it as much as heard it. "I'm sorry the class was so horrible. I should have practiced more. I was too distracted before, with everything…"

He took the fluffy uterus from her hands and spun her around. "Annie, I was worried no one would come. But the room was full. Then I worried they would run us out of the village. Talking about sex here is not like the United States." He held up his hands. "But we are still here. No pitchforks. You did a good job."

And she had. Her Spanish was sometimes hard to understand, and at one point her voice had grown so high and so loud he considered the logistics of giving all the students a hearing exam after the lecture. But Annie handled that arrogant teenager far better than Felipe would have.

When the kid stole that giant plantain, Felipe's instincts had braced him for Annie's temper tantrum. Something about how teenagers in America would never do such a thing. Instead, she had turned everything he thought he knew on its head. Again.

"Are you sure? You don't have to say that just because I let you cop a feel now and then." Her smile was small, but amusement flickered through her eyes.

"What is this policing a feel?" He lowered his forehead and kissed her top lip.

"No. Copping. Like this." She smacked him hard on the butt.

"I see." He smiled at her, counting the flecks of gold in her wide, brown eyes. "Actually, I do not see. I think you may need to explain this further. On our way to rounds." He slipped his hand into Annie's and tugged her toward the door.

She kept her feet planted. "You really think the class was okay? Because it felt like a total disaster to me."

"*Sí.* Next time we come to this village, they will be more open. They will participate more. And the time after that, the room will be so full we will have to move the class outside. When that happens, we will teach someone from the village to lead it. Probably Bianca. That is the woman in the purple clothes, she sat here in the front?" He waited for Annie to nod in recognition. "And then she will become the person everyone in this village goes to for questions about sexual education." If her questions today were any indication, being the sexual educator for the village would be the fulfillment of Bianca's every dream.

"Okay." Annie took a deep breath. "If you're sure."

"I am sure. It takes time."

Something cool and wet smacked the back of Felipe's neck as they hiked through the village, but he was so wrapped up in Annie—her wide smile, the curve of her cheekbone, the way her breath always caught under his touch—he didn't realize what was happening. Not until the rain drops dumped from the sky all at once, soaking him to the core.

The ground beneath them turned to mud, and they ran toward the cover of trees.

"You will like this woman. They say she has an abscess. But I hope not. She is one of my favorite patients." Felipe handed Annie his poncho, struggling to be heard over the drumbeat of the rain.

To the left, the woman's house sat slanted against the trees. But the rain came down so hard and fast in front of them that it was nothing but a blur of brown against a sea of green.

"There." He pointed to the house. "Ready?"

Her response was to barrel into the rain, head down as mud kicked up behind her.

Felipe ran behind, his fist raised to pound on the door the second they arrived.

No one came.

He thudded again, the edge of his balled fist beating against the wet wood. Every bit of him was drenched, and water dripped into his eyes. "*¿Buenas?*"

He cracked the door and poked his dripping head inside. The old woman sat on a bed in the corner. She seemed to be made entirely of loose skin propped up by a few bones. Far frailer than the last time Felipe had been up to see her. She nodded him in, and he ducked through the doorway. Rain dripped through the ceiling, creating a scattered maze of mud puddles. The scent of roasted corn and bonfire mixed with the sharp smell of rain.

Behind him, Annie peeled off the poncho, nearly as soaked through as Felipe. "*Hola*," she whispered.

The woman's expression stayed slack and still. He squatted on the floor in front of her and put on an easy smile. "*¿Cómo está?*"

She chewed on her thin, pale lips and opened her mouth, but nothing came out. Her shoulders lifted in a shrug, and Felipe rubbed the back of his neck. "*Doña* Godoy is one-hundred and three years old." His gaze flicked over her frail arms for signs of the abscess.

"Seriously?" Annie took a step forward. The disheveled knot on top of her head bobbed with the movement. "*¿Tiene ciento tres años?*"

Doña Godoy opened her mouth again and held her lips there, wheezing in and out between them. A few seconds later a faint "*sí*" escaped.

As she spoke, he found the lime-sized lump near her shoulder. Angry red streaks traveled from the abscess to her elbow and toward her neck. With a gentle finger, he pressed it. Her skin was hot and feverish, at least a few degrees hotter than the scorching midday air. She didn't move or acknowledge him, her eyes still trained on Annie. He pushed harder. This time the woman turned to look at him, her left eye hazy with cataracts.

"*¿Duele?*" he asked.

She nodded.

"*¿Qué pasó?*"

Her answer was a mix of broken thoughts and cracked phrases that made sense less than half the time. "I am not certain," he translated, "but I think this started as a bug bite. It got infected, and someone from the village tried to treat her with camphor."

"Camphor? Like the stuff that's in lip balm?"

"It is like a, how do you say…" He squinted, searching for the right English phrase. "Like a snake salesman. You got a bug bite? Camphor. You have a sunburn? Camphor. You have a headache? Camphor."

Her face went as blank as *Doña* Godoy's before it lit up again. "Snake oil salesman?"

He nodded. "Snake oil. What is this?"

"No clue." Annie shrugged, staring at the lump on the woman's arm.

"It did not work. Now she has this abscess. It needs to be drained, and she needs antibiotics."

"What do you want me to do?"

He handed her a stack of gauze packs. "Hold these. I am going to numb it." He prepped a syringe as he explained the procedure to their patient in Spanish. "But when I open it, I will need the gauze right away."

"Open it?"

"The abscess."

The previously inert woman jerked her arm away from him, scooting across the bed and waving her arms. "No, no." Her eyes shined with tears.

He put down the syringe and showed her his palms. "*Todo bien, Doña.*"

With newfound agility, she shoved her age-spotted hands under the jumble of pillows and sheets, her entire body shaking with the effort.

"We'll get her calmed down. Like we did Leonardo." Annie squatted in front of the woman. "*Todo bien.*"

"*¡No!*" Their patient whipped around, waving something in the air above her shock of white hair.

A steak knife. *Nothing like Leonardo.*

Its wooden handle was grayed with age, and years of use had dulled the serrated edge. But the old woman brandished it at them as if it were a freshly sharpened machete.

"Annie, back up."

But she was already scrambling away from the woman, backing herself into the corner of the room. "She has a knife? She's a million years old."

"That is why she has a knife," he whispered. "Stay here."

He crept forward, still keeping his hands near his face. At the other end of the bed, his scalpel and a syringe full of Lidocaine sat out in the open, and he put himself between the woman and his supplies. "Look, I have nothing," he said in firm but quiet Spanish. "*Nada.*"

She lifted the knife an inch higher.

"You remember me, yes? I was here three months ago. You gave me two mangoes when I left. Look." He inched toward his bag, and pulled out the mangoes he'd packed that morning. "And I brought these for you." He set them on the bed next to her, their red and yellow skin stark against the pale blue sheets.

Her eyes darted between the fruit and his face, and millimeter by millimeter she lowered the knife onto her lap.

"Give me your knife, and I will peel one for you."

"Go away."

Annie shuffled toward them. "Hey, what if I—"

Doña Godoy lurched forward, jabbing the knife in Annie's direction. "¡*No!* ¡*No!*"

"Get back." The words came out sharp and jagged, harsher than Felipe intended. "Please, Annie. Get back."

She took one step backwards, and the old woman lowered her knife.

"Your arm is infected. I want to help you." He moved the mangoes. "Can I sit?"

She stared without a word, and he sat beside her, careful to move at sloth speed. The lumpy mattress shifted, and the fruit rolled to his side. Felipe held one to his nose, breathing in the cloying scent.

He held out his other hand. "*Por favor?*"

She handed him the knife, and as she did, tears rolled down the crinkles in her face.

"*Gracias.*" Felipe peeled the mango, its sticky skin falling in a pile in his wet lap. "Here." He offered the woman a slice of the fruit, and she took it between trembling fingers.

"Do not cut me." Juice dripped down her arm. "I am tired. I do not want this."

Felipe froze, and the mango slipped between his fingers and tumbled onto the pile of peelings. "But if you do not let me help you, you will get very sick." He wiped his hands on his shirt. *And I will not be here to help you.* "You will die." The words stuck to the roof of his mouth, but he shoved them out before he swallowed them.

The woman shrugged, almost imperceptibly, and put the mango to her lips.

"What's she saying?" Annie whispered, inching closer.

It tore at him, having to tell her this. "She does not want treatment."

Her face fell. "What will happen if you leave it?"

He shook his head.

"Oh." She sat on the floor in front of them, her long legs tucked under her.

Felipe started peeling the mango again. It gave his hands something to do, and his eyes something to focus on besides Annie's mournful expression or the old woman's defiant one. "I can leave her some antibiotics, but I do not think that will be enough." He offered *Doña* Godoy another slice of mango. "If she will even take them."

They sat together in silence, listening to the rain and sharing slices of mango. Every so often, he would ask the old woman if she was sure. If this was really want she wanted. If she really understood what it meant. With every shake of her head, he became more and more convinced the woman knew what she was choosing. And every time she chose to die, he hated himself and his job a little more.

DAY SEVENTEEN

Annie had been awake since the sun cracked the horizon, hiking next to Felipe as the world woke up, then motoring along the rushing river to get to the next village. Neither of them had said another word about the woman they'd left alone in that cabin to die. But Annie felt it hanging around her neck, slowing her steps.

She pushed the woman's face from her mind, forcing her attention to the jagged handwriting in front of her. Around her, the clinic carried on in its usual state of controlled chaos. Children took nets from her table, and Annie ran through the sex ed lecture, trying to smooth out the bumps. She could hear the words in near-perfect Spanish, but when it came to forcing them from her throat, they became an epic Spanglish catastrophe.

A teenager with long limbs and a buzz cut tugged at her elbow. "*Hola.*" Annie smiled and handed him one of the nets.

He grasped the blue mesh, but it slid from his fingers a second later. "*Enfermo.*" He clutched his sides, and his mouth twisted into a grimace. His chipped front tooth tickled the recesses of her brain.

"Um, hurt? *Duele?*"

He nodded and staggered.

"Okay." Annie wrapped an arm around his thin waist, and his ribcage pushed against her fingertips. His skin was feverish, and she led the boy through the crowd waiting to see Felipe. "Hey," she said, interrupting his note-taking.

He straightened and smiled at her. "*¿Qué pasa?*"

"This kid doesn't look so hot." She pushed the boy forward, and Felipe's eyes widened then narrowed.

"Juan. Juan!" He grabbed the boy by the elbow, jerking him

away from Annie and pinning both bony arms behind the kid's back.

"Wait. What?" Annie shoved through the crowd, a dozen sweaty bodies closing in around her as she tried to keep up with Felipe's heavy footsteps. He shoved the boy outside, both of them ducking under the low doorway. Annie followed. Juan was at her heels. And so was every other person at the clinic. They congregated at the doorway, whispering behind cupped fingers, staring and pointing at Felipe and the teenager.

"What are you doing?" she asked, forcing her way through and squinting into the broiling afternoon sun.

Juan's feet appeared next to her, and the rest of the group backed away.

Annie craned her neck to look at him. He held a machete pointed at the ground, but this close, Annie saw the way the muscles in his forearm tensed, ready to swing it at any moment.

"What are you doing?"

Marisol appeared at her side. "You do not recognize him?"

"What?" Annie stared at the boy. His arms stayed twisted behind his back, while Felipe spoke over the kid's shoulder in hard, flinty Spanish. That chipped front tooth. Those sharp features. All he was missing was a rifle and two teenage cronies. The realization sent her staggering backward. "Oh my God." She turned to Marisol. "Do you think he was trying to rob us again?"

Her friend squinted, turning her ear toward Felipe and the kid. "Probably no. He says he ate something bad. Diarrhea, vomiting. Come, we need to get everyone inside." She turned and ushered the crowd into the clinic without waiting for Annie to respond.

When only a few gawkers loitered outside, Juan shoved the boy forward, following as he hobbled away from the clinic. Every few steps the kid doubled over, groaning and pressing his hands to his stomach. Three burly men stepped out of a nearby house and fell into step next to Juan.

Annie's insides twisted, and her heart beat too fast. She took a shaking step forward. Then another, evening herself with Felipe's angry, rigid form. "What's happening? Where are they taking him?

Don't we have to treat him?" The questions poured out of her.

"No. We must return to the clinic. Juan and the other men will make sure he leaves."

She shook her head but couldn't chase away her memory of the boy's expression. The way his lips turned up in agony. His skin, feverish and clammy. They hadn't been able to help the old woman the day before. But she didn't want help. This boy wanted help. He needed it. "But—"

Felipe turned toward the tiny building where the crowd waited. "It will be fine."

* * *

Felipe sent away his last patient and tugged at the striped bed sheet separating his exam room from the rest of the church. His eyelids felt like they were made of lead—ten tons of it—pressing toward sleep. He had been up all night as he thought of *Doña* Godoy, alone in that tiny house, letting the bacteria slowly carry her away. And now he had one more thing to sit on his conscience, to gnaw away at him as he lay in the hammock staring at the ceiling of whatever hut they would sleep in tonight. That stupid boy and his stupid illness. Assuming it was an illness. More likely, it was another ploy to steal drugs.

"Hey," Phillip interrupted Felipe's thoughts. "I'm glad you guys took care of that guy. Got him out of here, I mean."

"*Sí.* Me too."

"This is a great thing you've got going on here. At first, I was a little dubious—" He pushed the corn-yellow hair from his face.

"I do not understand."

"Your clinics. Top notch, man." He clapped Felipe on the back, hard.

Felipe stumbled forward, thrown off balance by the American's touch and his unexpected compliment. "*Gracias.*"

At this point on the last brigade, the three American men spent most of their time complaining about the bugs and judging the women in the villages for having more children than they could feed. They stopped interacting with Felipe and Juan for all but the most basic of necessities. Of course, they'd kept chit-chatting with Marisol. They always stayed friendly with Marisol.

But this time, Felipe was the one on good terms with the Americans. It was a disconcerting sort of relief. Like he'd been asked to carry a backpack full of rocks through the rainforest, only to misplace it halfway through the trip.

Something was different. Something big.

The realization hit him hard in the chest, like someone found that backpack full of rocks and smacked him with it. What if he stopped presuming the foreigners would fail? Quit expecting them to complain and push and moan their way through the trip? Abandoned the idea that they could never understand? How many brigades could have been better? For him and for all their patients? Not all, but some.

"Have you seen Annie?" he asked Phillip.

"Outside."

Felipe followed him out onto the church lawn, the overgrown green grass scratching at his ankles. The air was charged, and above them the thick clouds of another storm rolled by. A huddle of children stood outside the church. Two adult figures poked out among them. Annie's crazy hair was easy to spot, and next to her, Juan stood with his arms crossed over his chest.

"What is going on?" Felipe called over the mass of little people.

Annie flipped around to face him. In one hand, she held her purple notebook. She tugged at her shirt sleeve with the other. "Hey, I was coming get you."

Juan turned too, and the light reflecting off his machete blinded Felipe.

"Don't be mad, but after yesterday, I couldn't—" Annie started.

Felipe took another step forward, and the children parted. The teenage thief sat on the ground, the same grimace on his face. Sweat beaded the boy's forehead and upper lip.

"I thought they were going to send him away." Felipe rubbed

his temple and drew in a slow, steady breath. He raised an eyebrow at Juan. The old man shrugged and resumed watching the crowd.

"I know," Annie said, "but I asked them to stop. Look," she held open her notebook, "I went over these notes from last week. Remember the lady you thought might have appendicitis? Well, she didn't, but I think he does."

Felipe clenched his jaw and pushed down the frustration building in his chest. "You are not a doctor, Annie. This *muchacho* is dangerous."

"I know I'm not a doctor, okay? But look at him. Please. You can't turn sick people away. In America—"

"Annie," he closed his eyes, "we are not in America."

"Most of his pain is on the right side. And he has rebounding." The pages of her notebook flapped as she moved to stand in front of him. Her hair was wild in the breeze. "Remember when you told me about rebounding?"

"*Sí, sí.*" He took a deep breath, his resolve cracking. "I will examine him. You will take all those children inside and away from him, yes?"

"Thank you." She squeezed his hand as she walked by, ushering the *niños* ahead of her.

Juan kept his wide stance as Felipe squatted next to the teenager. A few questions and a couple of taps to the belly convinced him Annie was right. He pressed a fist against his thigh and let out a ragged breath.

"*Vamos,*" he said.

. . .

Disaster.

It was the only way Annie could describe her class. Five students and Annie had gathered in the back of the empty church, waiting for Felipe to join them. But after ten minutes of waiting in silence, the awkwardness grew too massive for her to ignore. She'd jumped in, reading the lecture in a sharp-voweled American accent, and prayed Felipe would show up soon.

Two people left in the first five minutes, sending snarls over their shoulders as they walked away. She wasn't sure if she'd inadvertently said something offensive, but she trudged through anyway, ignoring the churning in the pit of her stomach. Another person left as Annie picked up the decrepit package of birth control pills. And by the time she was ready for the condom on the plantain trick, every person in the class had bolted.

Shit, shit, shit, shit, shit. She inhaled through her teeth. *I'm screwing this up royally.*

"Annie?" Phillip stuck his head inside the church, his smile too bright in the dim light.

"Hey."

"We're going back for the night."

She picked up her box and followed him outside. Marisol stood alone in the yard, holding three duffle bags on one arm and two on the other. The combined weight of them was probably more than Marisol's total poundage.

Annie rushed over and took two from her, one for each arm. Phillip took two more. "Where did everyone go?" Annie asked.

"Juan and 'Lipe took that boy in the boat," Marisol said.

Annie's steps faltered, and she bumped into Phillip. "They did? Where were they taking him?"

"Rosita. To the hospital there."

"So did he have appendicitis? Was I right?"

"*Sí.*" Marisol smiled and nodded as they walked between tiny houses made of warped logs and thatched roofs. "*Mi Anita* is becoming a *doctora* right before my eyes."

"Yeah, good catch," Phillip added.

Annie stood taller, and some of the heaviness of her failed class lifted as they walked away from the clinic. "Thanks."

Their host greeted them with a small smile and a plate of rice and beans. Annie dropped the bags near the front door and sat. The lumps and ruts in the floor dug into her backside, and she shifted as she forced down the plate of bland mush.

"What's the first thing you want to eat when you get home?" Phillip asked, pushing around the rice on his plate.

"I think I want ice cream," Annie said. "Cookies and cream. Or a hot fudge sundae." She closed her eyes, biting back a whimper as she imagined the warm, sweet chocolate and cool, creamy vanilla mixing together on her tongue.

"I want a steak. No, bacon." He closed his eyes as he chewed. "A whole package of bacon."

Her mind flashed to the pigs swarming that poor diaperless little girl. "Even after—"

"Don't say it." He laughed.

Marisol pulled the fork from her mouth and pointed it at Phillip. "Have you told Annie about your girlfriend?"

"Girlfriend?" Annie wrestled the shock and judgment from her features. "Um…no?"

Phillip shook his head. "She wasn't my girlfriend. Well, she was when we were twelve." He put down his empty plate. "Lya was my neighbor, and her family was from Nicaragua. I was so in love with her. Or, I thought I was. We were kids. But we had some good times in college too. My twenty-first birthday, she bought me so many shots…"

Annie's stomach sank at his use of past tense. "What happened?"

"Car accident. Last summer. That's how I ended up here. Had some free time before classes restarted and…" He shrugged.

The light filtering in from the windows waned. The darker it grew inside the little hut, the sadder Annie became. *I was so in love with her*. His words wormed their way into her subconscious, playing again and again as she finished her meal. She shuffled into the other room to change and brush her teeth, again feeling sheepish and small for the way she had judged him.

She returned to the main room. Marisol and Phillip were tangled in the same hammock. Even in the falling darkness, Annie saw it rocking.

She cleared her throat. "Mari?"

"*¿Sí?*"

"How far is it to Rosita?" She tugged her shirt sleeves. So many days in and out of the boat had left her with little sense of where they were in relation to the cities. Not that she could have found Rosita on a map anyway. "They'll be okay, right?"

There was a pause and Marisol's flashlight clicked on. "Four hours. Maybe five, *depende* on the roads. It did not rain as much today, so probably four."

"So, it's been almost four hours. They should be back soon, right?"

"Four hours there. Four hours back."

"Oh." Annie bit her lower lip and sat in the hammock. "But they'll be okay. I mean, it's safe, right?"

"We will see them in the morning."

The flashlight clicked off, and a breeze rushed in through the cracks in the walls. Goosebumps rose on Annie's arms, and she pulled one of Felipe's scrub shirts from the top of his bag. It smelled like him, like comfort and medicine and earth. She snuggled into it, wondering how she would sleep two weeks from now, alone in her cold, air-conditioned bedroom, thousands of miles away.

DAY EIGHTEEN

The sound was so heinous, Felipe sat straight up, certain the world was ending. He threw his hands to his ears. But Juan increased the volume, singing loudly enough to wake everyone in Nicaragua. Maybe everyone in Honduras too.

"Okay. Okay." Felipe pulled his hands away from his ears long enough to smack the dentist in the leg. "I am awake."

Juan cackled and shuffled away, his song fading mercifully as he went. Felipe lay down, his eyes sliding closed before his head hit the yoga mat. After so few hours of sleep, the thin foam felt like a feather bed to his exhausted body.

He and Juan had returned to the village as the sun broke through the horizon. By the time they shuffled into the house, Felipe's eyes burned. But Annie was stretched out in the hammock, her mouth wide open with one arm dangling off the side. He couldn't bring himself to wake her and collapsed onto her purple mat, tumbling into sleep.

"Hey."

He pried open an eye as the sweet, yeasty smell of fresh bread pulled him further from unconsciousness.

Annie crouched next to him on the floor, her backpack hung over one shoulder and a lumpy roll of bread in one hand. "You awake?" she whispered. "I think we're getting ready to go."

"*Sí.*" The delicate skin on the inside of her elbow somehow made Felipe both sleepier and more awake. He pulled lightly, hoping she would curl up beside him. "Tired."

She hovered next to him for half a second, but she eased back on her heels and smoothed his hair with her free hand. Felipe's eyes fell closed.

"You'll be able to sleep on the boat." She nudged his hand with the bread. "This is yours."

"Annie?"

"Yeah?"

He pushed back his guilt and ran his hand down her arm. It was all he'd thought about on the way to the nearest hospital, as he and Juan sat in silence listening to the moans of the teenage robber—who they learned had a name, Marco, and a family, two sisters and a brother. As Marco eked out his answers to their questions, Felipe became more and more ashamed of the way he'd acted. And more grateful for Annie's unrelenting insistence. "I am sorry about yesterday." He took the bread.

Annie shook her head. A grin spread across her face, lit by the sun streaming through the open door. "It's like I was a real doctor. I mean, when you got there, did they confirm it? His appendicitis?"

Her giddiness was contagious. Felipe sat up and pulled her against him. Her lips were soft, and his fatigue faded, pushed out by the fervor of their kiss. "I did not wait to find out."

"Oh." She pulled away an inch, her shoulders sinking.

"Because you are here." He tilted her chin to look into her eyes. "I was not going to wait for three hours with a skinny teenager when I knew there was a beautiful woman waiting for me."

"I guess I can forgive you then." She gave him that smile. The one that made her nose crinkle and the gold flecks in her eyes glow. He took a bite of the roll, the warm, buttery dough falling apart on his tongue.

"It's *so* good, right?" Annie asked. "Or maybe it's because I haven't eaten anything besides rice and beans in almost three weeks."

He nodded and took another bite. "Here." Felipe handed her the other half, more interested in the way her eyelids fluttered closed as she took a bite than eating more himself.

"Hey man, Juan said to tell you that if you aren't outside in, like, five *minutos* he's going to start singing that song again." Phillip stood in the doorway, his face twisted into a grimace. "Please don't—"

"Okay, okay. Tell him I am coming." Felipe stood and pulled Annie next to him as Phillip strolled outside. "Maybe I should take six *minutos* to torture Phillip a little, yes?"

"I don't know." She picked up the yoga mat and began rolling it. "I kind of feel bad for him. Last night after my class—"

Felipe pulled a fresh scrub shirt over his head. "Your class. How was it?"

"You don't want to know."

"I do." He bent to kiss her, unable to stand the pout on her face. "What happened?"

"Well, for starters, I didn't have anyone to help with my Spanish." She gave him a pointed look. "And then everyone walked out. Just up and left. And I didn't even get to the part with the plantain."

"Well, you will have a rest from the class today."

"But Marisol said we were doing the clinic this afternoon, as soon as we get to the next village. Are we behind schedule?"

He shouldered his backpack as Juan's earsplitting ballad rushed in through the window. "We are coming, old man!" He turned to Annie and laced her fingers through his. "We are on time. But we will not do the class in this village."

"Why? Because I messed up yesterday? I have some ideas on how to fix it. I worked on it all night." She held out her journal. The edges were dirty and tattered from so much use. "And you'll be there this time, right? So the Spanish won't be as big of a problem."

The smile dropped from his face. "This village…I do not know how to say exactly. They are more closed than the others. Especially to foreigners."

"More closed?"

"They do not trust us as much as the others. We have not always been welcome here."

"Oh." She cocked her head to one side, and Felipe could see her mulling over the options. "And you don't think they would like me to whip out my giant banana penis?"

"No." He laughed imagining the horror on their faces. "You can practice taking blood pressures. I think Marisol would like help."

"Really? But if they don't want me…maybe I should stay behind the exam curtain with you."

He raised one eyebrow, and his mouth spread into a smirk. "Annie, I do not think the clinics are the time for—"

She shook her head and swatted him. "You know that's not what I meant."

"I think it is fine," he said. "Follow Marisol's lead. But do not ask many questions. Take the blood pressures and write them down on the cards. Then send the people to me, yes?"

She nodded.

"And later…" He smacked her curvy, perfect butt with a handful of paperwork.

Juan's singing reached new, horrendous heights as he stepped into the doorway. He'd found some substance to curl the ends of his mustache up toward his cheeks. It made him look like a pot-bellied circus master. Marisol stood beside him, one hand on her hip.

"We are right here," Felipe shouted. The singing died, leaving his ears ringing with the echo.

"You cannot do the blood pressures if you two do not hurry. We will miss the clinic." Marisol tapped her foot to the beat of Juan's now-dead song.

"How did you know I was going to take blood pressure?" Annie asked.

"Windows, *mi Anita*." She laughed then shuddered. "Knowing my brother is trying to seduce you is one thing. But hearing it as it is happening is much worse. He is not even good at it."

He rolled his eyes, enjoying the payback. He'd listened to his sister seduce guy after guy since she was thirteen.

"Mari," Annie wiped her sweaty forehead on her shirt sleeve, then glanced over her shoulder at Felipe, "he's really good at it. Like really, *really* good at it."

Felipe stood in the doorway, grinning and trying not to look like he was thinking about tearing Annie's clothes off. She and Marisol walked into the morning mist and melted into the blur of bodies and supply packs waiting for him at the river bank.

Juan poked him in the back with his finger. "Next time I will get out the hose."

• • •

After an endless day of perfecting her blood pressure reading skills, Annie dug into a bowl of rice and beans. She swiped bites of bread from the roll perched atop Felipe's plate. He put up a flimsy protest, but every time she pinched off another piece, he touched her. A nudge with his shoulder. A hand on hers, trying to steal it back and never succeeding. By the time she put one piece into her mouth, she was already planning the next theft.

Dusk rolled in, and their host, a middle-aged man with a perpetually red face, tended the bonfire in his backyard. Annie inhaled the scent of burning wood as the flames popped and hissed around them.

"Where is everyone?" Phillip asked, pulling Annie from her daze.

"What do you mean?" Marisol held her fork halfway to her mouth, and a bean tumbled onto her lap.

"Usually we have a crowd," Phillip said. "Like we're a traveling circus."

"Some will come." Marisol turned toward the red-faced man and shot off a barrage of Spanish.

He disappeared inside his round hut and came back with a decrepit guitar. Felipe gave Annie the last of his roll and traded his plate for the instrument. He tuned the guitar, smiling at her every few seconds. "*Mira.* Watch. You will get to see my fan club soon."

He strummed a few chords and nodded as a few bright faces poked out from the darkness. They were mostly children, with wide eyes, creeping out from their hiding places, as if drawn by the notes. But a few adults followed too, all women.

"Whoa," Phillip muttered. "I have to learn to play the guitar."

The miniature crowd closed in around Felipe and Marisol. Annie found herself being pushed further from the fire as the children scooted between, clapping and clamoring for his attention. She moved away, happy not to be the center of their curiosity for once.

Phillip plopped down beside her as a tiny girl appeared at the edge of the crowd. The hem of the girl's pink and white polka-dotted dress brushed against Annie's legs, and the child's crooked bangs hung into her eyes. Annie lifted a hand and waved, but the girl ducked behind her curtain of chocolate hair.

"*¿Cómo te llamas?*" Annie asked. The girl didn't answer. She slid into Annie's lap, her middle two fingers in her mouth.

"*Rosa. Ella es Rosa,*" a tall boy said, sitting beside them.

The girl snuggled into Annie's chest, humming as they listened to Felipe strum the guitar. Marisol sang in dewy, rolling Spanish, and Annie lost all track of time, listening to her friend's fierce and quiet voice. She'd forgotten how beautifully Marisol could sing.

Over the child's head, Annie glanced at Phillip. The way he stared at Marisol almost made Annie feel sorry for him. *Total goner.*

The songs varied between upbeat, choppy tunes that had every child singing and shaking to slow, quiet songs showcasing Marisol's low, soulful voice. Juan joined in, offering a bass line, and Annie could barely hold back her shock. Based on his spine-cracking performance that morning, she'd assumed he was one hundred thirty percent tone-deaf.

"What are you and Felipe gonna do when you leave?" Phillip asked as the music flowed through the yard.

"What do you mean?" She shifted Rosa, trying to regain feeling in her left arm and put off thinking about the question for a few precious seconds.

He shrugged, staring at the flickering fire. "Like with Marisol. At first it was this crazy, primal, sexual thing, but now…" His voice faded as they both watched Marisol sing and dance with a boy in the front row. Even though he looked to be all of ten years old, Annie could tell he was smitten with her friend. Almost as much as the blond, ex-reality star sitting beside her.

"I'm trying not to think about it." Annie ignored the lump in her throat. She rocked Rosa, wondering if she should tell Phillip about Marisol's parade of admirers. Wondering if she should tell him not to count on a relationship with her friend. As far as Annie knew, Marisol's longest actual relationship had lasted three months. And it only lasted that long because her boyfriend had mono and was absent from school for two-thirds of their relationship.

Felipe bent over the guitar. He mouthed the words as he played, and the way his fingers worked the strings made Annie flush. Before long she wasn't thinking about home or leaving or Marisol.

The music died out as the fire dwindled and the villagers drifted home. Soon, the only remaining guest was Rosa, out cold against Annie's chest. Their host gestured toward the girl and shook his head, muttering.

"Sorry, what? I mean, *no entiendo*," Annie said.

"Rosa's parents live across the street." The guitar strap still hung over Felipe's shoulder as he sat. "He will take her home."

The girl's little brown fingers curled under her chin. "Can I take her home?" Annie asked.

A deep wrinkle appeared between his eyebrows. "They are not kind people, Annie."

"I'll be okay." She stood and shifted the girl's weight to her hip. Rosa stirred and her eyelids fluttered, but she settled back into sleep. "You can come with me?" Annie pulled in her lips, hoping he read the words between her words. *And we can sneak into the woods to make out.*

"Ah, *sí*." He lifted an eyebrow and pulled the guitar strap over his head. "*Vamos*." He put a hand on the small of her back and led her down a windy path between the houses.

His flashlight illuminated the ground in front of them, and Annie's entire body hummed with his touch. Charged silence stretched between them, and her eyes kept drifting to his profile— his high cheekbones and the slope of his nose, a touch too long for his otherwise perfect face. And for once, she completely understood Marisol's live-in-the-moment, let's-get-drunk-and-get-it-on life philosophy. Because all Annie could think about was sneaking into the woods and ripping off Felipe's clothes.

"It is this one," he said when they reached a slight, narrow house at the end of the path.

He shined a flashlight in a darkened window, and before they could knock, the door swung open. A woman scowled at them, her face hard and streaked with lines. The blue fabric of her long dress shifted in the night breeze. Behind her, a disheveled man in a red t-shirt and briefs stumbled into view, a scuffed bottle in hand. He gave them all a toothless smile and slid into one of the chairs. Eyelids drooping, he called out, but his words were so slurred, Annie was certain she wouldn't understand them even if they'd been in perfect English.

"*Buenas*," Annie said, her heart stuttering. "*¿Su hija?*"

The woman pulled Rosa away and slammed the door, never uttering a word.

Annie's arms hung slack at her sides. She wondered how many of her belongings would need to stay behind to smuggle the girl home inside her suitcase.

Felipe slipped his hand in hers and tugged. "Come."

She took a deep breath and nodded, but a loud thwack rooted her feet to the ground. Rosa's wail sent Annie's stomach plummeting to her knees. Another thwack.

She thumped on the door with the heel of her hand. "Hey. Hey!"

Another thwack, louder this time. A hand clamped on her arm and pulled her away from the door. She swung around to Felipe. "What are you doing? Aren't you hearing this?" Her blood rushed by her ears.

"Annie, we need to go."

"You're kidding, right?" She turned away and pounded again.

He held her close, pinning her arms at her sides. "This isn't helping," he whispered.

She struggled, spinning to face him. "You need to call the police."

"Annie, there are no police here."

The door swung open, and Rosa's father lumbered out to them, slurring.

Annie shook as she stepped around him, stumbling into the house. She had to find Rosa. Had to. She wouldn't leave until she pried the sweet little girl from this poor excuse of a family. Anger built in a hard ball inside of her, growing so fast and so large it splintered and worked its way into every muscle.

Rosa lay on the floor. Silent sobs shook her petite body as a hand-shaped welt swelled on her cheek. Annie pushed past the girl's mother and swung Rosa over her hip. "Let's go." She expected Felipe to appear at her side and usher them away from these sick sons of bitches.

He pried the girl from her hands. "Annie, you cannot do this."

Rosa's father bumbled toward them, shouting and slurring and spitting curse words even Annie recognized.

Felipe set Rosa in front of the man and lifted his palms. "Annie, get out of here."

She glanced over her shoulder. Rosa's mother sat on the floor, her blue dress fanning out around her. Annie wasn't certain how the woman had ended up there—if Annie had pushed her to the floor in desperation to pick up Rosa or if she'd collapsed there amidst the chaos. But now she stared at the ceiling, silent.

Rosa scrambled over to the woman and buried her snot-streaked face in her mother's chest. The woman made no effort to comfort the child, and hot tears spilled down Annie's cheeks, leaking her fury and confusion and sadness across her face.

"Annie, I said to leave." Felipe's words came between clenched teeth.

"Are you serious right now?" She threw her hands up and wiped her nose on the hem of her shirt, trying to keep her voice from sprinting into hysterics.

"Leave."

• • •

Felipe heard the thunk of the man's fist smashing his shoulder before he felt it. Everything was numbed by his anger. He stumbled but gathered himself up, shoving the drunk's chest. The man was so *borracho* it took nothing to tip him over.

He stormed toward the door, but Rosa's cry was still fresh in his mind, and the things the man had threatened to do to Annie had him in a rage. He spun and snarled in the doorway. "You are disgusting," he spat in jagged Spanish. Outside, he jogged through the dark as a streak of lightning sliced through the sky. He whipped his flashlight from side to side, scouring the area for Annie's outline. But she was nowhere.

Please be at the house.

He moved faster, sprinting and looking over his shoulder every few steps. Once, he was certain the drunk was following him, but when he wheeled his flashlight around, there was nothing. He made it to the cooling bonfire, and Annie's hiccups and whimpers rang out as she told the story to Marisol and Juan.

"They're horrible. And we left her there. Left her!"

"It is okay. Shhh." Marisol stared at him, her eyes searing holes into his. "You are okay?" she mouthed.

Felipe nodded and slumped over, wheezing and shaking as the adrenaline left his body. He'd gotten so caught up in Annie that his common sense had disappeared. He should have known better than to let her go to that house. Known better than to ignore their host's warnings. And now they were all paying the price.

The shuffling of feet on damp earth sent him jolting upright, muscles wound tight and heart thudding in his ears. Someone clicked on a flashlight.

Rosa's father stood where the yard met the trail, leering. The light reflected off the spittle on his chin, and in his left hand he clutched a broken bottle.

Felipe's voice cracked. "Inside. *Dentro.*" He tried not to show his fear as Marisol ushered Annie and Phillip inside the hut.

Juan stood next to Felipe, and they watched as the man took one step toward them. Juan pulled out his machete, and the drunk tripped over his own bare feet. The girl's father scrambled backward, slicing his palm on the bottle. It took two tries before he made it up on swaying legs, the bloody shard of glass forgotten on the ground. The man spat and sneered, then turned toward home as if nothing had ever happened.

"We will leave in the morning," Juan said, tucking the long knife into the holster at his hip. "Sunrise."

Felipe nodded. Both men turned toward the house, but the tumbling rush of footsteps came again. The child's father lurched forward, running and falling, running and falling until he was within striking distance. He swatted and swung, and Juan put his hand on the machete. Felipe's legs and arms were heavy and slow, but he worked his way to the left, drawing the furious *borracho* away from the house.

The door swung open, and Marisol stepped out. Marco's confiscated rifle trembled in her hands. "Leave us. Leave us!" Each time she repeated the phrase, her words filled with more fervor.

The lush raised his hands and stumbled backward, catching himself a moment before he tumbled into the remains of the fire. Cursing and spitting, he threw the first thing he found into the dying flames before bumbling off into the night.

Felipe ran to the fire and tried to rescue the sex ed supplies, but with new fuel, the fire grew, engulfing it all. The fuzzy uterus shriveled and turned to ash as the furious orange flames lapped at his feet. He raised his eyes from the fire to find a gathering crowd.

"Do not ever come back!"

"You are a disgrace!"

"Please do not go. My baby is sick!"

Shouts came from all sides. The mass of people closed in around them, turning the air hot and furious. Felipe grabbed the supply bags, tossed a few to Juan, and they jogged into the hut with Marisol. Their host shoved a heavy log against the door.

Phillip blinded Felipe with a flashlight, and chaos erupted. Felipe cursed and dropped the bags. Marisol forced Phillip's light to the ground, and eventually the shouts from outside faded. In the corner, Annie sat with her arms folded across her chest.

"Are you okay?" he asked, stopping his shaking legs a few feet in front of her.

She shook her head, mouth set in a firm line. "This fucking place…"

Felipe sank against the wall, drowning in his emotions.

"How could you do that?" Annie's voice was small, but her words were pointed.

Half his mind remained outside, processing the villagers' irate shouts. "¿Qué?"

"Send her back to those people. How can you send a child back to…to a monster? Like you didn't even think it was wrong. Like, no problem, here in Nicaragua it's okay to beat your kids."

"Are you serious?" Felipe's fury threatened to erupt. He'd put Annie in danger. He'd put the entire brigade in danger, taking her to that house. And he could tolerate her being angry with him for that. But this—

"Yes."

"What do you want me to do?" He stood, his fists tight at his sides.

Marisol grabbed the flashlight and made her way over to them. The yellow light illuminated Annie's red-rimmed eyes and the fat, ugly tears streaking her cheeks.

"'Lipe." Marisol tugged at his arm. "Ven. Not now."

"You want me to kidnap her? Kidnap every child here who has awful parents? Sorry, Annie. That is not going to happen." He shook off his sister's grip. "And Rosa. You made things worse for her. Do you think her dad went home and said, 'Oh, I am so sorry now because the American girl showed me the error of my ways?'"

"Felipe, shhh." Marisol pulled at him again.

"You handed her off to those people and walked away." Annie smacked a hand against the dirt floor. "You knew what would happen, and you took her home anyway. How sick is that?"

"Do you know how many nights I had to sit around this fire playing the damn guitar before they would let us vaccinate their niños? Do you have any idea how many times we came out here only to have every person in the village ignore us?" The words ran out of his mouth, piling up in the space between them, pushing them further apart.

"So that makes it okay to let someone beat the shit out of a little girl?"

"No. How can you say that?" He started to walk away but flung himself around after a few steps. "Being a good doctor means making hard choices, Annie. Maybe one day you will see." He took a deep breath, thinking of her bright future, probably working in the best hospitals in America. Never wanting for supplies or equipment or money. "But maybe not."

Annie's face crumbled then went slack. For a second he regretted every word. Her hands trembled as she pulled at the ends of her hair. "I want to go home." She raised her eyes, furious tears working their way down her face. "I'm not staying here."

Marisol pushed him off into another corner before he could spit out a response.

Juan stepped in front of him, cutting off Felipe's view of Annie. "What now?" Juan asked.

Their host jabbed a finger at Felipe's chest. "You must go. Once the people are gone. I cannot have these risks. I have family."

When they were certain the last of the angry mob had retreated for the night, Felipe loaded his aching body with bags and led the group down the path. Juan and the rifle took the rear, and no one said a word as they slipped out of the village in the darkness.

DAY NINETEEN

Annie pulled out her journal, and her shoulders slumped over the blank page. *Brown is never going to happen anyway. Not now.* She shoved the cap between her clenched jaws as she pressed her pen to the page. The tip tore through the edge of the paper and still she pushed harder, letting the ink bleed through to the next page.

Day 19: Get me the hell out of this place.

"Are you okay, *mi Anita?*" Marisol stood over her. Dark circles ringed her eyes.

"Mari, I really need to go home."

"I do not understand."

"I *need* to go home. I can't stay here and do this. I can't…I can't." Annie bore down on the words, forcing them out with less hysteria than she felt.

Marisol sighed. "You can. You must. We are too far away from the roads."

A cold rush of panic hit her skin. Marisol was right. She couldn't leave. She was trapped in the rainforest, in this heat, with these mosquitos, covered in a perpetual layer of bug spray and sweat, following around a doctor who let drunks beat their daughters. And the only way out was time. Nine more days to be exact.

Nine. I have to make it through nine more days.

Marisol uncapped a lancet, pricked her finger, and smeared a drop of blood on one of her test strips. "I need to eat something."

Annie had heard those words hundreds of times in the early months of their friendship. Marisol had just received her pump, and finding the right dosage of insulin had been tricky. Especially since all the training had been given in English.

"Do you have something in here?" Annie picked up Marisol's pack and began digging. "Geez, Mari, how many books did you bring?" She pulled out three paperbacks before her fingers closed around the slick cylinder of glucose tabs. "Here."

"*Gracias.*" Marisol sat and popped open the package, cramming two orange tabs into her mouth at once. "We have to wait for them to come get us."

Annie wrinkled her forehead, wondering if her friend's blood sugar had gone too low. "Who?"

"The people from the next village. They will meet us here and take us with them. It is inland. I think you will feel better after that. What happened last night," she shook her head, "it was bad. But only a bump. We still have many days left to have fun together." Her eyes brightened, and Annie could tell the sugar was working its way through her bloodstream.

"Okay. Do I have time to show—" Annie shook her head. "To wash off?"

Marisol pursed her lips. "Are you okay?"

She shrugged and nodded, her shoulders refusing the lie her head told. Her face felt puffy and raw, and anger still boiled in her chest. All morning she'd wondered about Rosa. Whether she sat huddled in a corner somewhere bruised and broken. Whether she was playing with her friends as if nothing happened. Whether Felipe was right about one thing—if she had made things ten times worse for the girl, for the whole village.

"Go ahead," Marisol said.

Annie grabbed her pack and tore toward the water, her sadness and anger growing like a malignancy in her chest. She rounded a corner, and soon a line of trees stood between her and the others. She dropped her pack and collapsed on the ground, hanging her head between her knees. The sobs she'd held in all morning eased their way out in silent, searing pain.

When her tears dried, she stripped down, not bothering to pull her towel free of the mess in her bag, and jumped into the cool river. The water numbed her, and for a blissful few minutes she was able to scrub yesterday from her skin without being so deep inside her own head.

She sloshed her way to the shore and stood dripping next to her bag. As she rifled for her towel, the beat of footsteps came from her right.

"I'm naked!" Her voice carried through the trees. "Please wait." She rummaged faster, yanking her towel around her as Phillip poked his head around the corner.

"Well, that's no way to keep people away, yelling about how you're naked." His smile was wide and goofy, but his hands covered his eyes.

"Decent people would stay away."

"Burn. Can I open my eyes now?"

She pulled the towel tighter around her. "Sure."

"Do you want to talk?"

"I want to get dressed."

"Are you sure? That chick on *Barnyard* said I was a great listener."

She turned her back to him.

"Okay, you might hurry though. The horses are here."

"Horses?"

He'd disappeared by the time she turned around.

She wrung out her hair and slipped into a different set of clothes. The edges of her t-shirt grew more tattered each day, and the stiff and unyielding fabric chafed her sun-soaked skin.

By the time she trudged to the campsite, their group had grown by nine—three men and six horses. The animals were rough and scarred but well-fed and strong. As they paced, the muscles rippled in their haunches. She dropped her pack and inched forward, offering her palm to the nearest one—a bay paint, with a splotch of white across the nose. He snorted and nuzzled her hand. She scratched his neck, and her breathing slowed.

It was only after she buried her face in the horse's mane—its rough hairs tangled and knotted at the ends—that she saw who was perched atop.

Felipe.

She took two giant steps back, and her pulse throbbed in her temples. "We're going to ride?" she asked.

"*Sí.*" Marisol put a leg in the stirrup and threw the other over the saddle. Phillip slipped in behind her, wrapping his arms around her waist and pulling her unnecessarily close.

Annie clenched her jaw so tightly her eye sockets ached. She was the only one left on the ground. The three strange men were already saddled, their horses loaded with bags. And she wasn't about to ride with someone she didn't know. Not after last night. Juan sat perched atop a mule, and there was no way it could carry both of them.

"Mari," Annie stepped close to her friend's horse, a lanky white thing with a beige mane, "let me ride with you. Please. I can't do this. Not today."

"You can. Just a bump, Annie. You will ride together into the sunset and make all your fighting disappear."

She turned to the bay paint. She breathed deep, taking in the horses' grainy smell. "I guess I'm riding with you."

Felipe stared at her, embers of anger still burning in his expression. Without a word he offered her a hand.

Annie shook her head. *No way I'm riding with my arms wrapped around him. No fucking way.* "I need the saddle."

"Do you know how to ride a horse?"

"Yes."

They squared off, and the more time Annie spent there on the ground, grinding her teeth and seething, the louder the voice in the back of her mind became. *Home. Home. I want to go home.*

Finally, Felipe slid to the ground, and she threw herself over the animal's back.

She leaned forward as he climbed on, putting as much space between them as possible, but there was no getting around the way his thighs pressed against her hips. Her skin scorched at his touch, but Annie ignored her body's betrayal. "Let's go boy." She followed the others into the jungle.

The animal's walk was clipped and purposeful. He did all the work, turning before Annie told him to and easing into the quick jumps over the gullies they crossed. "He must take this run a lot," she muttered, relaxing into his trot as the breeze pulled the sweaty hairs from the back of her neck.

"*Sí.*"

Felipe's breath warmed her skin, and Annie's stomach churned. For three blissful seconds, she'd managed to forget he was behind her. The horse stiffened his movements to match hers, and they stopped, the distance between them and the others growing. She exhaled and nudged the animal forward. He took a single step. "Look." She twisted around. "Don't talk to me, right now. It's making me all tense and—"

"I thought you knew how to ride horses."

Annie dug her heel into the animal's side. They tore off, and Felipe fumbled backwards, his hands finding her waist and gripping for dear life. She drove the horse faster, not caring that the brush tore at her arms and legs. Every scrape and scratch reminded her of Rosa. Reminded her of the way he'd pried the poor girl from her arms, then acted as if she was the one who did something wrong.

Nine more days.

DAY TWENTY

Felipe rose out of his hammock before the sun climbed fully in the sky. All night, he'd stared at the ceiling of the tiny house, worrying while he listened to Juan's deafening snores. Worrying about Rosa. Whether news of the near riot would follow the brigade, seeping distrust into the other villages. About the fight brewing with his mother—even if she didn't know it yet.

The last brigade had included a prominent surgeon from Seattle with a big forehead and an even bigger ego. Things had gone downhill fast, and by the halfway point in the trip, the man had stopped speaking to everyone. When the group returned to *Ahora* headquarters, Dr. Big Head refused to participate in the post-trip debriefing and instead checked himself into the hotel down the street. A month later, he mailed Melinda a letter with a detailed list of complaints. Number one: the "angry child" in charge. The letter also hinted that he would like his sizeable pre-trip donation returned in full. Melinda had pulled the funds from Felipe's salary and given him a "last chance" lecture that left him queasy and outraged for days.

Already, he could picture how this lecture would go. Even a hundred kilometers from home, he could hear his mother's voice— sharp as the broken glass the drunk had clutched in his fingers— see her heavy sigh, feel her disappointment. She'd sigh and shake her head when they arrived home, rambling on about how he needed to be more flexible. That he needed to understand more about how the world works and the people in it. He would beg her once again to stop parading the Americans through the jungle, mucking up everything in their wake. And then she'd fire him from these trips, severing his last remaining ties to the place he'd been born. Felipe dropped his bags to the ground and sat outside the hut while everyone else slept. Around him, people left their houses for morning chores. They waved and welcomed him as they passed, and Felipe breathed a little deeper. Either they did not care about what had happened, or the news had not made it this far. Yet.

The hard, cracked dirt dug into his backside, and with each passing minute, the sun rose higher, pounding down on his skin. He ran through excuse after excuse, searching for any explanation that could possibly satisfy his mother and finding none.

"What are you doing?" Marisol's shadow blocked the sun.

"Thinking."

"Everyone is ready to go to the clinic…"

"And?"

"Except Annie. She does not feel well. But I think it is—"

"If she is sick, she should not come." He stood and picked up the bags at his feet, refusing to meet his sister's eye.

"'Lipe, you know—"

"No, I do not know. If she wants to stay here, she can stay here." He swallowed something hard and bitter in his throat. "We do not need her."

Marisol threw a duffle bag at his feet. It hit the ground with a thud, stirring up dust around his ankles. "You will do the nets then?"

They stared at each other, Marisol's nostrils flaring.

"Fine." He picked up the bag and tossed it over his shoulder with the others. As he turned, a crop of messy red curls poked out from the doorway, and his eyes landed on Annie's. The mix of emotions boiling inside him was so acrid the words flew out of his mouth before he could stop them. "We do not need you anyway."

She stared at him, unmoving, unblinking. But the hurt was etched into her features, and it only made his anger burn and blister deeper.

"You are so stupid, 'Lipe." Marisol's words hit him in the back, shoving him forward. He kept walking, ignoring the cold, hard lump of pain in his throat.

DAY TWENTY-ONE

The fine spray of river water made goose bumps rise on Annie's forearms. Thick, slate-gray clouds overhead blocked every ounce of sunlight, and the breeze created by the boat ride was almost enough to make her teeth chatter. For the first time since she left the airport in Managua, Annie was cold.

Beside her, Marisol droned on, asking question after question about their old classmates. Annie knew her friend was trying to keep her mind off of what had happened. "And the girl with all the earrings in her face? I do not remember her name, but she had very long hair."

"I think her name was Jen." Annie stared out at the river. Looking at Marisol meant seeing Felipe's annoying broad shoulders. It meant seeing the way Phillip looked at Mari, all infatuation and puppy love. And not standard puppy love. It was starving-puppy-rescued-from-a-mill-and-given-a-sirloin, puppy love.

"Does she still live in St. Louis?"

"No, she moved away in eleventh grade. But she still had all the piercings then."

"Probably more." Marisol nudged Annie with her shoulder. "Remember when her tongue earring got stuck to the gym teacher's whistle?"

The memory rushed back, forcing out a smile. "She kept screaming, 'Thluck! Thluck!'" Annie waved her hands in panicked circles, mimicking the poor girl's movements. "And Coach Roberts kept saying, 'Quit moving, Martin. Quit moving!'"

"I never believed the she-dropped-a-pen-under-the-desk story."

"That sounds like the best school ever," Phillip said. "Stuff like that never happened at mine. But the teachers were all nuns, so…"

Ahead of them, Felipe shook his head, and even though Annie couldn't see his expression, she could picture it perfectly. All judgment and annoyance. Steely superiority.

"You look like you're about to murder someone's grandma. Relax." Phillip gave Annie his trademark blinding smile. "We've got another week here to live *la vida loca* or whatever. Might as well try to have a good time."

"Yes, because nothing helps someone relax more than being *told* to relax. God. Do you ever think before you open your mouth?" Annie's last tiny bit of happiness splintered inside her, turning to shards of bitterness and reaching out to stab anyone in her way. "Probably not. That's why everyone but you knows this little fling with Mari has been doomed from the beginning, so no big deal. Just relax, right?"

Phillip's calm, cool, good looks morphed into something so sad and pathetic Annie could barely stand it.

"Look," she said. "I'm sorry. I—"

He turned away before she could finish.

"What is wrong with you?" Marisol's harsh whisper twisted the knife of regret deeper into Annie's stomach.

She couldn't find the words to explain what was wrong with her. Everything was wrong. The overcast sky. The sour taste on her tongue. Felipe's stupid cowlick. Rosa's cries. "I don't know."

Marisol turned her face to the gray sky for a long moment, then looked at her palms, pointedly ignoring Annie's silent pleas for forgiveness.

The first rain drops fell, and Annie didn't bother to dig for a poncho. She let the rain hit her face and mix with her tears, trying not to think about how she was all alone.

• • •

Under the cover of his poncho, Felipe alternated between staring out at the water and closing his eyes. He was grateful for the smacks of rain hitting the plastic, blocking out Annie's voice. Even sitting at the tip of the boat, as far from her as he could get, there had been no escape. The conversation behind him was muffled, but earlier, when her laugh rang out, diving into the murky water and swimming to the next destination felt like his only option.

Maybe a long swim against the torrential current was a terrible idea, but it would certainly let him forget the look she gave him that night. At least for a little while. Forget the way she'd accused him of being some kind of accomplice to child abuse. How she assumed it didn't tear him into agonizing shreds to leave Rosa there with her parents. His head drooped, suddenly heavy, and everything seemed disheveled and out of place. He had to do something, anything to quiet his mind.

"Juan," he turned and raised his voice above the rain and the engine, "I want to drive." He waited as Juan stared at him from the back of the boat. The old man never let anyone drive. Ever.

But Juan gave a single nod and steered left. A second later, he cut the engine and grabbed onto a tree trunk as they floated by the shore. The boat jerked to a halt.

"You are going to drive?" Marisol's mouth fell open. "Do you know how to drive this thing?"

The boat rocked and jerked as Felipe rose and stepped between his sister and Phillip, avoiding Annie's eyes as he moved. He grabbed onto the tree trunk and waited as Juan took the seat at the front of the boat.

With the engine roaring behind him, it was easier to construct a wall. It was easier to stay angry at the back of her head than it was with her voice and laugh knocking him in the gut every few minutes. And when he was angry, it was easier to convince himself that she was wrong.

She'll be gone in a week. One more week.

"*¡Cuidado!*" Juan shouted.

The boat shuddered to the right, then left, making a horrible thumping noise as they pitched from side to side. Felipe struggled for control, and waves of brown water crashed over the side, soaking them all with the smell of fish and decay. He yanked them in the opposite direction, narrowly avoiding a midstream boulder.

Felipe blinked droplets from his eyes and wiped the river water from his lips. "*Todo bien.*" The lie was for himself as much as anyone. But before anyone could respond, another log came rushing through. And without warning, they were in the river, their belongings bobbing alongside them.

Felipe pounded a fist on the bottom of the boat, barely feeling the sting of his hand smacking the aluminum. Between the rain pelting his face, the whoosh of the river rushing by, and the taste of rotting leaves lingering in his mouth, there was little room for anything else. He grabbed onto the cool, hard lip of the boat and heaved. But no matter where he pushed or twisted, he couldn't get the damn thing to flip over.

Annie stood at the other end. The river came to her hips, and she stared at him as the others grabbed the bags. "Ready?" she asked.

He nodded without looking her in the face.

"One, two, lift." Together they flipped it over.

"This. This is why I do not let you drive." Juan shook his head, water flying from his hair.

"No offense man, but I think we should let Juan drive from now on." Phillip flipped back his sun-drenched locks. Something was missing from his usual everything-is-so-awesome-bro expression, and Felipe assumed it had been replaced by judgment. *Of course.*

"*Verdad,*" Marisol agreed, heaving herself over the edge of the boat.

Felipe turned, expecting Annie's jab next. The river rushed past him, and raindrops plastered his hair to his forehead. Already soaked, he ripped off his poncho. "Do not bother," he spat. "I already know you think this is my fault."

"Yes, you already know everything, don't you?"

"I know you do not understand."

"Right, because I'm American. You almost let me forget that for like, what, thirty seconds?"

"This is not some vacation. Some way for you to feel good

about yourself before you go home and forget it all."

"I promise this is the *last* place I'd spend my vacation."

The rain came down harder with every passing second, and each drop solidified Felipe's certainty that he was right: Annie was just like all the others.

DAY TWENTY-TWO

Annie stared at the spider web, waiting. It stretched from the low, bowed ceiling to the wall, draping her tiny corner of the hut with a glistening canopy. She held perfectly still, praying its eight-legged owner would stay away.

The soft rub of turning pages drew her attention from the web. To her right, Marisol's hammock rocked, and over the crest of the fabric, Annie saw the red flash of a book cover.

Annie rolled off her mat and tiptoed toward her friend. "Mari?"

Another page turned.

"Mari? Please. I'm really sorry." She waited, looming over the hammock, but Marisol's eyes never left the book. "I shouldn't have said those things to Phillip. I was angry, and I took it out on you guys. I was stupid. I'm sorry."

For half a second, Marisol's eyes met hers, then her friend licked her index finger and turned another page.

"Come on, Mari. I'm not leaving here until you talk to me. I'll stand here like a total creeper while you read."

The hammock next to Marisol shifted, and Phillip mumbled something too full of sleep to be intelligible. Annie froze, waiting to see if she'd woken him, but he rolled over with his eyes still closed.

"Come." Marisol shot out of her hammock and stomped outside, her plaid shorts twisted around her waist.

Annie scrambled behind her and into the morning sun. "Mari, please. I'm so stupid sometimes. I'm sorry. What can I do to fix this?"

Her friend stayed silent.

Annie waited, staring at her bare feet. The wet blades clung to her ankles, and tiny clumps of dirt dotted the tops of her toes.

"What is wrong with me?" Marisol's voice cracked.

"What? Nothing. Nothing is wrong with you. It's me. My fault. I was upset about what happened. And things with your brother. And…" She shook her head. "No excuses. I'm sorry."

"But that is the problem. You are so upset with my brother. But Phillip could leave here and start a harlem with all the women in this village, and I would not care. There is something wrong with me."

Annie squinted, trying to make sense of her friend's jumbled thoughts. "There is nothing wrong with you. You're not attached to Phillip. It's a fling. Nothing wrong with that." She brushed a long strand of hair behind Marisol's ear.

"But it is not only Phillip. I do not care about any of them. It is fun for a little while, then I am bored. I read these books about butterflies and happiness and trust. I see you care about my brother so much that when he makes you mad, you want to tear his head off and eat it like a praying manatee."

"Oh, Mari." Annie wrapped her arms around her friend. "There's nothing wrong with you. You're perfect."

She pulled back, her eyes rimmed red and her cheeks splotchy. "But I cannot care about anyone. I am empty inside."

Annie looked her right in the eye. "You care about your brother. I see it in the way you guys take care of each other. And your mom, right? And I can't believe you would be out here doing this every three months if you didn't care about all the people in these villages." She shook her head, amazed by her friend. "And me. I know you care about me. I would never have survived the last few weeks without you."

Marisol wiped her tears with the back of one hand. "But that is not what I mean."

"I know. But you do care about people. You just haven't found the right guy to give you all those butterflies, yet. You will."

Marisol shrugged.

"And in the meantime, you can still have fun trying. Right, Cupid of Nicaragua?"

A hint of a smile emerged on her friend's lips.

"I'm sorry I ruined your fun with Phillip, though."

"It is okay. I think he was getting too suctioned to me anyway."

"Suctioned?"

Marisol nodded. "Like too much wanting to be with me all of the time. Too much of everything." She shook her head.

"Ah. Too attached."

"*Sí*. I need to check my blood sugar. It is making my brain slow." She leaned against the side of the house.

"Okay. Stay here. I'll get your stuff. Front pocket?" Annie had watched Marisol shove her cow print case in that same place dozens of times since they'd set out, and she was already halfway inside the house when Marisol nodded.

A minute later, she sat at her friend's side, watching her prick her finger and chew another chalky glucose tab. The artificial orange smell was so strong it made Annie's stomach rumble.

"Better?"

Marisol nodded.

"Good. Because I'm not sure I can handle being called a praying manatee ever again."

"That is the bug, no? The one where the woman has sex with the man and rips off his head after they are done?"

"Mantis. Praying mantis. Manatees are these cute things with wrinkly faces."

Marisol's giggle cut through the last remaining strings of tension between them. "I have been saying praying manatee for years and no one has corrected me. You must swear to always tell me when I say something like this."

"I swear. Which is why I'm going to tell you it's harem, not Harlem. Harem is a bunch of women. Harlem is an area of New York City."

"Oh! Yes, that one I know. The Globetrotters!" Marisol lifted both of her hands to the sky. "I love the Globetrotters."

"What? How?" Annie rolled onto her back. "Never mind. I don't want to know. I love that you love the Globetrotters."

Marisol lay beside her as the sun rose higher in the sky. The morning air was still light and cool, and the sweet tang of someone cooking plantains drifted on the breeze.

"You will help me today," Marisol said.

"What do you mean? What about the mosquito nets?"

"*¿Qué?*"

"The nets."

She waved Annie off. "We will make Felipe do it."

"Um, I doubt he'll go for that."

"He never argues with me. Trust."

"What do you want me to do? I can put kids in the scale thing."

"I am going to teach you to give vaccines," Marisol said. "It will look better on your applications, no?"

"I think my applications are a lost cause."

Marisol waved her off. "Do not be stupid."

"I don't think I'm allowed to give vaccines. And there's no point anyway. This trip was supposed to be my chance to help my application." She blew out a breath.

"*¿Y?*"

"And," her voice was strained, "look what happened. No way Felipe will write a letter of recommendation for me after all this. Not that I want him to." She sighed. "Sorry, I know he's your brother."

"You think Felipe was going to write the letter? What do you think he would say? Annie is very good at making the sex?"

"Stop." Her face flamed. "We didn't—"

"My mother writes the letters. And I tell her what to say. If Felipe had to write the letters…" Marisol shook her head. "Help me with the vaccines, and I will make sure my mother tells the American doctors how you saved *all* the Nicaraguan children from mumps."

"Seriously?"

"No, you did not really save them all."

"No. Your mom writes the letters? But she isn't even on the trip."

"You think the big shot American doctors will care what Felipe says? No, my mother is much more important."

"And if Felipe wrote them, he would just say bad things

about Americans."

"Probably." Marisol looked at her hands. "But you are being too hard on him."

"Doubtful." But even as Annie said it, she glanced over her shoulder into the doorway. From this angle all she could see was the outline of his shoulder blade and his smooth, perfect arm dangling from his hammock.

"Yes, look at him," Marisol said. "Sleeping in a hammock, waking before the sunrise to take care of poor people. He is so terrible."

• • •

Felipe dug through his supplies, throwing them down haphazardly. The line of patients waiting to get into the clinic coiled around the pavilion, twice as long as the last time he'd visited. "Juan?" He waited while the dentist strolled across the rectangular building, his hands stuffed into the pockets of his dental apron. "Do you have the bag with the extra supplies? I think we will need them here."

"Your sister." Juan twisted his mustache.

Over the man's shoulder, Marisol and Annie huddled together, passing something small and green between them. *So Annie has decided we are good enough to help this time.*

"Mari?"

"*¿Sí?*" She didn't turn.

"Mari?"

At last, she looked up and rolled her eyes, stomping across the dirt toward them with a bag in her arms. "What?"

"What are you doing?"

"Teaching Annie to give vaccines."

"Why?"

"So she can help me. Look at all the people waiting."

He snuck a glance at Annie. Her t-shirt hung off one shoulder, taunting him with all the freckles there as she jabbed a lime with a needle. This was not how it was supposed to go. She was supposed to spend the last few days moping and ignoring the clinics, like she had at the last village. "No."

"I am in charge of the vaccines, yes?"

Juan chuckled, his belly bouncing with the sound.

Felipe ignored him. "Who will do the mosquito nets?"

"You." She dropped the bag at his feet and gave him her I-dare-you-to-tell-me-no stare.

"Fine." He picked up the bag and rearranged his things to make room for the nets. He expected Marisol to wander back to Annie and for Juan to bumble over to his array of dental torture instruments. But they both stayed glued to the floor in front of him.

"What? Juan, do you want Annie to help you instead? Pull a couple of teeth? Sure!" He threw his hands up, knocking two mosquito nets to the ground. "Why not?"

"'Lipe, you are being too hard on her," Marisol said.

"And not in the good way." Juan wagged his eyebrows between guffaws.

"Annie was doing the thing she thought was right. You were doing the thing you thought was right." Marisol looked at him with her gigantic brown eyes. "You two are making these last days *terrible* for all of us." She rolled her r's, stretching out the word.

"Do not look at me like that."

"Like what?" She widened her eyes.

"You know."

"I do not. You mean the I-almost-died-three-times-when-we-were-children-so-you-must-give-me-whatever-I-want look?" She dropped the façade and stared at him, as if daring him to defy her.

"We need to start seeing patients now."

Marisol crossed her arms and tapped her foot on the hard dirt floor of the pavilion. "Fine. But Annie is giving vaccines. And after, she will do her sexual education class." More foot tapping. Another I-dare-you look.

"No. She can do the vaccines, but—" His throat closed, suffocating his voice.

"So, I uh…" Annie appeared beside his sister. Her fingers

twisted several sheets of lined notebook paper, and she kept her gaze far from his. "Where I can set up for my class?"

"You cannot do the class."

She stopped moving and looked between Marisol and Felipe. "Mari said I was doing it in this village. That it's okay here."

He gritted his teeth. "All the supplies were burned, no?"

Annie's eyes shifted to the pages in her hand. "I can still do it. Mari helped me with it this morning." She handed him the papers as his sister and Juan slunk away.

He unfolded it and stared at Annie's delicate, precise handwriting. The entire lecture was there in Spanish, with English notes scrawled in the margins. Most of the spelling was phonetic, but it wasn't bad. It was good. Better than his original. "Do you have a pen? You have mixed up some of your conjugations."

"Oh."

Felipe leaned over the table, correcting the errors in her notes. There was a buzz of satisfaction every time he scribbled out something she'd written. But there was something else there, weighing down his anger. Something that felt a lot like doubt and a little like regret.

The silence rolled on. His skin prickled under her stare, and he handed her the paper without meeting her eyes. "¡Atención!" The crowd hushed and turned toward him. "Después de la clínica hay una clase de educación sexual. Todos están invitados."

He turned to Annie. "I told them there would be a class—"

"After the clinic," she finished. "Okay. Mari said she'll help translate, so you don't have to."

"Annie?"

"Yeah?"

The things he wanted to say withered in his throat. "There are corn tamales for lunch. In the pan on the back table."

She nodded and walked away. And even though the pavilion was small and narrow, it felt like she was already home. Unreachable.

DAY TWENTY-THREE

Felipe tried to shut it out, willing his mind to unhear the sounds trailing in through the open window. But it was futile. He jerked out of his hammock, his feet sinking into the warm earth as he searched for the source of the retching.

Flashlight in hand, he slipped by the old wooden panel that served as the door, expecting one of the villagers—someone who'd hiked to get there and was early. Maybe a wandering cow or a hungry, stray dog.

It was Annie.

She raised a hand, shielding her eyes from his flashlight beam.

Felipe crossed the thick grass and stopped a few feet away. "You are sick?"

"I'm fine." She shook her head. "A stomachache. You can go back to sleep."

A smattering of fat raindrops hit his forearm. He stepped closer. The beam of the flashlight reflected off the grass, illuminating the flush in her face and the sheen of sweat on her forehead. "It is raining. Come inside."

"It's too hot in there. I'll wake everyone."

"What are your symptoms?"

"I'm okay," she said.

Felipe squatted beside her. "Annie, as the doctor responsible for your health—"

"Vomiting. Nausea."

"Do you have a rash?"

"No."

"Are you sure?"

"No."

He took a deep breath and readied himself for the torture. "May I?"

She closed her eyes and nodded.

Felipe dragged the flashlight beam over her legs looking for the telltale sign of dengue fever. He swiped it over her arms. *Nada.* "Can you lift your shirt, *por favor?*"

She kept her eyes closed as she did it, and the grimace that weighed down her lips didn't escape his notice.

No rash.

"You can put it down now."

She dry heaved.

"You are taking malaria preventative, *sí?*"

"Every Monday." Her eyes flew open. "You think I have malaria?"

"No." He put on his best nothing-to-worry-about smile. "I think you ate something that did not agree with your stomach. It happens sometimes on these trips. What was the last thing you ate?"

"Lunch, I guess. I didn't have anything for dinner. Once we got off the boat my stomach was upset. I thought it was seasickness or whatever." She shrugged. "So those corn tamales, I guess."

"Did you bring any ciprofloxacin? It is an antibiotic."

"It's in my bag." The rain was a constant drizzle now.

"We will go inside then, yes?"

She nodded but didn't stand. Felipe wrapped an arm around her waist and pulled her to her feet. He cleared his throat and tried to ignore the feel of her skin against his as he walked her into the hut.

Juan snored from his hammock, but the rest of the crew was silent. Only the shuffle of their footsteps on the dirt and the hum of night insects filled the tiny house. "Where is your medicine?" he asked.

"Here." She pointed at her bag. "I'm going—" She stood and ran back out into the rain.

Felipe dug through the bottles and papers and pens in her bag until he found the medication. He grabbed Annie's water and pulled a poncho from his own belongings, then darted outside.

She leaned against the side of the house. Bent in half, her hair fell around her face like dozens of wild springs.

"Here." He held out the water and a pill. She gulped it, and he slipped the poncho over her head.

"Thank you."

"Drink all of it, *por favor.*"

"I will."

He stared at her a moment longer, waiting for the right words to come to him. But his mind stayed blank.

"I'm okay." Her voice cracked. "You can go back to bed."

"I know." He waited a beat, trying to pull together the courage to say the thing he needed to say. The thing that had been pulling and tugging at his conscience for the last several days. The thing that made him so angry at himself and the world and Annie. That she was brave. Braver than him. "Do you know if anyone else ate the tamales?"

"Me, Mari, and Juan." She chewed her bottom lip. "Phillip didn't have any. Said he had to watch his carbs or something?"

Felipe shook his head. "Did he mention his washing machine when he said it?"

"Yeah. Lifted his shirt and everything." She took another sip of water. "But I think, really, he didn't feel like eating."

"Why?" He leaned beside her, the rough logs digging into his back and the rain hitting his face.

"He really likes Mari. But you know." She shrugged and glanced at him from the corner of her eye. "And we're leaving soon anyway, so…"

He nodded, but her words raked through his insides.

Overhead, the rainclouds moved by, quick and furious, and for an all too brief second, the moonlight reflected the curve of Annie's lips. "I can't stopping thinking about her. About Rosa," she said.

"I know."

"I wish I could throw something in with the sex ed classes. Like, if you do get knocked up, try not to abuse your kid when it comes out." She lifted both hands to her face and rubbed her cheeks.

The rain came down in sheets around them, and Annie's words looped through his mind. Before long, an idea sank its roots into his chest. *Five more days.*

• • •

Annie groaned and rolled over, burying her face into the hammock. A hint of something sweet and spicy drifted into her subconscious. *Felipe.* She sank deeper into the fabric, clinging to the last flickers of sleep as she stretched her arms then her legs.

"Ooof." Her tailbone hit the floor first, and she flopped to the ground like a murder victim waiting to be outlined.

Where am I?

She remembered sitting outside in the rain while another storm waged its way through her intestinal tract. She remembered vomiting in front of him—again—and then taking the antibiotic, praying it would work its voodoo magic before her body could force it up. Everything after that was a dark, dehydrated blur.

She forced her eyes open, squinting into the blazing sun coming in the windows. The hammocks around her hung empty, stiff and unmoving. Cotton-mouthed and nauseated, she crossed the room and looked out the window. A football field away, a line of patients curved around the outskirts of a thatched roof.

She grabbed her water bottle, taking small, anxious sips until her mouth stopped feeling like it was stuffed with sand. An orange prescription bottle sat on top of her bag along with a two-pack of little blue pills. Imodium. Felipe's scrawled handwriting was on the paper next to them. "*Por si acaso.*" Just in case.

Her insides tried to climb inside themselves, as if it would make her as small as possible. "In case I want to fling myself off a cliff," Annie muttered.

She downed the blue pills and another antibiotic. One change of clothes, two mouthfuls of toothpaste, and a three-inch thick slather of deodorant later, she shuffled her way toward the clinic.

The crowd outside had dissipated, but there were still one or two stragglers.

"*¿Clínica de Ahora?*" she asked.

They nodded, staring and smiling.

She slipped in the open door, and a small brown hand grabbed her elbow.

"You are feeling better, yes?" Marisol whispered. Her hair clung to the rounded edges of her face, heavy with sweat, and her sienna skin lost color before Annie's eyes.

"I think. Mostly. Are you okay?" she asked.

Marisol shrugged. "I think the tamales were *no bueno*. But I will be fine. Nicaraguan stomach is stronger than *Americana*." Marisol raised one dark eyebrow, but the rest of her expression was so droopy, it made her look like a terminally ill pirate. Minus the eye patch.

"Are you sure you're okay?"

Marisol didn't answer. The hum of voices faded into silence as Felipe stepped to the front of the room.

"If you want to do the sex ed lecture here, you need to stop him." Marisol nodded toward her brother.

"What?"

"He is going to do your lecture. Because you were sick."

She turned to the front, her eyes following Felipe as he greeted the people, shaking hands and kissing cheeks. People who knew him. Trusted him.

He looked up, and his eyes locked on hers. "You want?" he mouthed.

The thought of standing there in front of all those people and trying to speak Spanish while beating down nausea was too much to handle. "No," she mouthed back.

He jumped straight into the lecture. Annie did her best to follow, but her stomach was still full of rocks and knots. His words blurred.

After a few minutes, Marisol groaned through pale lips. "Corn tamales."

"Seriously." Annie guided her out the back door. "Come on, I'll walk with you."

She dragged her friend to her hammock, praying Marisol wouldn't throw up on the way. Annie was certain her own stomach wasn't solid enough yet. It would be puke dominoes.

"Here, drink." She handed Marisol some water. "Do you want me to get something for you? Crackers? Medicine?"

"'Lipe has them." Marisol shot out of her hammock and ran outside. Her retching filtered in through the windows, and Annie plugged her ears, ignoring the nausea building inside her.

"I'm going to get you some medicine." Annie didn't wait to see if her friend responded. She shuffled toward the clinic building, squinting and shielding her eyes from the too bright sun.

"How are you feeling?" Felipe's silhouette appeared in front of her.

"Okay. A little better." She tugged at her shorts, heat inching up her cheeks. "Mari isn't feeling well either. She said you have something she can take? I didn't know because of her diabetes—"

"*Sí*." He took three long strides toward the hut.

"Felipe?" She reached for his elbow, and he froze. Her nerves frayed as she touched his warm, smooth skin. "Thank you. For taking care of me, I mean."

He took another step. "I am a doctor, Annie. It was for nothing."

Annie nodded and followed him inside, wishing it was for something.

DAY TWENTY-FOUR

The words ran together on the page, blurred by Felipe's exhaustion and his own terrible handwriting. Around him, everyone else slept, but each time he closed his eyes he saw Annie. The way her nose scrunched up as she laughed. The tight line of her jaw as she scowled at him while she stood in the middle of the river. The soles of her shoes, climbing up the stairs to the plane and out of his life forever. He kept his eyes open and pushed through, scribbling more notes in the margins. More ideas. More questions. All triggered by Annie's offhand middle-of-the-night remarks.

One more clinic. A sharp breeze blew through the window, cooling his skin and swirling up all his mixed emotions. He folded the paper in half and tucked it into his backpack, trying to stay quieter than the din of insects and Juan's snores.

"*Aquí.*" Marisol's voice was rumpled and heavy, and she let out a noise that was half sigh, half whimper.

Felipe froze. He snapped his eyes shut and prayed for sleep. The deep, tumbling-into-a-dreamless-pit kind of sleep that would keep him from hearing his sister's make up session with Phillip. But the noises carried on, slowly at first and growing louder and more excruciating as the minutes crept by.

Felipe rolled over and reached into his bag for a spare shirt. He wasn't sure if he intended to throw it at his sister or pull it over his ears to drown out her moans, but he never made it that far. An arm's length away, Annie sat on her yoga mat, rubbing her eyes and squinting in Marisol's direction.

"I guess they made up," she whispered.

It would be so easy to fall back into their old conspiratorial ways, to poke good-natured fun at his sister, as if their laughter had been a rope holding them together.

He rolled over and stared at the ceiling. "You only have to make it through one more clinic."

· · ·

The moonlight poured in through the window and cast shadows into every corner of the room. Annie peered into them, taking in the details of the tiny hut as she tried to forget Felipe's words. *One more clinic.* That sentence echoed in her mind, filling it with promises of air-conditioning and her father's famous homemade vanilla ice cream. Hot showers and cuddling with her cat. But it also meant going back to her boring, insignificant life. Watching reality television while people here lived without access to clean water. Worrying about classes and sorority gossip, while Felipe worried about children with dengue fever.

Felipe. At least she'd only have to deal with his glowering for one more clinic.

Annie rolled over, burying her face in the damp yoga mat. The foam stuck to her cheek, and she closed her eyes, hoping sleep would clean all her festering wounds. But Marisol's grunts started again as Annie began to slip into unconsciousness.

Again? Seriously?

She flung a hand to her ear, debating whether she should throw something at them or take Juan's make-your-ears-bleed approach. She began to turn away when the shadows shifted, illuminating a shock of blond hair.

Phillip wasn't in Marisol's hammock. He was tucked solidly into his own, with one tanned arm dangling from the side.

Her friend groaned again, and this time its familiarity made Annie's pulse roar in her ears. She'd heard these noises before. And they weren't the ones she got used to her freshman year, when her roommate would bring her long-distance boyfriend up to visit every other weekend.

Annie sprung to her feet. "Mari? Hey, Mari?" She tried to keep her voice down as she scrambled toward her friend's hammock.

Sweat covered Marisol's face and beaded on her upper lip. Her right cheek twitched.

"Okay. Sugar. Need sugar." Annie dropped to her knees and dug through her friend's bag, not caring where the clothes and books landed. "Where is it?" Finally, her trembling fingers closed around the cylinder of glucose tabs. "Here, Mari." She flipped open the lid and tried to shake an orange coin free.

Empty.

Annie's fingers and toes went cold even though the humidity and the temperature both approached the hundred mark. "Felipe. Wake up." Her voice was so sharp and frantic it shredded her throat.

"¿Qué?" He shot up.

"Mari. She needs sugar. Where is her icing? Does she still keep a tube of icing?" Annie knew she was loud enough to wake the entire village, but she could barely hear it over the pounding of her own heart.

He threw his legs over the side of his hammock. "Get my bag. There is candy there. Front pocket." He sprinted toward Marisol.

Annie ruffled through his backpack, dumping everything into a pile at her feet. A crumpled sheet of notebook paper stuck to her ankle, and she pulled it away. Across the top, in his familiar, slanted chicken-scratch was her name.

It made her heart thud harder, and Annie shoved the paper to the bottom of the pile. As she did, her fingers brushed the plastic bag of Smarties. "Here." She ran the few feet to her friend's hammock, holding a package of the candy out in front of her.

Marisol knocked it away with a grunt and a sneer.

• • •

The tiny pieces of candy clattered to the ground, leaving a rainbow of sweets at Felipe's feet. He shoved his sister to her side as she smacked at his arms and face. "Hold her arms." In those first months after his sister had been diagnosed, he'd shot cake icing into her mouth more than once. And even a few times as adults, but usually Marisol had perfect control of her blood sugar. Especially during the brigades.

Annie dropped the bag of candy and grabbed Marisol's wrists, giving him a reprieve from the attack while he turned off her pump.

"She gets like this when her sugar is too low," he said.

"I remember." Annie picked up another tube of Smarties. "What do we do?" Her fingers never stopped moving, twisting and untwisting the piece of plastic in her hands.

Felipe glanced at Marisol's sweaty face. Her eyes seemed to focus on him for a half-second, then they slid up to the ceiling.

"I will hold her, and you put some in her mouth."

"Won't she choke?" Annie asked.

He shook his head. "She is still here enough to swallow. Tuck it inside her cheek." Felipe grabbed Marisol's arms an inch below the elbow. She squirmed and kicked, and her sweaty skin made a good grip difficult, but he held tight. "Be careful. She might bite you."

Annie pinched three pieces of pink candy between her fingers. "Okay." She pulled Marisol's cheek and dropped the candy in.

Half of it came up as she spat.

"Break it," he said.

"Break what?"

His voice cracked, letting some of his fear escape. He took a deep breath and swallowed it back. "The *dulce*. If it is powder, it is harder for her to spit out."

"What's going on?" Phillip's eyes bugged as he bolted toward them.

"Her blood sugar is too low," Felipe said.

Annie grabbed a new roll and stomped on it. The sugary pieces crumbled, and she held the wrapped powder between her fingers. "Do I dump it in?"

"*Sí.* Try to hold her mouth closed this time. Like," his forehead crinkled as he remembered that picture in her photo album, "like your cat, Mr. Flowers. Do you ever give him medicine?"

"Got it." Annie grabbed Marisol's lower jaw and dug her fingers into her friend's cheeks. When her mouth opened, Annie popped the broken candy inside. She pushed up on Marisol's chin and rubbed her throat until she swallowed.

A handful of breaths later, Marisol's face stopped twitching. Her eyes were still hazy, but there was less anger there.

"You okay?" Phillip pushed the sweaty hair from Marisol's forehead, but she didn't answer.

"One more?" Annie crushed another package of candy under her flip flops.

His sister opened her mouth voluntarily, and Annie dropped the sugar inside.

Felipe let go of Marisol's arms and waited while her mouth worked over the sweets. Beside him, Annie shook, and the plastic bag in her hands crinkled as she trembled.

"She is okay, Annie." Without thinking, he put a hand on her back. For a moment, the shaking stopped, but then it returned worse than before. He tore his hand away.

Marisol eased herself up as Juan shuffled over to join them.

"I turned off your pump," Felipe said. "Where is your meter?"

She pointed to the mess under her hammock, and he crouched to dig.

"Here." Annie nudged him out of the way. "She keeps it in this pocket." She grabbed the black and white case and held it out to him.

Outside, the sun appeared over the horizon, throwing soft, pink light through the room. This close to her, Felipe could see exactly where each of her long, pale eyelashes ended. Her hair slumped half out of her ponytail, and her gold-flecked eyes bore into him.

"*Gracias.*" He took the meter and shot up, afraid he would lose what little composure he still had.

Juan's voice came from behind him. "Everything is okay?"

Felipe handed his sister her meter. "*Sí.*"

"*Bien.*" The man cleared his throat, and Felipe turned around to face him. "Because I looked through my bag for the extra sugar tablets, but I found only this." He held up an enormous pair of underwear, and the red fabric flapped in the morning breeze.

There was a long beat of silence before Marisol coughed. "I am glad you did not try to shove those in my mouth," she whispered.

DAY TWENTY-FIVE

Annie looked at the exposed wood ceiling and the wide, fingerprint-smudged windows at the back of the room. The screech and thump of children playing echoed through the cabin. "This place is really neat. What did you call it?"

"The *Casa del Niños*," Marisol said.

"Like an orphanage?" Phillip asked.

"Not so much orphans. More like their parents cannot take care of them," Marisol said.

A knot of children swarmed the group, and the press of little hands and legs threw Annie off balance. She stumbled as a boy stuck a finger into a hole in her shirt, and someone lifted the supply bag from her shoulder. She turned, expecting an overeager child. Instead, she found herself staring at Felipe.

Juan shoved a bag in Phillip's hands and dragged him toward the door. "I will do my exams in the sleeping room. It is bigger."

"I will go do the organizing. So Annie can do lots of observations for her last clinic, yes?" Marisol didn't wait for an answer, sashaying out of the room with a trail of children in tow.

Real subtle, Mari. Annie pulled down her ponytail and redid it twice, her fingers refusing to stay still. "Is that okay?"

Felipe nodded but kept setting out supplies. She wondered if it really was okay. If being alone together was as terrifying for him as it was for her. She pushed out her doubts. The last clinic. Her last chance to bolster her med school application. *Last chance.*

Their first pint-sized patient sprinted in, and Felipe lifted her onto a heavy oak table that took up most of the space in the room. He looked in the girl's ears and eyes. He shined a light down her throat then pulled out his stethoscope.

"Do you want to listen?" he asked.

"Really?"

"*Aquí.* Tell me what you hear." He put the stethoscope in her ears and moved the round end of the device around the girl's back.

Annie's smile spread like wildfire. "Her lungs."

"And? Do you hear anything concerning?"

She closed her eyes and listened again. The sound of deep, clear breaths filled her ears. "No. I don't think so."

"*Muy bien.*" He lifted the girl off the table. She wrapped her tiny arms around him, muttering into his waist.

"What is she saying?" Annie watched them, imagining the girl was begging him to stay or to take her away from this place.

"She wants a Band-Aid."

"Oh." Annie dug in a bag and produced a Snoopy Band-Aid. "Here." She unwrapped the bandage and stuck it to the child's hand.

The girl fell into a fit of giggles and tore out of the room.

"How many are left?"

"Many," he said as the next child shuffled in. Felipe shined a light into the chubby boy's throat. The boy's left eye pointed toward the floor while the right looked straight ahead. "Come look at this."

She took the black penlight from Felipe's hand. "What am I looking for?"

"Shine it in his right eye first. Then the left." He stood behind her, guiding the light between her fingers.

"Go slow. Look at his pupil."

She moved the light back and forth between his eyes. Only his right one shrank under the beam. The left eyelid drooped, as if the boy was exhausted. "This one isn't reacting. Or," she moved the light again, "the left one is a lot slower."

Felipe forced the light toward the floor. "Do not blind him."

"Sorry." Annie stepped away. "What does it mean?"

"He has damage to the oculomotor nerve."

Her chest constricted. "That sounds bad. Do you want me to get someone?"

"No. It is okay. He has been injured since birth. I want to take him to Managua to see about surgery for his eyelid, but so far we have not been able to raise the money."

Annie fumbled for words as she helped the boy off the table.

A girl with a prosthetic leg and a smile so wide it took up half her face came scrambling into the room. "*¡Doctor! ¡Doctor!*" She rapped on her fake leg, the pale plastic shocking against her dark skin.

"*Dios mío, ahora puedes correr más rápido que los muchachos.*" Felipe's smile was wide enough to match the girl's.

Annie's heart ached. "Did you tell her she can run faster than the boys now?"

"*Sí.* Your Spanish is getting very good." He tugged at the girl's ponytail. "This is Mariana. One of *Ahora's* donors helped her get a new leg last year."

"*Hola.*" She squatted and smiled at the child.

The girl waved, and Felipe lifted her onto the table in front of them. "When we are done here, I want to talk to you, Annie." He closed his eyes as he rubbed the crease in his forehead. "*Por favor.*"

Annie handed the girl a Band-Aid, ignoring the torrent of emotions swirling inside her. "Okay."

• • •

Working next to Annie had grown more fluid with each child. They moved and talked and examined in the tiny quarters, handing out Band-Aids like stickers. But in the tight space, there were a dozen accidental touches and a handful of looks that lingered a second too long.

"I think that is the last of them." Felipe packed up his supplies. "Last clinic. You survived Nicaragua." He hated the bitter taste of the words.

"Barely."

Silence ran between them, interrupted only by the shuffle of little feet in the hallway.

Felipe pulled the crinkled sheet of notebook paper from his

bag and held it out to her. She reached out, but he jerked it back to his chest. "I am sorry. For the things I said. For yelling. For all of it."

She frowned, and a few tiny lines sprung up on her forehead. He wanted to reach up and smooth them away.

"And I have an idea. But I am not sure of all the details." He tucked the page into her hands. "I wanted to ask for your help before you leave."

Her frown deepened as she stared at the paper, her eyes narrowed and focused. His stomach sank. *She hates it.*

"Child vacations?" She squinted up at him. "Your handwriting is terrible."

"No. Child abuse education. Maybe a class, like your sexual education classes?"

"Really?"

"*Sí*, I think so. I will have to talk with my mother. We have not done things like this before. Things that are not so much physical health."

"This is great." Annie's face cracked into a brilliant smile, sending a wave of relief through him. "But I don't think you need me for anything."

Felipe stomped out the urge to say he needed her for everything. Even if everything only spanned a few more days. "I do. When we go back to my mother's house, I will have to tell her what happened." He wiped the sweat from his brow. "She will not be happy—"

"Because of me." Annie's shoulders sank.

"No. Because I let you go to that house. Because we were chased away. Because I made you feel bad for trying to help. Because of all of it." He willed away the gut-twisting memories. "But if I can show her a plan and tell her I have learned something, she will not be so upset."

"You think she might give you *Ahora*? If she likes it?"

He shook his head. "No. But she might let me keep going on the brigades."

"She wouldn't keep you from them, right? You're too good."

"After the last one, she threatened…" The words wouldn't come.

"Then we're coming up with a plan." She tugged a supply pack over her shoulder. "Let's go." They hiked to their temporary home as fireflies flickered in the distance. She smiled and waved her arms as she threw out idea after idea for the class.

"You are a real *Nica* now," he said the third time her elbow jabbed his forearm.

"What?" She cocked her head, and a clump of hair clung to the sweat on her forehead.

He pushed it away and forced his thumb not to trace her cheekbone. "You talk with your hands now. *Mucho*."

"Ha. I think I got used to no one understanding me. This. Seems. To. Help." She accented each syllable with a random gesture.

By the time they reached the house, everyone else had finished dinner. Juan, Phillip, and their host played a game of UNO by flashlight, and Marisol had her face in a book. Annie and Felipe made themselves plates of lukewarm *gallo pinto* as they brainstormed.

"Like with the lady who was *really* into the sex ed classes?" Annie asked between bites.

"*Sí*. Bianca." He sat next to her on the yoga mat. "If we have an educator in the villages, the people will be more open. Because the information is coming from someone they trust."

Annie's face puckered, and he could practically see her brain spitting out the ideas. "Maybe you should have two educators in each village. I mean, if they're going to be dealing with people like Rosa's dad, they might want to have some backup."

"*Bien*. Do you still have the paper? Write that down."

She smoothed the crinkled page and printed the words in her perfect handwriting. "Oh! Idea." She looked up at him with a grin so wide he nearly kissed her. "What if—"

"You are funny."

"No, I'm excitable."

"I cannot read with all your excitability, *Anita*." Marisol kept her eyes focused on her book. "You should go outside."

"Sorry," Annie whispered. She plucked the flashlight from Felipe's hands and tucked the pen and paper under one arm. "Let's go. Bring the yoga mat." She darted out the door before he had time to stand up.

Marisol finally put down her book and looked him straight in the eye. "*De nada.* Do not waste your last moments, *hermano.*" She pulled the pages up to her nose without waiting for him to respond.

Outside, Annie paced back and forth, tapping the pen to her lips. Her perfectly curved, soft lips. Felipe threw down the yoga mat and sat. His sister's words spun in his mind. "Tell me your grand ideas, *Americana.*"

She sat beside him, and his skin buzzed as her knee brushed up against his.

"So what if…"

"…We could have a…"

"…No, that won't ever work…"

"…Money. It is always a problem…"

"…It's a fundraiser…"

They went on and on, throwing out ideas and scribbling the best on their single sheet of paper. Sleep weighed on Felipe as Annie talked, but he didn't want to lose this moment. He stretched out, staring up at the sky with the damp grass tickling his neck.

Annie lay beside him, and he was acutely aware that no part of her was touching him. Her ideas slowed, and the silence between them stretched on.

"I think we have a very good plan," Felipe said.

"Yeah." Her voice softened at the end, and he could tell she was fading into sleep.

Last moments. He took a deep breath, and his throat went dry. There was no reason this should be so hard. No reason he should be so worried. No reason he should be so wrapped up in a girl who was leaving in a few days. "Annie?"

She didn't respond, and he turned to look at her. The flashlight still lay in her palm, pointed limply at her feet, and the steady rise and fall of her chest told him she was already dreaming.

Felipe clicked off the flashlight. "I miss you already," he whispered.

DAY TWENTY-SIX

The sun was bursting on the horizon, and a low cover of thick fog hung over the damp grass. A bird sang in a nearby tree, and Annie honed in on the sound. She'd been awake for a while now, reliving last night's brainstorming session and making mental notes to add ideas to their list. But between thoughts, she found herself staring at Felipe. Memorizing the line of his jaw and the smooth curve where his neck met his shoulder.

"Good morning." His face dipped into a sleepy, dazzling smile.

It was her undoing. Her heart thumped against her ribcage, begging her to both stop and go. To kiss him and to run away.

"Annie, I—"

She pressed her lips to his, giving in to the loudest of her body's demands. And after half a stunned second, he kissed her back. And then he was pulling her on top of him, all hands and warmth moving against her.

"I missed you," she said.

He pulled her top lip between his teeth, and she pressed harder against him. Her skin felt electric and frenzied, like she might combust if she couldn't lay her bare chest to his.

"You are beautiful." His fingers inched up her side, until he stroked the sensitive skin beneath her breasts. Their tongues explored each other, and Annie forgot where she was or who she was. The smell of morning dew and the taste of Felipe's mouth and the feel of their skin sticking together combined to overwhelm her senses and her mind.

"You should go into the woods. Or at least do not lie in the way of the *baño*." Juan's voice trailed behind him as he stepped over their

214

wild tangle and headed toward the outhouse.

Annie rolled off of Felipe, scrambling to find her composure. "We can't do this."

Felipe sat up beside her and brushed the curls from her forehead. "Why not? I do not care that you are leaving. I care about right now. This." He slipped his hand around the back of her neck and traced her cheekbone with his thumb.

She grinned, even though his eyes were soft and serious. "No. Not that. He's coming back." She jerked her head toward the outhouse, where Juan had reemerged. His whistling grew louder and more obnoxious with each second. But he stepped around them and into the tiny house without a word.

"He's going to wake everyone."

Felipe nodded, still running his thumb along her cheek.

"Do you think he's trying to get us back? For the underwear thing?"

"No." Felipe chuckled. "He will do something worse, I think."

"We'll maintain constant vigilance." Annie leaned forward and kissed him again, softly this time, trying not to lose herself or this moment in the taste of his lips.

"Annie?"

"Yeah?" She kept her eyes closed as she nuzzled into his shoulder. Behind them, the sound of the others waking and shuffling around made her stomach sink.

"Tomorrow, Marisol and I will go to a resort. We go there after every brigade for a few days. Come with us. We can cancel your hotel in Managua, and you can go to the airport from the resort. It is beautiful there. I want you to see it." He swallowed, and Annie felt the movement along her forehead. "I want one more day with you."

"Really?"

"*Sí.*"

"Will Mari mind? Is it like a sibling tradition?"

He laughed. "I think my sister will murder me in my sleep if I do not invite you."

"We can't have that." She kissed him one last time before she stood. "It's a date."

• • •

The house was exactly as they'd left it four weeks ago. Exactly as Felipe had left it six years ago when he moved across the country. Fans perched on every open space. The worn couch with its faded blue pinstripes and sagging cushions. It was all the same. But something felt different…off, like this was a replica of his old home rather than the real thing.

As he stared at the awards lining the walls, it hit him. For the first time since he started going on the brigades, Felipe wasn't relieved to return home. He wasn't happy to dump off the Americans and have a week off to rest and relax away from the worry of medicine. Instead, he was nervous and excited and energized. And he would have gladly hopped back in the boat if it meant another month to put his plan into action. Another month with Annie.

His mother jumped up from her desk to greet them and knocked a stack of forms to the floor. "¡Hola! I am so happy to see your faces." She hugged every one of them, enveloping them in her familiar scent. Felipe dug through a pile of envelopes on the rickety kitchen table, and Annie lingered with his mother.

"Can I use your phone to call my dad?" Annie asked.

"Of course. Let's have a debriefing afterward. Everyone all together. I'm sure there are things you want to talk about." A debriefing meant telling his mother what had happened. Every last detail. Felipe's shoulders crept toward his ears, and he could already hear his mother's pointed lecture.

"Okay." Annie slipped outside with the phone.

"*Madre.*" Felipe put down the mail, and gathered up his courage. "Before we have a group debriefing—"

Her face sank. "What happened?"

"It is okay. We had some trouble in one of the villages."

"Trouble? What kind of trouble? Felipe, I don't know—"

"We should wait for Annie." Without her at his side, bubbling over with her excitement and ideas, Felipe wasn't sure he could pull it off.

"Why?"

"Because…" The anxious pit in his stomach grew deeper, swallowing his voice box. "I will go check on her." He rushed out the door without waiting for a reply.

Annie sat on the front stoop with Phillip, the phone dangling at her side.

"No worries. I'll get back to school. There'll be plenty of chicks to choose from there. And if not, there's talk of doing a *Barnyard* spinoff. *The Farmer's Wife* or something like that. They've already asked me to audition."

"Sounds great. But I shouldn't have said anything. It was between you and Mari."

Annie's voice trembled a little at the end, and it made Felipe want to scoop her up and kiss away her nerves.

"I guess it wasn't anything I didn't already know. I mean, she lives here. I live in America. It's not like it could have been anything, right?"

Felipe's hands went numb, and his heart sprinted harder. He didn't want to hear Annie agree, even if he already knew Phillip was right. "Annie? Did you get ahold of your father? My mother wants to talk about the class, and…" He swallowed hard. "And I need you."

She shot up. "No answer. I'll try again tonight. You think everything's okay, right?"

Felipe could practically see the medical terms swirling through her mind. Decompensation. Shortness of breath. Ejection fractions. "I am sure he is fine."

"Okay." She slipped her hand into his and squeezed.

He led her inside, and his mother made no effort to hide her shock at their intertwined fingers.

"This is new." She motioned to the chair across the table. "Sit."

Annie perched on the edge of her chair and let go of his hand. Felipe slid in beside her.

He stayed silent for a long second, his pulse thudding in his temples.

"Anything you want to share?" his mother asked.

"No." Felipe relaxed a bit. "Well, yes. We had some trouble—"

"I got us run out of a village." The words spilled from Annie's mouth, and she tugged at the hem of her t-shirt. "I'm so sorry, Melinda."

"Annie that is not the entire story." Felipe leaned in closer to his mother. "We—"

"Wait." Melinda's forehead creased. "Which village, Annie? Start at the beginning, please."

"There was this little girl. Her name is Rosa…" The story tumbled out, all jumbled together and full of heavy sighs. Felipe interjected when he could, but once Annie got started, it was hard to fit a word into the conversation.

His mother's face was indecipherable.

"*Madre*," Felipe began. "We can work our way back into the village. We have done it before. And you always say there is no way to know how many people we impact with our actions." He glanced at Annie and nodded. "When Annie stood up to that *borracho* some of the people were on her—our—side. I heard the things they said. Those are the people we want to start with."

"Start with?" Melinda sat back in her chair. Felipe's stomach turned over. He waited, expecting her to tell him this was the end for him. That he didn't have the personality or the right skillset to lead a multicultural group into the rainforest. But she stayed silent.

"*Sí.*" Felipe laid out their plan for child abuse education classes, unfolding the creased sheet of paper where they'd jotted it all down. "We start with the people who believe it is wrong. Give them the information so they can teach the others. This is our way, no?"

"Hmmm."

Annie jumped in, pouring out her ideas and throwing around words like grants and fundraisers and social workers. Felipe clenched and unclenched his fists as they awaited the verdict. As he waited to see whether he would lose his dreams.

Melinda zeroed in on Annie. "So you think your reaction was the wrong thing to do?"

"Yes. No. I don't know." She chewed her bottom lip. "I wish I had handled it differently, I guess. The thought of all of those kids going without medical care now makes me sick." Tears streaked her face, and Felipe squeezed her knee under the table.

Melinda scribbled on one of the many papers in front of her, the scratching of her pen and the hum of the fans the only sound in the room. The tension stretched tighter with each passing second. Finally, she looked up. "When I write up your letter of recommendation, I will tell them how you matured during this trip." She bent her head and wrote something else.

"I'm sorry?" Annie blinked and looked at Felipe. He shrugged.

"Annie," his mother smiled, kind crinkles forming at the corners of her eyes, "this is hard work. There is no right or wrong answer. It's nothing but gray around here. You understand that, and it shows great maturity. And somehow, in a month, you taught my son the lesson I've been trying to drill through his thick skull for years." She shook her head and tossed her pen at Felipe.

He let out an audible breath, then smiled and threw the pen back at his mother.

"You are still in trouble, *hijo*."

Felipe's body went cold. "I should not have let anyone go near the home in that village. I know we agreed—"

"Yes, we did." His mother picked up the crumpled paper and looked over their notes again.

He waited, silently willing Annie to leave while he suffered whatever lecture was headed his way. But she didn't move.

"I trust you won't do that again." Melinda squinted at the page.

"I will not."

"Your handwriting is horrible. Especially in English." She turned the paper sideways. "Go clean up. We will do our debriefing at Alma's, yes?"

Relief flowed through him, and every muscle relaxed, leaving him exhausted. "*Sí.*" He stood and tugged Annie up next to him. "You probably want a shower?"

"Oh, God, yes." She grinned, and he saw the relief in her eyes.

"You'll take separate showers." Melinda still didn't look up from the page. "Don't get any ideas."

Felipe ignored her, and at the top of the stairs, Annie gave him one of her nose-scrunching smiles. "It's going to take her so long to read your handwriting, she probably wouldn't know..."

"Tomorrow," he whispered into her hair.

"Promise?"

"Promise." He laughed and nudged her into the bathroom. "Do not use all the hot water."

DAY TWENTY-SEVEN

Annie closed her eyes. The salt and roar of the Pacific Ocean filled her lungs. From the front, the resort was a simple, three-story, white rectangle with a dash of palm trees lining the lawn. But beyond the building, there was nothing but blue-green waves.

"You sure you don't want to stay?" Annie asked Juan.

"No, no." Juan ran a hand along his now clean-shaven upper lip. Without the handlebar mustache, he looked ten years younger. "There will be too much lovesickness. It will turn my stomach, and then Felipe will have to take care of me. And you will be angry because he is taking care of me instead of you." He waggled his eyebrows.

Annie laughed. "Get out of here." She wrapped her arms around his shoulders and squeezed. "Thank you for everything."

She forced her eyes to the clear, perfect sky, hoping it would stave off her tears. No dice.

"You are good people, Annie." He let go and ducked into his tiny red car.

"Email me?" Phillip handed her a slip of paper with his address printed in block letters.

"You have an AOL address?"

"It was the only one that didn't have Barnyard Bro taken. I guess all the other guys got to them first." He shook out his blond hair. It had grown too long over the last month, and it flopped over his eyes.

"I'll email you. And you're not that far away, maybe we can meet in the middle somewhere and do lunch. Bacon for you. Ice cream for me."

She expected a laugh, but he was silent. His gaze strayed over her head, and Annie didn't need to turn around to know who'd captured his attention.

"Go say goodbye to her. You guys are—"

Phillip pushed past Annie, and in three resolute steps he'd wrapped his arms around Marisol's waist. He dipped her into a low, deep kiss that made Annie's eyes bug out of her head.

"Gross," Felipe said.

"Let's go. Give them some time." She slipped the email address into her pocket and tugged him toward the lobby. At the doorway, she waved to Juan one last time. "And we made it through without Juan getting us back for the underwear. I think that means we won, right?"

"You won. I am sure he is leaving right now to do something terrible to my house." Felipe held open the door, and she slipped in under his arm.

The resort wasn't as open and ornate as some of the lobbies she'd seen on spring break trips to Cancun or even on jaunts to New York with her father. But there was air conditioning. Sweet, precious, thank-you-baby-Jesus air conditioning. And that made this seem like the most luxurious place she'd ever stayed.

"Feels so good." Marisol's voice echoed off the tile. She lifted her arms and spun like a ballerina—once, twice, three times—until she reached the front desk. After a short conversation that involved a lot of suggestive leaning on the desktop, she pirouetted back to them. "He gets off at five. Here are the keys."

Felipe took a set from her and shook his head.

"¿Qué?" Marisol asked.

"Nothing." Annie didn't give him time to explain, afraid it might set off Marisol's insecurities again. "Let's go."

They circled to the back of the resort, and Marisol peeled off to her room. "I will be at the pool."

Annie chewed the inside of her left cheek. They hadn't discussed where she would sleep, but she knew where she wanted to wind up at the end of the night. And it wasn't with Marisol and the guy from the lobby.

"Stay with me." Felipe's hand slid around her waist, pulling her to the other end of the breezeway. "*Por favor.*"

She couldn't have protested if she wanted to. Not with his hands roaming along her hips like that. "Since you asked nicely." She raised up and pressed her lips to his. The way he smiled when she pulled away lit her insides on fire. She pulled out her cellphone, trying to regain her composure. "But I really need to call my dad."

Felipe unlocked the door and tucked the keys into her free hand. His index finger lingered in her palm. "I will be in the room."

Annie grinned so hard her face hurt. "I'll be quick." She pressed the numbers haphazardly, her brain still thinking about the shower she'd been promised. The one that came with hot water and an even hotter, naked doctor.

"Yellow?"

She fumbled and nearly dropped the phone. "Hi, Dad."

"Annie! How are you?" He coughed, and her jaw clenched.

Dozens of terrifying thoughts shot through her at once, careening into one another and leaving her heart pounding. "How are you feeling?" she asked.

"I'm fine, kiddo. I'm not the one who's been running through the jungle for the last month. How are *you* feeling?"

"Pretty good actually." She paced along the tile.

"I knew it. And I take it they all saw how wonderful you are?"

"Something like that." She fiddled with handle of her suitcase. "Are you really okay?"

"Really," he said, and her heart took it down a notch. "I checked your flight schedule online this morning. Times are the same."

"You did?" Her father was Internet-disabled.

"I had Susan check."

"Susan?"

"My home health nurse. She's a looker, Ann."

"You have a home health nurse now?" She stopped moving and stared out at the courtyard, not seeing anything.

"It's fine. Nothing to worry about. Thought it would be good to have someone around while you were gone." He coughed again. "Is that Mike character picking you up? He's been calling here."

"Mike?" Annie's toes went numb.

"Yeah, called twice. Asked what time your flight was getting in. I figured—"

"No, he's not picking me up." She laughed at the idea of sitting in a confined space with that level of douche-baggery. "If he calls again, tell him."

"Okay?"

She ignored the question. "When I get home, let's have dinner at your house."

"You got it. Love you, kiddo."

"Love you. See you tomorrow."

Tomorrow. The word rang out as she hung up. Tomorrow she'd be home. Tomorrow she'd return to life in St. Louis with her friends and her classes and her medical school applications. *Tomorrow I'll be gone.*

"Annie?" Felipe poked his head into the hallway.

"Yep." She moved to the doorway, but he stood still, blocking her entrance.

An unruly patch of hair jutted across his forehead, and she brushed it back. It was so easy and familiar to touch his face. To stand close enough to count the crinkles at the corners of his dark eyes. Felipe ran a finger down her shoulder, pausing at the crook of her elbow, then lingering at her wrist.

Her stomach grumbled.

"You are hungry?" He didn't wait for her to respond. "Come. The restaurant here is very good. But I am not sure they will serve your favorite food. We will ask."

"My favorite food?"

"Armadillo." His grin lightened the weight on her chest, and she shoved her suitcase into the room and followed him down the stairs.

• • •

They made trip after trip to the beach-side buffet—sampling shrimp, a plate of fruit, half a roast chicken. Annie smiled every time a bite passed her lips, and Felipe couldn't stop watching her.

"I never thought I'd miss mashed potatoes so much." She stole a spoonful from his plate. A dot of potato strayed to the corner of her lips. He wiped it away with his thumb, letting his hand linger against her skin. She laughed. "You know, I would be embarrassed, but I'm so sick of eating rice and beans, I don't even care."

After his third glass of Merlot and Annie's second helping of chocolate cream pie, he stood and offered her a hand. They walked the length of the beach, nothing but perfect sand for one long stretch after another, until it turned to hulking boulders and an inky cliff face jutting into the horizon. Felipe stayed silent as they walked, memorizing the whip of salt on his skin and the constant in and out of the waves. He committed every inch of Annie's soft curves and her ridiculous laugh to his memory. Each time a thought of tomorrow crept in, he swatted it back by pulling her into a long kiss. When his mind was foggy with want, the sting faded.

"My dad and I are having dinner tomorrow when I get home."

"Good."

"I'm going to ask him about the fundraiser."

"You do not have to do that."

They reached the boulders, and Felipe began to turn back, tugging Annie with him. But she dropped his hand and climbed, scaling the rocks in bare feet. She towered over him.

"I can see up your skirt from here," he said.

"You cannot." She crossed her legs anyway. Curls swatted her cheeks, and the six or seven feet between them seemed unbearably vast.

He found his way up the slippery rock and stood behind her, his hands draped on her hips. He kissed her collarbone. And her neck. And her ear. She turned, lifting her chin so their lips met.

"It's going to work. My dad will love the idea. And you'll have a nice chunk of money to start the program."

Since they'd started brainstorming, she'd thrown this idea at him again and again. A fundraiser put on by her sorority and her father's old medical practice. Something about "philanthropy points" and wealthy, old doctors. Felipe couldn't follow it all, and he didn't try.

"Annie, people leave here, and they forget." He felt her sharp intake of breath. "I am not saying *you* will forget. But if so many people who *have* been here forget after a few months, why would people who have never known us give their money?"

"I can't explain it. I just know. Trust me."

Felipe bent to kiss her again. He'd do nearly anything to keep from talking about what it all meant—that she'd be gone tomorrow.

She stepped back. "What's wrong? The idea is brilliant. Your mother loves it. Seems like *Ahora* is in your hands if you want it."

"No. She will not budge on the Master's degree."

"Okay, but still." Annie squeezed his hand. "You can do that. If you made it through medical school, what's another year or two?"

He ran a hand through his hair, trying to find the words. "I…" He sighed as the realization hit. "I am scared."

"Of what?"

"That I will forget. That I will get my Master's degree, and it will be too easy to forget the brigades and the villages when I am in a classroom. And when I am done, I will want a job at a private hospital where everything is easy. Or at least easier." He'd never given voice to his fears before. He wasn't even sure he'd known what they were before now. Before Annie.

"Even if you never went on another brigade for the rest of your life—which I'm sure you will—you can't forget something like this."

He pulled her close. She was right, he wouldn't forget. Not the brigades. Not Annie. Not any of it.

She pressed harder against him. "Do you want to go back the room? Would that cheer you up?"

"*Sí.*" Felipe's tongue explored hers, and a fire crackled inside him. He pulled back, groaning. "But I promised Marisol we would go dancing."

"Dancing? Let's go." She grinned up at him one last time before she zipped down the rock.

Felipe hopped down and caught up with her in two lengthy strides. Her hair whipped around her face, swatting her forehead and eyes. He pulled her in for another kiss, and his hands roamed up her dress, catching on the thin fabric of her underwear.

He dipped down until her lips were half an inch from his. "After dancing, I am taking you back to the room." He dropped her dress. "And we are not coming out until tomorrow."

DAY TWENTY-EIGHT

In the early morning, the DJ cut off the music, and Annie strolled up the pathway to their room. Her arms and legs were Jell-O, and her ears rang from the blast of the speakers. Sweat beaded her hairline and chest, and she was so damn thirsty. But she beamed. With one arm looped through Marisol's and the other intertwined with Felipe's, her heart overflowed.

They stopped in the breezeway. "What time do you leave?" Marisol asked.

"Six," Annie said. Her stomach sank. *Five hours.*

"I will be up."

"No, you won't."

"*¿Qué?* I will." She pulled her key from her bra. "But if I am not, wake me up."

Annie wrapped her arms around Marisol's neck. "No way." She squeezed her tiny friend, and tears edged their way into her laugh.

"*Mi Anita.* No crying. I am going to email you all the time. And I will come for a visit so you can introduce me to a whole fraternity of American boys, yes?" Marsiol pulled away and grinned.

"An entire fraternity? They'll never know what hit them."

"Good." Marisol hugged her again. "If I do not let you go now, my brother will never forgive me," she stage-whispered. They both turned to Felipe, who rolled his eyes and took Annie's hand. With a kiss on each of her cheeks, Marisol was gone, the door clicking shut behind her.

Felipe guided Annie across the hallway, and before he could unlock the door, she fell into him, wrapping her arms around his waist. "I don't want to go."

He chuckled and kissed the top of her head. "Of course you do. Cable television. All the hot water you can ever use."

"Sometimes it *does* run out you know."

"Well, you are not leaving yet. I still have you for a little bit longer." He pried her body from his and tugged at the ends of her hair, but his smile didn't stretch all the way to his eyes.

Seeing him fight his own feelings to keep her sadness at bay made Annie want him more. Until that moment, she'd hadn't been sure that was possible. As they'd pressed together on the dance floor, her body screamed at her. All *yes, yes, yes* and *more, more, more*. But now, standing in front of their hotel room, she expected to be overcome with doubt. She expected her mind to race through all the reasons she shouldn't sleep with him. To pull all her fears front and center.

But as she looked into his half smile, Annie realized she had none. And she was certain that if she didn't rip Felipe's clothes off and pull him on top of her, she'd regret it for the rest of her life.

She raised up, putting them eye-to-eye, nose-to-nose, lip-to-lip. "However will we fill the time?"

His hands were on the knob and then on her. Felipe picked her up, and she wrapped her legs around his waist as he kicked the door closed. Pinned against the heavy door, Annie shivered as his hands slid up her dress. He grabbed her thighs as his tongue found hers. Somehow they wrangled the fabric over her head, and her flip-flops hit the ground.

Felipe carried her to the bed, stumbling as his lips stayed pressed to hers. He laid her down and took a step back. His Adam's apple slid in his throat, and Annie squirmed under his stare.

"What?" she asked.

"*Nada.*" He crawled onto the mattress.

Their lips met, charging into one another. Annie could still taste the wine on his bottom lip as her fingers undid the smooth buttons on his shirt. When his bare chest finally touched hers, he moaned into her mouth, and a rolling fire worked its way to her core. She ran her hands down his stomach, and his muscles tensed beneath her touch. Smiling, Annie dipped her fingers below the waistband of his pants, enjoying the low rumble of his groans. She slid her palms over his shoulders and into his hair. He was hard against her, and she arched her back, desperate for friction.

He circled his hands around her waist and lifted, pulling her to the edge of the bed. Annie's legs dangled off the mattress. "What are you doing?" she asked, her voice broken by laughter and lust.

Felipe bent low to her ear, and Spanish rolled off his tongue, so deep and visceral Annie didn't need a translator to understand. She shuddered as he hovered over her, planting kisses from her neck to the valley between her breasts. Every touch left a trail of fire along her skin. He kept going until his lips were an inch below her navel. She gasped and tilted her hips, savoring the feel of his hands on her thighs as he worked her underwear to the floor.

Naked from the waist down, desire made her arms and legs heavy. Felipe's hand was at her knee, pushing outward as his lips grazed her inner thigh. He worked his mouth to her folds, and his tongue flicked and kneaded and explored. When she tilted her hips, his mouth moved faster, and his fingers worked their way inside her. Her mind went blank, but every other part of her burned.

She leaned her head back and let a moan escape. Felipe's warm breath between her thighs was at once unbearable and vital for her very existence. She struggled to sit up and unfastened her last piece of clothing. The bra fell to the ground, and his eyes traveled up her naked body.

Annie unbuckled his belt, savoring the way he looked at her. The way his eyes lit with desire. The way his eyes slid closed when her fingers brushed his skin.

With another tug, she had his pants around his ankles. Felipe fell onto the bed, pulling her on top of him. She threw a leg over his hips, straddling him.

"Annie," he panted. "We should… I mean, if…" He groaned as she rubbed herself against the length of him.

"Do you want to stop?" she whispered.

"No."

"Me either."

The look on his face made her body ache and tense further. Felipe rolled out from under her and dug through the crumpled pile of clothes on the floor. *"Aquí."*

She took the condom and pushed him onto the pillows, sliding the latex over him.

"You are beautiful," he murmured.

She buried her face into his neck and straddled his hips. "I've been thinking about doing this for the last…" Her voice trailed off as a nervous giggle bubbled up inside her. "Since I attacked you at the airport."

"Annie?" He looked up at her from under heavy eyelids. "I have been thinking about doing this since I was seventeen." He cupped the underside of her breasts and rolled a finger over her hardened nipples. "So thank you for attacking me at the airport." He pulled her closer, his teeth grazing her earlobe.

A groan slipped from her lips, and she guided him into her, forcing herself to inch slowly around him. If this was going to be their first and last time, she was going to savor every single second, even if her body demanded everything move faster and deeper and harder.

But Felipe's hands worked her hips back and forth, building the friction between them to an unbearable pleasure, and all her plans tumbled out the window. Soon her gasps were fast and loud, and she was useless to stop them.

Felipe shifted his weight, rolling on top of her. Annie wrapped her legs high on his waist, forcing them closer. And soon his shudders rocked through her.

"Annie?" His lips grazed her neck. "You are amazing."

She peeled back her heavy eyelids, confounded and mesmerized by the ways this trip was leaving its marks on her. And all at once, she knew she wouldn't have it any other way. Battle scars and all.

● ● ●

Felipe's throat was thick with the things he wanted to tell her. She was beautiful. She was amazing and smart and funny. Her crazy laugh made him dizzy. She was certainly some kind of sex goddess, and he would follow her to the ends of the earth to make love to her like that every day. He wanted to beg her to stay for one more day. Or two. A week. Another month.

But the silence was too loud.

Annie pulled on a pair of shorts and slid her arms into his crumbled shirt. The blue cotton hung like a coat from her frame. The sight of her in his clothes left his heart exposed and raw.

"Do you want help with this?" he asked, pointing to the mounds of her belongings at their feet. Clothes spilled from her suitcase, and papers littered the floor.

Annie shook her head and climbed onto the bed. He slipped on a pair of pajama pants and followed, turning off the bedside lamp. Their arms and legs weaved together in the dark, but he felt like he couldn't get close enough to her.

"When is your next brigade?" she asked.

"September." His eyes closed.

"What will you do until then?"

"I have one more week off. Then I will go back to the clinic."

"What will you do during your week off?"

"Miss you."

Silence rose up in the space between them, filling in the cracks and pushing outward, until he felt they were already thousands of miles apart. She nuzzled into his chest, and her breathing slowed. But he stared at the ceiling and inhaled her coconut scent until, too soon, the shrill of their alarm clock sounded.

She pulled a pillow over her head. "Turn it off."

Felipe ducked under the pillow and snuggled into her neck. "You have to get up, or you will miss your flight."

She grumbled, and he rolled out of bed. Annie's clothes and soaps and shoes lay scattered on the floor around her suitcase, and one by one he picked them up and tucked them into her bag. "How do you have more things now than when you first arrived?" he asked. "This does not all fit in your suitcase."

She nudged him out of the way and shoved everything inside her suitcase, nothing folded or rolled. She tugged the zipper but it wouldn't budge, and stray shirt sleeves poked out from under the lid. With a sigh, she pulled the top layer of things out and tossed them on the floor. The zipper closed, and she threw her hands up in the air. "Ta da!"

"And these things?" A bottle of shampoo rolled along the carpet and a handful of t-shirts lay at his feet.

"Those shirts are so gross, I'll never be able to wear them again. And I have more shampoo at home."

He wrapped his arms around her hips, and his fingers dug into the soft curves. Every second seemed to rush by as he stood there, staring at her, trying to figure out how to stop time, or at least to find the words to tell her how he felt.

Their phone rang, and his chest tightened. "Your cab must be here."

"Yeah." She tilted her chin up, and he pressed his mouth to hers, pulling her against him.

The phone kept ringing.

"I miss you already."

And with the click of the door, she was gone.

DAY THREE HUNDRED AND FOUR

Annie's insides twisted and tangled with every exhale. She tugged at the hem of her dress for the tenth time and tried not to stare at the door.

"You could have gone to the airport, kiddo."

"Too much to do here." She pushed her father's wheelchair to the other end of the room, weaving around the banquet tables. The starched, white tablecloths fluttered as they went by. Catering staff hovered at the edges of the room, putting out place settings and straightening fruit trays. "Speech, decorations, making sure you don't embarrass me."

"Embarrass you? That's what fathers are for."

"I should wheel you into the coat closet and leave you there." She shook her head and picked up her index cards. By now the bullet points of her speech were seared into her memory, but it kept her mind occupied. If she let it wander to everything that was scheduled to happen in the next few hours, she'd end up in the fetal position with a bottle of tequila in her hands.

"What time was their flight supposed to land?"

Annie glanced at her phone. "An hour ago."

"An hour must be how long it takes to get here."

Her eyes darted to the open door. Melinda was first, dressed in a sleek, gray suit that was miles from the loose, aging hippy clothes Annie remembered. Marisol came next, ridiculously gorgeous in a black lace dress. She squealed and shuffled across the plush carpet of the banquet center.

"¡Anita!"

Annie wrapped her arms around her friend and squeezed. "I'm

so glad you could come."

"How could we not come?" Melinda asked. "This is an amazing fundraiser. I don't know how you pulled it off, but *Ahora* is never going to be able to repay you."

"Funny thing," her father said, "when you're sick, people will do pretty much anything you want."

Annie started to explain how they had really done it, but Felipe walked through the door, dragging a wheeled suitcase behind him. His suit hugged his body in all the right places, and his green tie set off his skin and eyes. The words clung to the inside of her mouth, refusing to come out.

"We made him carry everything." Marisol cackled.

"Hi." Annie wasn't sure what to do with her hands or her feet. Every part of her felt loose and weak and heavy. All the Skyping in the world couldn't have prepared her for the emotions fluttering around inside her. It was nothing like having him in person, in front of her, close enough to touch. To kiss.

"*Hola.*" He smiled, and everything shifted into place. "Mr. London." He offered her father a handshake.

"I understand you have some not-so-chaste feelings for my daughter."

"Oh my God. Dad, no." Annie knew her cheeks had to be the same color as her hair. She'd spilled far more than she intended her first night back in the States, and her father hadn't let her live it down.

"Let's give them some privacy." Melinda dragged Marisol away, pushing the wheelchair as they went.

They hadn't defined their strange, long-distance relationship in the nine months since she'd left Nicaragua. The first time he left on a brigade, her roommates dragged Annie out on a few double dates. But none of it mattered, because when she came home, all she could think about was Felipe.

"You're really here."

"I am really here." His hands circled her waist, and the kiss was all new again and somehow like slipping into her favorite t-shirt.

Annie's heart stuttered and fumbled over the soft eagerness of his mouth, and she began to rethink who she wanted to escort to the coat closet.

"Did you make your final decision?" he asked, pulling away half an inch. His features went blank, and it took her a second to figure out what he meant.

"For school?"

He nodded.

"I told you already. Brown. Once they said yes, there was no competition."

"But did you pay your down payment?"

"Deposit? Two weeks ago." She smiled, and something fluttered inside her chest. "Thank you again for the letter of recommendation, by the way."

"I have something for you." He hefted the suitcase onto one of the chairs and reached into the front pocket. A thin strip of fire-engine red fabric fell out, the sequins glinting under the florescent lights.

She picked it up and turned the fabric between her fingers. "What *is* this, the world's skimpiest man-thong? Did you decide to give up medicine to become a stripper?"

Felipe rolled his eyes. "Juan." He plucked the G-string from her hands and replaced it with a tattered, purple notebook. A giant muddy thumbprint streaked the back.

"My journal!" In her mad packing crunch, Annie had left it on the floor of the resort with all her torn t-shirts.

During application season, Felipe had typed up the entries she needed and sent them to her. It took her an email or two to get over the mortification of him flipping through her most private thoughts, but he deadened the pain by adding ridiculous stories to each one. Sometimes it was Annie being attacked by a swarm of monkeys. Once, he wrote an entire page about her falling so in love with *gallo pinto* that she swore to eat nothing but rice and beans for the rest of her life. He added bits in Spanish she had to translate and ended each email the same way. *I miss you.*

She thought the day of the banquet would never come.

"Open it." His face was still blank.

Annie chewed her bottom lip. This wasn't quite the reunion she had dreamed of every night since they'd set the date of the fundraiser. "Is everything okay? You don't seem—"

"Open it." He ran a hand through his hair.

She pulled back the cover. On the front page was a collapsed fortune teller. Typed words ran across the page in every direction. "Hey, you finally figured it out. Did you make it on the plane?"

Felipe shifted his weight and jammed his hands into his pockets. "Unfold it."

"What? That's not how it works."

"Annie."

"Okay, okay." She set the journal on the table and unfolded the paper with shaky hands, careful to keep it from tearing. Her eyes skimmed over the page, the words swirling.

"I am tired of missing you all the time," Felipe said. "But I will not come if you do not want—"

She held up a hand to stop him, still dizzy with disbelief, and read the words a second time. It was all there in heavy black type, unchanged.

Dear Dr. Felipe Gutierrez: Welcome to the Brown University School of Public Health.

Annie let the paper flutter to the ground and pressed her forehead to his. The words tangled in her throat, but she forced them out. "I definitely want." Somehow, some way, they'd stolen a little more time together, and there was nothing she wanted more.

AUTHOR'S NOTE & ACKNOWLEDGEMENTS

Years ago, I spent a summer in Sahsa, Nicaragua, a real place, filled with real people, in the North Atlantic Autonomous Region of Nicaragua. I volunteered with a public health organization, traveled with a medical brigade, saw beautiful rainforests, and learned the words to dozens of Sandinista songs. To the people I met that summer, especially Don José and Edith, I will be forever indebted— in more ways than one. And, as much as Sahsa is a real place filled with real people, many of the communities in Without Borders are fictional. Created for story purposes but inspired by the places I visited and the people who welcomed this sunburned gringa into their homes time and time again, feeding me armadillo (armadillo is seriously tasty, folks) and giving me a place to sleep at night. I hope I did justice to these communities (both the fictional and the real), but I am human. And flawed. And sometimes (a lot of times) I screw things up. If I did that here, I am truly sorry.

Turning a bunch of words into an actual book is a group effort, and I'm lucky to have a lot of fabulous people in my corner. My agent extraordinaire, Jessica Watterson, who promised me we'd make this happen and somehow made it so. Everyone at Diversion Books who had a hand in bringing this story to life, but especially Randall Klein, Beth Brown, Sarah Masterson Hally, and Trent Hart. The world's best writing group, The Pen Gangstas—Heather, Laura, Stephanie, Larry, and Cortez—there would be no book if it weren't for you guys. Of that I am certain. And the critique partners— Debbie, Nicole, and Marty—who helped me make these characters come alive.

Even though this is a group effort, publishing can be

exceptionally lonely sometimes. Without my author friends, I would have lost what little sanity I have long ago. Special thanks to the NAC—Jamie, Wenphia, Marie, Annika, Jessica, Tegan, Meredith, Ara, Diana, Marnee, Kate, and Laura—for your friendship, support, and Facebook threads full of hot guys. Also, so much love to the ladies of the Life Raft—Samantha, Kelly, Anise, Tara, Colleen, Brenna, Emily, Heather, and Kimberly—you've kept me afloat more times than I can count. (And extra thanks to my pop culture soul mate, Brenna, who made her husband fix my Spanglish. Boomer, you're the best.)

Many thanks to Karen Sander, who first inspired my wanderlust years ago and let me pick her brilliant bilingual brain to put the final touches on this story. To my parents, who kept me flush in Baby-Sitters Club books, even though it wasn't always cheap or easy. To Keegan-Michael Key, who sits firmly at the top of my celebrity crush list—people who skim this will now think we know each other. Score. Finally, all the thanks to my husband, Matt, who's my biggest fan, favorite plotting partner, and best proofreader.